RANDOM
HOUSE
LARGE
PRINT

The Good Guy

Also by Dean Koontz
available from Random House Large Print

The Husband
Velocity
Life Expectancy
The Taking
Odd Thomas
From the Corner of His Eye
False Memory
Dark Rivers of the Heart
Icebound
Intensity
Sole Survivor
Ticktock
Brother Odd

DEAN KOONTZ'S FRANKENSTEIN
Book One: Prodigal Son • with Kevin J. Anderson
Book Two: City of Night • with Ed Gorman

DEAN KOONTZ

The Good Guy

This is a work of fiction. Names, characters, places, and incidents either are the product of the author's imagination or are used fictitiously. Any resemblance to actual persons, living or dead, events, or locales is entirely coincidental.

Published in the United States of America by Random House Large Print in association with Bantam Dell, New York.
Distributed by Random House, Inc., New York.

Library of Congress Cataloging-in-Publication Data
Koontz, Dean R. (Dean Ray), 1945-
The good guy / by Dean Koontz.—1st large print ed.
p. cm.
ISBN 978-0-7393-2725-8
1. Large type books. I. Title.
PS3561.O55G66 2007b
813'.54—dc22
2007015349

www.randomhouse.com/largeprint

FIRST LARGE PRINT EDITION

10 9 8 7 6 5 4 3 2 1

This Large Print edition published in accord with the standards of the N.A.V.H.

To Mike and Mary Lou Delaney,
for your kindness, for your friendship, and
for all the laughter—even if a lot of the time
you don't know why we're laughing at you.
With you. Laughing **with** you. We love you guys.

I shall tell you a great secret, my friend.
Do not wait for the last judgment, it
takes place every day.

—Albert Camus

The Good Guy

Part One

The Right Place at the Wrong Time

One

Sometimes a mayfly skates across a pond, leaving a brief wake as thin as spider silk, and by staying low avoids those birds and bats that feed in flight.

At six feet three, weighing two hundred ten pounds, with big hands and bigger feet, Timothy Carrier could not maintain a profile as low as that of a skating mayfly, but he tried.

Shod in heavy work boots, with a John Wayne walk that came naturally to him and that he could not change, he nevertheless entered the Lamplighter Tavern and proceeded to the farther end of the room without drawing attention to himself. None of the three men near the door, at the short length of the "L"-shaped bar, glanced at him. Neither did the couples in two of the booths.

When he sat on the end stool, in shadows

beyond the last of the downlights that polished the molasses-colored mahogany bar, he sighed with contentment. From the perspective of the front door, he was the smallest man in the room.

If the forward end of the Lamplighter was the driver's deck of the locomotive, this was the caboose. Those who chose to sit here on a slow Monday evening would most likely be quiet company.

Liam Rooney—who was the owner and, tonight, the only barkeep—drew a draft beer from the tap and put it in front of Tim.

"Some night you'll walk in here with a date," Rooney said, "and the shock will kill me."

"Why would I bring a date to this dump?"

"What else do you know but this dump?"

"I've also got a favorite doughnut shop."

"Yeah. After the two of you scarf down a dozen glazed, you could take her to a big expensive restaurant in Newport Beach, sit on the curb, and watch the valets park all the fancy cars."

Tim sipped his beer, and Rooney wiped the bar though it was clean, and Tim said, "You got lucky, finding Michelle. They don't make them like her anymore."

"Michelle's thirty, same age as us. If they don't make 'em like her anymore, where'd she come from?"

"It's a mystery."

"To be a winner, you gotta be in the game," Rooney said.

"I'm in the game."

"Shooting hoops alone isn't a game."

"Don't worry about me. I've got women beating on my door."

"Yeah," Rooney said, "but they come in pairs and they want to tell you about Jesus."

"Nothing wrong with that. They care about my soul. Anybody ever tell you, you're a sarcastic sonofabitch?"

"You did. Like a thousand times. I never get tired of hearing it. This guy was in here earlier, he's forty, never been married, and now they cut off his testicles."

"Who cut off his testicles?"

"Some doctors."

"You get me the names of those doctors," Tim said. "I don't want to go to one by accident."

"The guy had cancer. Point is, now he can never have kids."

"What's so great about having kids, the way the world is?"

Rooney looked like a black-belt wannabe who, though never having taken a karate lesson, had tried to break a lot of concrete blocks with his face. His eyes, however, were blue windows full of warm light, and his heart was good.

"That's what it's all about," Rooney said. "A wife, kids, a place you can hold fast to while the rest of the world spins apart."

"Methuselah lived to be nine hundred, and he was begetting kids right to the end."

"Begetting?"

"That's what they did in those days. They begot."

"So you're going to—what?—wait to start a family till you're six hundred?"

"You and Michelle don't have kids."

"We're workin' on it." Rooney bent over, folded his arms on the bar, and put himself face-to-face with Tim. "What'd you do today, Doorman?"

Tim frowned. "Don't call me that."

"So what'd you do today?"

"The usual. Built some wall."

"What'll you do tomorrow?"

"Build some more wall."

"Who for?"

"For whoever pays me."

"I work this place seventy hours a week, sometimes longer, but not for the customers."

"Your customers are aware of that," Tim assured him.

"Who's the sarcastic sonofabitch now?"

"You still have the crown, but I'm a contender."

"I work for Michelle and for the kids we're gonna have. You need somebody to work for besides who pays you, somebody special to build something with, to share a future with."

"Liam, you sure do have beautiful eyes."

"Me and Michelle—we worry about you, bro."

Tim puckered his lips.

Rooney said, "Alone doesn't work for anybody."

Tim made kissing noises.

Leaning closer, until their faces were mere inches apart, Rooney said, "You want to kiss me?"

"Well, you seem to care about me so much."

"I'll park my ass on the bar. You can kiss that."

"No thanks. I don't want to have to cut off my lips."

"You know what your problem is, Doorman?"

"There you go again."

"Autophobia."

"Wrong. I'm not afraid of cars."

"You're afraid of yourself. No, that isn't right, either. You're afraid of your potential."

"You'd make a great high-school guidance counselor," Tim said. "I thought this place served free pretzels. Where're my pretzels?"

"Some drunk threw up on them. I've almost finished wiping them off."

"Okay. But I don't want them if they're soggy."

Rooney fetched a bowl of pretzels from the backbar and put them beside Tim's beer. "Michelle has this cousin, Shaydra, she's sweet."

"What kind of name is Shaydra? Isn't anyone named Mary anymore?"

"I'm gonna set you up with Shaydra for a date."

"No point to it. Tomorrow, I'm having my testicles cut off."

"Put them in a jar, bring them on the date. It'll be a great ice-breaker," said Rooney, and returned to the other end of the bar, where the three lively customers were busy paying the college tuition for the as-yet-unborn Rooney children.

For a few minutes, Tim worked at convincing himself that beer and pretzels were all he needed. Conviction was assisted by picturing

Shaydra as a bovine person with one eyebrow and foot-long braided nose hairs.

As usual, the tavern soothed him. He didn't even need the beer to take the sharp edges off his day; the room itself did the job, though he did not fully understand the reason for its calming effect.

The air smelled of stale beer and fresh beer, of spilled brine from the big sausage jar, of bar wax and shuffleboard powder. From the small kitchen came the aroma of hamburgers frying on a griddle and onion rings crispening in hot oil.

The warm bath of agreeable scents, the illuminated Budweiser clock and the soft shadows in which he sat, the murmurs of the couples in the booths behind him and the immortal voice of Patsy Cline on the jukebox were so familiar that by comparison his own home would seem to be foreign territory.

Maybe the tavern comforted him because it represented, if not permanence, at least continuance. In a world rapidly and ceaselessly transforming, the Lamplighter resisted the slightest change.

Tim expected no surprises here, and wanted none. New experiences were overrated. Being run down by a bus would be a new experience.

He preferred the familiar, the routine. He would never be at risk of falling off a mountain because he would never climb one.

Some said he lacked a sense of adventure. Tim saw no point in suggesting to them that intrepid expeditions through exotic lands and across strange seas were the quests of crawling children compared to the adventures waiting in the eight inches between the left ear and the right.

If he made that observation, they would think him a fool. He was just a mason, after all, a bricklayer. He was expected not to think too much.

These days, most people avoided thinking, especially about the future. They preferred the comfort of blind convictions to clear-eyed thought.

Others accused him of being old-fashioned. Guilty as charged.

The past was rich with known beauty and fully rewarded a look backward. He was a hopeful man, but not presumptuous enough to assume that beauty lay, as well, in the unknown future.

An interesting guy came into the tavern. He was tall, although not as tall as Tim, solid but not formidable.

His manner, rather than his appearance, made him interesting. He entered like an animal with a predator on its trail, peering back through the door until it swung shut, and then warily surveying the premises, as though distrusting the promise of refuge.

When the newcomer approached and sat at the bar, Tim stared at his Pilsner glass as if it were a sacred chalice, as though he were brooding on the profound meaning of its contents. By assuming a devotional demeanor, rather than a pose of sullen solitude, he allowed strangers the option of conversation without encouraging it.

If the first words out of the newcomer's mouth were those of a bigot or a political nut, or the wrong kind of fool, Tim could morph from a pose of spiritual or nostalgic reverie to one of bitter silence and barely repressed violence. Few people would try more than twice to break the ice when the only response was a glacial chill.

Tim preferred quiet contemplation at this altar, but he enjoyed the right kind of conversation, too. The right kind was uncommon.

When you initiated a conversation, you could have a hard time putting an end to it. When the other guy spoke first, however, and revealed his nature, you could shut him down by shutting him out.

Diligent in the support of his yet-to-be-conceived children, Rooney arrived. "What'll it be?"

The stranger put a thick manila envelope on the bar and kept his left hand on it. "Maybe . . . a beer."

Rooney waited, eyebrows raised.

"Yes. All right. A beer," said the newcomer.

"On tap, I have Budweiser, Miller Lite, and Heineken."

"Okay. Well . . . then . . . I guess . . . Heineken."

His voice was as thin and taut as a telephone wire, his words like birds perched at discreet intervals, resonant with a plucked note that might have been dismay.

By the time Rooney brought the beer, the stranger had money on the bar. "Keep the change."

Evidently a second round was out of the question.

When Rooney went away, the stranger wrapped his right hand around the beer glass. He did not take a sip.

Tim was a wet nurse. That was the mocking title Rooney had given him because of his ability to nurse two beers through a long evening. Sometimes he asked for ice to enliven a warm brew.

Even if you weren't a heavy drinker, however, you wanted the first swallow of beer when it was at its coldest, fresh from the tap.

Like a sniper intent on a target, Tim focused on his Budweiser, but like a good sniper, he also had keen peripheral vision. He could see that the stranger had still not lifted the glass of Heineken.

The guy did not appear to be a habitué of taverns, and evidently he didn't want to be in this one, on this night, at this hour.

At last he said, "I'm early."

Tim wasn't sure if this was a conversation he wanted.

"I guess," said the stranger, "everyone wants to be early, size things up."

Tim was getting a bad vibe. Not a look-out-he's-a-werewolf kind of vibe, just a feeling that the guy might be tedious.

The stranger said, "I jumped out of an airplane with my dog."

On the other hand, the best hope of a memorable barroom conversation is to have the good luck to encounter an eccentric.

Tim's spirits lifted. Turning to the skydiver, he said, "What was his name?"

"Whose name?"

"The dog's."

"Larry."

"Funny name for a dog."

"I named him after my brother."

"What did your brother think of that?"

"My brother is dead."

Tim said, "I'm sorry to hear it."

"That was a long time ago."

"Did Larry like sky-diving?"

"He never went. He died when he was sixteen."

"I mean Larry the dog."

"Yeah. He seemed to like it. I bring it up only because my stomach is in knots like it was when we jumped."

"This has been a bad day, huh?"

The stranger frowned. "What do you think?"

Tim nodded. "Bad day."

Continuing to frown, the skydiver said, "You **are** him, aren't you?"

The art of barroom banter is not like playing Mozart on the piano. It's freestyle, a jam session. The rhythms are instinctual.

"Are you him?" the stranger asked again.

Tim said, "Who else would I be?"

"You look so . . . ordinary."

"I work at it," Tim assured him.

The skydiver stared intently at him for a

moment, but then lowered his eyes. "I can't imagine being you."

"It's no piece of cake," Tim said less playfully, and frowned to hear a note of sincerity in his voice.

The stranger finally picked up his drink. Getting it to his lips, he slopped beer on the bar, then chugged half the contents of the glass.

"Anyway, I'm just in a phase," Tim said more to himself than to his companion.

Eventually, this guy would realize his mistake, whereupon Tim would pretend that he, too, had been confused. Meanwhile, there was a little fun to be had.

Sliding the manila envelope across the bar, the guy said, "Half of it's there. Ten thousand. The rest when she's gone."

As he finished speaking, the stranger turned on his stool, got to his feet, and headed toward the door.

As Tim was about to call the man back, the terrible meaning of those eleven words clarified for him: **Half of it's there. Ten thousand. The rest when she's gone.**

First astonishment—and then an uncharacteristic clutch of fear—choked off his voice.

The skydiver was intent on bailing out of

the bar. He quickly crossed the room, went through the door, fell away into the night.

"Hey, wait a minute," Tim said, too softly and too late. "Wait."

When you skate across the days, leaving a wake as thin as spider silk, you're not accustomed to shouting or to chasing after strangers with murder on their minds.

By the time Tim realized pursuit was obligatory and got up from his stool, a successful chase could not have been mounted. The quarry had covered too much ground.

He sat again and finished his beer in one long swallow.

Foam clung to the sides of the glass. Those ephemeral patterns had never before seemed mysterious to him. Now he studied them as if they embodied great meaning.

Feeling disoriented, he glanced at the manila envelope, which looked as portentous as a pipe bomb.

Carrying two plates of cheeseburgers and fries, Liam Rooney served a young couple in one of the booths. No waitress worked on a slow Monday.

Tim raised a hand to signal Rooney. The tavern keeper didn't notice; he returned to the bar gate at the farther end of the room.

The envelope still had an ominous significance, but already Tim had begun to doubt that he had correctly understood what had happened between him and the stranger. A guy with a sky-diving dog named Larry wouldn't pay to have someone killed. All this was a misunderstanding.

The rest when she's gone. That could mean a lot of things. It didn't necessarily mean when she was **dead.**

Determined that the world would quickly be put right, Tim pried up the prongs of the brass clasp, opened the flap of the envelope, and reached inside. He withdrew a thick wad of hundred-dollar bills bound together with a rubber band.

Maybe the money wasn't greasy, but that was how it felt. He returned it at once to the envelope.

In addition to the cash, he found a five-by-seven photograph that might have been taken for a driver's license or passport. She appeared to be in her late twenties. Attractive.

A name had been typed on the back of the photo: LINDA PAQUETTE. Under the name was an address in Laguna Beach.

Although he had just finished a beer, Tim's mouth was salt-dry and lemon-sour. His heart beat slowly but unusually hard, booming in his ears.

Irrationally, he felt guilty looking at the photo, as though he had somehow participated in the planning of this woman's death. He put away the picture. He slid the envelope aside.

Another man entered the bar. He was nearly Tim's size, with brown hair cropped short like Tim's.

Rooney arrived with a fresh beer and said to Tim, "You keep chugging them at that pace, you won't qualify as furniture anymore. You'll be a real customer."

A persistent feeling of being caught in a dream slowed Tim's thinking. He meant to tell Rooney what had just happened, but his tongue felt thick.

The newcomer approached, sat where the skydiver had sat, with an empty stool between him and Tim. He said to Rooney, "Budweiser."

As Rooney went to draw the beer, the stranger stared at the manila envelope, and then met Tim's gaze. He had brown eyes, just as Tim did.

"You're early," said the killer.

Two

A **man's life can pivot on the smallest** hinge of time. No minute is without potential for momentous change, and each tick of the clock might be the voice of Fate whispering a promise or a warning.

When the killer said, "You're early," Tim Carrier noticed that the Budweiser clock showed five minutes shy of the hour, and he made an educated guess: "So are you."

The hinge had turned. The door stood open, and it could never be closed again.

"I'm no longer sure I want to hire you," Tim said.

Rooney brought the killer's beer, and then answered a call to the farther end of the bar.

A trick of light, reflecting off the mahogany, gave the contents of the glass a rubescent cast.

The stranger licked his chapped lips, and drank. He had a deep thirst.

When he put down the glass, he said amicably, "You can't hire me. I'm no one's employee."

Tim considered excusing himself to the men's room. He could call the police on his cell phone.

He worried that the stranger would interpret his departure as an invitation to take the manila envelope and leave.

Carrying the envelope to the lavatory would be a bad idea. Under the assumption that Tim wanted privacy for the transaction, the guy might follow him.

"I can't be hired, and I'm not peddling anything, either," said the killer. "You sell to me, not the other way around."

"Yeah? What am I selling?"

"A concept. The concept of your world profoundly changed by one . . . alteration."

In Tim's mind rose the face of the woman in the photo.

His options weren't clear. He needed time to think, so he said, "The seller sets the price. **You** set the price—twenty thousand."

"That's not the price. It's a contribution."

This conversation made no less sense than typical bar talk, and Tim found its rhythm.

"But for my **contribution** I get your . . . service."

"No. I have no service to sell. You receive my grace."

"Your grace."

"Yes. Once I accept the concept you're selling, your world will be profoundly changed by my grace."

Considering their ordinary color, the killer's brown eyes were more compelling than they should have been.

When he had sat down at the bar, his face had appeared hard, but that had been a mistaken first impression. A dimple adorned his round chin. Smooth pink cheeks. No laugh lines. No furrows in the brow.

The whimsical quality of his half-smile suggested that he might be remembering a favorite childhood story about fairies. It appeared to be his default expression, as if he were not entirely connected to the moment, perpetually bemused.

"This is not a business transaction," said the smiling man. "You petitioned me, and I'm the answer to your prayers."

The vocabulary with which he discussed his work might have been an indication of caution, a technique to avoid incriminating himself.

When delivered with a persistent smile, however, his genteel euphemisms were disquieting if not in fact creepy.

As Tim opened the manila envelope, the killer warned, "Not here."

"Just chill." Tim removed the photo from the envelope, folded it, and put it in his shirt pocket. "I've had a change of heart."

"I'm sorry to hear that. I was counting on you."

Sliding the envelope in front of the empty stool that stood between them, Tim said, "Half of what we agreed. For doing nothing. Call it a no-kill fee."

"You'd never be tied to it," the killer said.

"I know. You're good. I'm sure you're good at this. The best. I just don't want it anymore."

Smiling, shaking his head, the killer said, "You want it, all right."

"Not anymore."

"You wanted it once. You don't go as far as wanting it and then not want it anymore. A man's mind doesn't work that way."

"Second thoughts," said Tim.

"In a thing like this, the second thoughts always come **after** a man gets what he wants. He allows himself some remorse, so he feels better about himself. He got what he wanted and he feels good about himself, and a year from now it's just a sad thing that happened."

The brown-eyed stare disturbed, but Tim dared not look away. A lack of directness might inspire in the killer a sudden suspicion.

One reason those eyes were compelling became clear. The pupils were radically dilated. The black pool at the center of each iris appeared to equal the area of surrounding color.

The light at this end of the bar was reduced but not dim. The pupils were as dilated as they might have been in perfect darkness.

The hunger in his eyes, the greed for light, had the gravity of a black hole in space, of a collapsed star.

A blind man's eyes might be perpetually dilated like this. But the killer was not blind, not blind to light, although perhaps to something else.

"Take the money," Tim said.

That smile. "It's **half** the money."

"For doing nothing."

"Oh, I've done some work."

Tim frowned. "What have you done?"

"I've shown you what you are."

"Yeah? What am I?"

"A man with the soul of a murderer but with the heart of a coward."

The killer picked up the envelope, rose from the stool, and walked away.

Having successfully passed himself off as the man with a dog named Larry, having for the moment spared the life of the woman in the photograph, having avoided the violent confrontation that could have ensued if the killer had realized what had gone wrong, Tim ought to have been relieved. Instead, his throat tightened, and his heart swelled until it seemed to crowd his lungs and crimp his breath.

A brief dizziness made him feel as if he were spinning slowly on the bar stool. Vertigo threatened to revolve into nausea.

He realized that relief eluded him because this incident was not at an end. He didn't need tea leaves to read his future. He clearly foresaw the prospects for tragedy.

With only a glance at any stone courtyard or driveway, he could name the pattern of the pavement: running bond, offset bond, coursed ashlar, basket weave, Flemish bond. . . . The pattern of the road before him was chaos. He could not know where it would lead.

The killer walked with a light step that

could be achieved only by someone not weighed down with a conscience, and went out into the night's embrace.

Tim hurried across the tavern, cautiously cracked the door, and peered outside.

Behind the steering wheel of a white sedan parked at an angle to the curb, half veiled by a windshield that reflected the tavern's blue-neon sign, sat the smiling man. He riffled the packet of hundred-dollar bills.

Tim withdrew his slim cell phone from his shirt pocket.

In the car, the killer rolled down a window. He hung an object on the glass and cranked up the window to hold it in place.

Blindly feeling his way across the cell-phone keypad without looking at it, Tim began to dial 911.

The object pinched between the window frame and the glass was a detachable emergency beacon, which began to flash as the car reversed away from the curb.

"Cop," Tim whispered, and hesitated to dial the second 1.

He risked stepping outside as the sedan pulled away from the tavern, and he read the license-plate number on the back of the dwindling vehicle.

The concrete underfoot seemed to have no more surface tension than the skin of water on a pond. Sometimes a skating mayfly, eluding birds and bats, is taken by a hungry bass rising from below.

Three

In the downfall of golden light from the dragon lamp, a simple iron railing guarded the rising concrete steps. The concrete had been worked with a screed when it was bleeding, and as a consequence, some edges had scaled badly; some treads were as crazed as crackle-glazed pottery.

Like a lot of things in life, concrete is unforgiving.

Through four framed panels, the copper dragon, still bright but greening at the edges, serpentined against a luminous backdrop of lacquered mica lenses.

In the wash of ruddy light, the aluminum screen door appeared to be copper, too. Behind it, the inner door stood open to a kitchen rich with the aromas of cinnamon and strong coffee.

Sitting at the table, Michelle Rooney

looked up as Tim arrived. "You're so quiet that I **felt** you coming."

He eased the screen door shut behind him. "I almost know what that means."

"The night outside quieted around you, the way a jungle does when a man passes through."

"Didn't see any crocodiles," he said, but then thought of the man to whom he had given the ten thousand dollars.

He sat across from her at the pale-blue Formica-topped table and studied the drawing on which she worked. It was upside-down from his point of view.

Out of the jukebox in the tavern downstairs rose the muffled but lovely voice of Martina McBride.

When Tim recognized the drawing as a panorama of silhouetted trees, he said, "What's it going to be?"

"A table lamp. Bronze and stained glass."

"You'll be famous someday, Michelle."

"I'd stop right now if I thought so."

He looked at her left hand, which lay palm-up on the counter near the refrigerator.

"Want a cup?" she asked, indicating the coffeemaker near the cooktop. "It's fresh."

"Looks like something you wrung out of a squid."

"Who in his right mind wants to sleep?"

He poured a mugful and returned with it to the table.

As was true of many other chairs, this one seemed like toy furniture to him. Michelle was petite, and the same kind of chair appeared large under her, yet Tim was the one who felt as if he were a child playing at coffee klatch.

This perception had less to do with chairs than with Michelle. Sometimes, all unaware, she made him feel like an awkward boy.

She finessed the pencil with her right hand, holding the drawing tablet steady with the stump of her left forearm.

"ETA on the coffeecake," she said, nodding toward the oven, "is ten minutes."

"Smells good, but I can't stay."

"Don't pretend you've gotten a life."

A shadow danced across the table. Tim looked up. A yellow butterfly fluttered at the silvered hooves of the leaping bronze gazelles in a small chandelier by Michelle.

"It slipped in this afternoon," she said. "For a while I left the door open, tried to chase it out, but it seems at home here."

"Why wouldn't it be?"

A tree branch whispered into existence between the pencil point and the paper.

"How did you make it up the stairs, carrying all that?" Michelle asked.

"All what?"

"Whatever it is that has you so weighed down."

The table was the blue of a pale sky, and the shadow seemed to glide behind it, a graceful mystery.

"I won't be coming around for a while," he said.

"What do you mean?"

"A few weeks, maybe a month."

"I don't understand."

"There's this thing I have to take care of."

The butterfly found a perch and closed its wings. As though the shadow were the quivering dark reflection of a burning candle, it vanished as suddenly as a flame from a pinched wick.

"'This thing,'" she echoed. Her pencil fell silent on the paper.

When his attention rose from the table to Michelle, he found her staring at him. Her eyes were a matched blue and equally convincing.

"If a man comes around with a description of me, looking for a name, just say the description doesn't ring a bell with you."

"What man?"

"Any man. Whoever. Liam will say, 'Big

guy on the end stool? Never saw him before. Kind of a smart-ass. Didn't like him.'"

"Liam knows what this is about?"

Tim shrugged. He had told Liam no more than he intended to tell Michelle. "Nothing much. It's about a woman, that's all."

"This guy who comes around to the bar, why would he also come up here?"

"Maybe he won't. But he's probably thorough. Anyway, you might be down in the bar when he comes around."

Her left eye, the artificial one, the blind one, seemed to pierce him more thoroughly than did her right eye, as if it were possessed of major mojo.

"It's not about a woman," she said.

"It really is."

"Not the way you're implying. This is trouble."

"Not trouble. Just embarrassing."

"No. You'll never embarrass yourself. Or a friend."

He looked for the butterfly and saw it perched on the chain from which hung the gazelle chandelier, slowly flexing its wings in the warm air rising from the incandescent bulbs.

"You don't have the right," she said, "to go it alone, whatever it is."

"You're making too much of this," he assured her. "It's just an embarrassing personal thing. I'll deal with it."

They sat in the silence of the stilled pencil, no music on the jukebox in the tavern below, no sound issuing from the throat of the night at the screen door.

Then she said, "What are you now—a lepidopterist?"

"Don't even know what that is."

"A butterfly collector. Try looking at me."

He lowered his gaze from the butterfly.

Michelle said, "I've been making a lamp for you."

He glanced at the drawing of stylized trees.

"Not this. Another one. It's already under way."

"What's it like?"

"It'll be done by the end of the month. You'll see it then."

"All right."

"Come back and see it then."

"I will. I'll come back for it."

"Come back for it," she said, and reached out to him with the stump of her left arm.

She seemed to hold tight to him, as if with ghost fingers, and she kissed the back of his hand.

"Thank you for Liam," she said softly.

"God gave you Liam, not me."

"Thank you for Liam," she insisted.

Tim kissed the top of her bent head. "I wish I had a sister, and I wish she was you. But you've got this trouble thing all wrong."

"No lies," she said. "Evasions, if it has to be that way, but no lies. You're not a liar, and I'm not a fool."

She raised her head and met his eyes.

"All right," he said.

"Don't I know bad trouble when I see it?"

"Yes," he acknowledged. "Yes, you know it."

"The coffeecake must be nearly done."

He glanced at the prosthesis on the counter by the refrigerator, palm turned up, fingers relaxed. "I'll get it from the oven for you."

"I can manage. I never wear the hand when I'm baking. If it burned, I wouldn't feel it."

Using oven mitts, she transferred the cake to a cooling rack.

By the time Michelle took off the mitts and turned from the cake, Tim had moved to the door.

"I'll look forward to seeing the lamp," he said.

Because her lacrimal glands and tear ducts had not been damaged, both her living eye and the dead one glimmered.

Tim stepped onto the landing at the head of the stairs, but before he let the screen door fall shut behind him, Michelle said, "It's lions."

"What?"

"The lamp. It's lions."

"I bet it'll be terrific."

"If I do it right, you'll get a sense of their great hearts, their courage."

He closed the screen door and descended the steps, seeming to make no noise on the scaling concrete.

Gliding by in the street, the traffic surely was not quiet, but Tim remained deaf to its chorus. Headlights approached and taillights receded like luminous fish in the silence of an oceanic abyss.

As he neared the bottom of the steps, the noise of the city began to rise to him, softly at first, but then loud, louder. The sounds were mostly made by machines, yet they had a savage rhythm.

Four

The woman marked for death lived in a modest bungalow in the hills of Laguna Beach, on a street that lacked a money view but that was being gentrified nonetheless. Compared to the aging structures, the land under them had such value that every house sold would be torn down regardless of its condition and its charm, to make way for a larger residence.

Southern California was shedding all its yesterdays. When the future proved to be a cruel place, no evidence of a better past would exist, and therefore the loss would be less painful.

The small white house, huddled under tall eucalyptuses, had plenty of charm, but to Tim the place looked embattled, more bunker than bungalow.

Lamplight warmed the windows. Sheer curtains made mysteries of the rooms beyond.

He parked his Ford Explorer across the street from—and four doors north of—Linda Paquette's property, at another house.

Tim knew this place: three years old, in the Craftsman style, with stacked stone and cedar siding. He had been the head mason on the job.

The walkway was random flagstone bordered by a double row of three-inch-square cobbles. Tim found this combination unattractive; but he had executed it with care and precision.

Owners of three-million-dollar homes seldom ask masons for design advice. Architects never do.

He pressed the doorbell once and stood listening to the faint susurration of the palm trees.

The offshore flow was less a breeze than a premonition of a breeze. The mild May night breathed as shallowly as an anesthetized patient waiting for the surgeon.

The porch light came on, the door opened, and Max Jabowski said, "Timothy, old bear! What a surprise."

If spirit could be weighed and measured, Max would have proved to be bigger than his house.

"Come in, come in."

"I don't want to intrude," Tim said.

"Nonsense. How could you intrude in a place you built?"

Having clasped Tim's shoulder, Max seemed to transfer him from porch to foyer by some power of levitation.

"I only need a minute of your time, sir."

"Can I get you a beer, something?"

"No, thank you, I'm all right. It's about a neighbor of yours."

"I know them all, this block and the next. I'm president of our Neighborhood Watch."

Tim had expected as much.

"Coffee? I have one of those machines that makes it a cup at a time, anything from cappuccino to plain old plain old."

"No, really, but that's very kind, sir. She lives at fourteen twenty-five, the bungalow among the eucalyptuses."

"Linda Paquette. I didn't know she was going to build. She seems like a solid person. I think you'd enjoy working with her."

"Do you know her husband, what he does?"

"She isn't married. She lives there alone."

"So she's divorced?"

"Not that I'm aware. Is she going to tear down or remodel?"

"It's nothing like that," Tim said. "It's a personal matter. I was hoping you'd speak to her about me, let her know I'm okay."

The bushy eyebrows rose, and the rubbery lips stretched into an arc of delight. "I've been a lot of things, but never before a matchmaker."

Although he should have foreseen this interpretation of his questions, Tim was surprised by it. He hadn't dated anyone in a long time. He had assumed that he'd lost the telltale glint of eye and had stopped producing whatever subtle pheromones might have allowed him to be mistaken for a man still in the game.

"No, no. It's not that."

"She's easy on the eyes," said Max.

"Truly, it's not that. I don't know her, she doesn't know me, but we have a . . . mutual acquaintance. I have some news about him. I think she'll want to know it."

The rubbery smile loosened only a little. Max didn't want to let go of the image of himself as a facilitator of true romance.

Everyone, Tim thought, had seen too many movies. They believed that a meet-cute relationship awaited every good heart. Because of movies, they believed a lot of other improbable things, as well, some of them dangerous.

"It's a sad business," Tim said. "Some depressing news."

"About your mutual acquaintance."

"Yes. He's not a well man."

This could not be counted as a lie. The skydiver was not physically ill, but his mental condition was suspect; and his moral health had fallen to disease.

Consideration of death relaxed all the delight out of Max Jabowski's smile. His mouth shrank to a grim shape, and he nodded.

Tim expected to be asked the name of the mutual acquaintance. He would have had to say that he didn't want to provide it for fear of alarming the woman before he could be at her side to comfort her.

The fuller truth was that he had no name to give.

Max did not ask for a name, sparing Tim from resorting to that deception. Bushy brows beetling now over solemn eyes, he once more offered coffee, and then went away to call the woman.

The coffered ceiling and wood-paneled walls of the foyer were dark, and the limestone floor was so light, by contrast, that the support it provided seemed illusory, as if he might at any moment fall through it like a man stepping out of a plane in flight.

Two small chairs flanked a console, above which hung a mirror.

He did not look at his reflection. If he met his eyes, he would see the hard truth from which he preferred to remain diverted.

Directly met, his gaze would tell him what was coming. It was the same thing that was always coming toward him, that always would be, as long as he was alive.

He needed to prepare for it. He did not need, however, to dwell on it.

From elsewhere in the house arose Max's muted voice as he spoke on the phone.

Here at the center of the foyer, Tim stood straight, and felt as if he were suspended from the dark ceiling, like a clapper in a bell, with empty air below him, in silent anticipation of a sudden tolling.

Max returned and said, "She's curious. I didn't say much, just vouched for you."

"Thanks. I'm sorry to have bothered you."

"It isn't any bother, but it is kind of peculiar."

"Yes, it is. I know."

"Why didn't your friend call Linda and vouch for you himself? He wouldn't have to tell her why he's sending you around—the bad news."

"He's very ill and very confused," said Tim. "He knows the right thing to do, but he doesn't any longer know how to do it."

"That's maybe the thing I fear the most," said Max. "The mind going, the loss of control."

"It's life," Tim said. "We all get through it."

They shook hands, and Max walked him out onto the porch. "She's a nice woman. I hope this won't be too painful."

"I'll do my best for her," Tim said.

He returned to his Explorer and drove to Linda Paquette's bungalow.

The herringbone brick of the front walkway had been laid on a bed of sand. The air was fragrant with eucalyptus essence, and dry leaves crunched underfoot.

Step by step, urgency overcame him. Time seemed to quicken, and he sensed trouble coming sooner rather than later.

As he climbed the front steps, the door opened, and she greeted him. "Are you Tim?"

"Yes. Ms. Paquette?"

"Call me Linda."

In the porch light, her eyes were Egyptian green.

She said, “Your mama must have had a hard nine months carrying all of you around.”

“I was smaller then.”

Stepping back from the door, she said, “Duck your head and come on in.”

He crossed the threshold, and after that nothing was ever the same for him.

Five

Golden honey poured wall to wall, a wood floor so lustrous and warm that the humble living room appeared spacious, quietly grand.

Built in the 1930s, the bungalow had either been meticulously maintained or restored. The small fireplace and flanking wall sconces were simple but elegant examples of Art Deco style.

The glossy white tongue-and-groove ceiling lowered over Tim, but not unpleasantly. The place felt cozy instead of claustrophobic.

Linda had a lot of books. With one exception, their spines were the only art in the room, an abstract tapestry of words and colors.

The exception was a six-by-four-foot image of a television with a blank gray screen.

"Modern art baffles me," Tim said.

"That's not art. I had it done at a photo shop. To remind me why I don't own a TV."

"Why don't you?"

"Because life is too short."

Tim gave the photo a chance, then said, "I don't understand."

"Eventually you will. A head as big as yours has to have some brains in it."

He wasn't sure if her manner indicated a breezy kind of charm or a flippancy bordering on rudeness.

Or she might be a little screwy. Lots of people were these days.

"Linda, the reason I'm here—"

"Come along. I'm working in the kitchen." Leading him across the living room, she said over her shoulder, "Max assured me you're not the type to stab me in the back and rape my corpse."

"I ask him to vouch for me, and that's what he tells you?"

As he followed her along a hallway, she said, "He told me you were a talented mason and an honest man. I had to squeeze the rest of it out of him. He really didn't want to commit to an opinion about your possible homicidal and necrophilic tendencies."

A car was parked in the kitchen.

The wall between the kitchen and the two-car garage had been removed. The wood floor had been extended throughout the garage, as had the glossy white tongue-and-groove ceiling.

Three precisely focused pin spots showcased a black 1939 Ford.

"Your kitchen is in the garage," he said.

"No, no. My garage is in my kitchen."

"What's the difference?"

"Huge. I'm having coffee. You want some? Cream? Sugar?"

"Black, please. Why is your car in your kitchen?"

"I like to look at it while I'm eating. Isn't it beautiful? The 1939 Ford coupe is the most beautiful car ever made."

"I'm not going to argue for the Pinto."

Pouring coffee into a mug, she said, "It's not a classic. It's a hot rod. Chopped, channeled, fully sparkled out with cool details."

"You worked on it yourself?"

"Some. Mostly a guy up in Sacramento, he's a genius at this."

"Had to cost a bunch."

She served the coffee. "Should I be saving for the future?"

"What future did you have in mind?"

"If I could answer that, maybe I'd open a savings account."

His mug had a ceramic parrot for a handle, and bore the words BALBOA ISLAND. It looked old, like a souvenir from the 1930s.

Her mug was doubly a mug, in that it was also a ceramic head of President Franklin Delano Roosevelt biting on his famous cigarette holder.

She moved to the '39 Ford. "This is what I live for."

"You live for a car?"

"It's a hope machine. Or a time machine that takes you back to an age when people found it easier to hope."

On the floor, on a drip pan, stood a bottle of chrome polish and a few rags. The bumpers, grill, and trim glimmered like quicksilver.

She opened the driver's door and, with her coffee, got behind the steering wheel. "Let's go for a ride."

"I really need to talk to you about something."

"A virtual ride. Just a mind trip."

When she pulled the door shut, Tim went around the coupe and got in through the passenger's door.

Because of the chopped roof, headroom

was inadequate for a tall man. Tim slid down in his seat, holding the parrot mug in both hands.

In that cramped interior, he still loomed over the woman as though she were an elf and he a troll.

Instead of mohair upholstery, common to the 1930s, he sat on black leather. Gauges gleamed in a checked-steel dashboard billet.

Beyond the windshield lay the kitchen. Surreal.

The keys were in the ignition, but Linda didn't switch on the engine for this virtual ride. Maybe when her mug was empty, she would fire up the Ford and drive over to the coffee brewer near the oven.

She smiled at him. "Isn't this nice?"

"It's like being at a drive-in theater, watching a movie about a kitchen."

"The drive-in theaters have been gone for years. Don't you think that's like tearing down the Colosseum in Rome to build a mall?"

"Maybe not entirely like."

"Yeah, you're right. There never was a drive-in theater where they fed Christians to lions. So what did you want to see me about?"

The coffee was excellent. He sipped it, blew on it, and sipped some more, wondering how best to explain his mission.

Crunching through dry eucalyptus leaves on the front walk, he had known how he would tell her. When he met her, however, she was different from anyone he expected. His planned approach seemed wrong.

He knew little about Linda Paquette, but he sensed that she did not need to have her hand held while receiving bad news, that in fact too much concern might strike her as condescension.

Opting for directness, he said, "Somebody wants you dead."

She smiled again. "What's the gag?"

"He's paying twenty thousand to get it done."

She remained puzzled. "Dead in what sense?"

"Dead in the sense of shot in the head, dead forever."

Succinctly, he told her about the events at the tavern: first being mistaken for the killer, then being mistaken for the man hiring the killer, then discovering that the killer was a cop.

She listened open-mouthed at first, but her astonishment faded rapidly. Her green eyes clouded, as if his words stirred long-settled sediment in those previously limpid pools.

When Tim finished, the woman sat in silence, sipping coffee, staring through the windshield.

He waited, but finally grew uneasy. "You do believe me?"

"I've known a lot of liars. You don't sound like any of them."

The pin spots, in which the car gleamed but also darkled, did not much brighten the interior. Though her face was softly shadowed, her eyes found light and gave it back.

He said, "You don't seem surprised by what I've told you."

"No."

"So . . . then you know who he is, the one who wants you dead?"

"Not a clue."

"An ex-husband? A boyfriend?"

"I've never been married. No boyfriend at the moment, and I never did have a crazy one."

"A dispute with someone at work?"

"I'm self-employed. I work at home."

"What do you do?"

"I've been asking myself that a lot lately," she said. "What did this guy look like, the one who gave you the money?"

The description didn't electrify her. She shook her head.

Tim said, "He has a dog named Larry. He once went sky-diving with the dog. He had a brother named Larry, died at sixteen."

"A guy capable of naming his dog after his dead brother—I'd know who he was even if he'd never told me about Larry or Larry."

This was not playing out in any way that Tim had imagined it might. "But the skydiver can't be a stranger."

"Why not?"

"Because he wants you dead."

"People are killed by strangers all the time."

"But nobody **hires** someone to kill a perfect stranger." He fished the folded photograph from his shirt pocket. "Where did he get this?"

"It's my driver's-license picture."

"So he's someone with access to the DMV digital-photo files."

She returned the photograph. Tim put it in his shirt pocket again before he realized that it belonged to her more than to him.

He said, "You don't know anyone who'd want you dead—yet you aren't surprised."

"There are people who want **everybody** dead. When you get over being surprised about that, you have a high amazement threshold."

Direct, intense, her green gaze seemed to fillet his serried thoughts and to fold them aside like layers of dissected tissue, yet somehow it was an inviting rather than a cold stare.

"I'm curious," she said, "about the way you've handled this."

Taking her comment as disapproval or suspicion, he said, "I'm not aware of any other options."

"You could have kept the ten thousand for yourself."

"Somebody would have come looking for me."

"Maybe not. Now . . . for sure someone will. You could have just passed my photo to the killer, with the money, and done a fade, got out of the way and let things unfold as they would have done if you'd never been there."

"And then . . . where would I go?"

"To dinner. To a movie. Home to bed."

"Is that what you'd have done?" he asked.

"I don't interest me. You interest me."

"I'm not an interesting guy."

"Not the way you present yourself, no. What you're hiding is what makes you interesting."

"I've told you everything."

"About what happened in the bar. But . . . about you?"

The rearview mirror was angled toward him. He had avoided his eyes by meeting hers. Now he looked at his narrow reflection, and at once away, down at the ceramic parrot choked in his right hand.

"My coffee's cold," he said.

"Mine, too. When the killer left the tavern, you could have called the police."

"Not after I saw he was a cop."

"The tavern's in Huntington Beach. I'm in Laguna Beach. He's a cop in a different jurisdiction."

"I don't know his jurisdiction. The car was an unmarked sedan. He could be a Laguna Beach cop for all I know."

"So. Now what, Tim?"

He needed to look at her and he dreaded looking at her, and he didn't know why or how, within minutes of their meeting, she should have become the focus of either need or dread. He had never felt like this before, and although a thousand songs and movies had programmed him to call it love, he knew it wasn't love. He wasn't a man who fell in love at first sight. Besides, love didn't have such an element of mortal terror as was a part of this feeling.

He said, "The only evidence I have to give the cops is the photo of you, but that's no evidence at all."

"The license number of the unmarked sedan," she reminded him.

"That's not evidence. It's just a lead. I know someone who might be able to trace it for me and get me the driver's name. Someone I can trust."

"Then what?"

"I don't know yet. I'll figure something."

Her gaze, which had not turned from him, had the gravitational force of twin moons, and inevitably the tide of his attention was pulled toward her.

Eye to eye again with her, he told himself to remember this moment, this tightening knot of terror that was also a loosening knot of wild exaltation, for when he realized the name for it, he would understand why he was suddenly walking out of the life he had known—and had sought—into a new life that he could not know and that he might come desperately to regret.

"You should leave this house tonight," he said. "Stay somewhere you've never been before. Not with a friend or relative."

"You think the killer's coming?"

"Tomorrow, the next day, sooner or later, when he and the guy who hired him realize what happened."

She didn't appear to be afraid. "All right," she said.

Her equanimity perplexed him.

His cell phone rang.

After Linda took his coffee mug, he answered the call.

Liam Rooney said, "He was just here, asking who was the big guy on the last stool."

"Already. Damn. I figured a day or two. Was it the first or second guy?"

"The second. I took a closer look at him this time. Tim, he's a freak. He's a shark in shoes."

Tim remembered the killer's persistent dreamy smile, the dilated eyes hungry for light.

"What's going on?" Liam asked.

"It's about a woman," Tim said, as he had said before. "I'll take care of it."

In retrospect, the killer had realized that something about the encounter in the tavern had not been right. He had probably called a contact number for the skydiver.

Through the windshield, the kitchen looked warm and cozy. On a wall hung a rack of cutlery.

"You can't freeze me out like this," said Rooney.

"I'm not thinking about you," Tim said, opening the door and getting out of the coupe. "I'm thinking about Michelle. Keep your neck out of this—for her."

Carrying both coffee mugs, Linda exited the Ford from the driver's door.

"Exactly how long ago did the guy leave?" Tim asked Rooney.

"I waited maybe five minutes before calling you—in case he might come back and see me on the phone, and wonder. He looks like a guy who always puts two and two together."

"Gotta go," Tim said, pressed END, and pocketed the phone.

As Linda took the mugs to the sink, Tim selected a knife from the wall rack. He passed over the butcher knife for a shorter and pointier blade.

The Pacific Coast Highway offered the most direct route from the Lamplighter Tavern to this street in Laguna Beach. Even on a Monday evening, traffic could be unpredictable. Door to door, the trip might take forty minutes.

In addition to a detachable emergency beacon, maybe the unmarked sedan had a siren. In the last few miles of approach, the siren would not be used; they would never hear the killer coming.

Turning away from the sink, Linda saw the knife in Tim's fist. She did not misinterpret the moment or need an explanation.

She said, "How long do we have?"

"Can you pack a suitcase in five minutes?"

"Quicker."

"Do it."

She glanced at the '39 Ford.

"It's too attention-getting," Tim said. "You should leave it."

"It's my only car."

"I'll take you wherever you want to go."

Her green gaze was as sharp as a shard of bottle glass. "What's in this for you? Now you've told me, you could split."

"This guy—he'll want to waste me, too. If he gets my name."

"And you think I'll spill it, when he finds me."

"Whether you spill it or not, he'll get it. I need to know who he is, but more important, I need to know who hired him. Maybe when you've had more time to think about it, you'll figure it out."

She shook her head. "There's nobody. If the only thing in this for you is the chance I'll figure who wants me dead, then there's nothing in this for you."

"There's something," he disagreed. "Come on, pack what you need."

She glanced at the '39 Ford again. "I'll be back for it."

"When this is done."

"I'm going to drive it all over, to wherever there's something left from those days, something you can still see that they haven't torn down yet or desecrated."

Tim said, "The good old days."

"They were good and they were bad. But they were different." She hurried away to pack.

Tim turned off the kitchen lights. He went down the hall to the living room, and he switched off those lights, too.

At a window, he pulled back a sheer curtain and stood watching a scene that had gone as still as a miniature village in a glass paperweight.

He, too, had been glassed-in for a long time, by choice. Now and then he had lifted a hammer to shatter through to something, but he had never struck the blow because he didn't know what he wanted on the other side of the glass.

Having strayed from a nearby canyon, perhaps emboldened by the round risen moon, a coyote climbed the gently sloping street. When it passed through lamplight, its eyes shone silver as if cataracted, but in shadows its gaze was luminous and red, and blind to nothing.

Six

As if following the spoor of the now vanished coyote, Tim drove north. He turned left at the stop sign and headed downhill toward the Pacific Coast Highway.

He repeatedly checked the rearview mirror. No one followed them.

"Where do you want to stay?" he asked.

"I'll figure that out later."

Still in blue jeans and a midnight-blue sweater, she had added a camel-colored corduroy jacket. She held her purse on her lap, and her carryall was in the backseat.

"Later when?"

"After we've seen the guy you can trust, the one who can trace that license-plate number."

"I figured to go to him alone."

"Aren't I presentable?"

She was not as pretty as she had been in the photo, yet she struck him as somehow better looking. Her hair, such a dark brown that it seemed black, had been shorter than this, and calculatedly shaggy, when she had stood before the DMV camera.

"Totally presentable," he assured her. "But with you there, he'll be uneasy. He'll want to know more of what it's about."

"So we tell him whatever sounds good."

"This isn't a guy that I lie to."

"Is there one?"

"One what?"

"Never mind. Leave it to me. I'll shine him up something he'll like."

"Not you, either," Tim said. "We walk the line with this guy."

"Who is he—your dad or something?"

"I owe him a lot. He's solid. Pedro Santo. Pete. He's a robbery-homicide detective."

"So we're going to the cops, after all?"

"Unofficially."

They headed north along the coast. Southbound traffic was light. A few cars rocketed past them in excess of the speed limit, but none featured an emergency beacon.

To the west, the house-crowded bluffs descended to unpopulated lowlands. Beyond coastal scrub and wide beaches, the Pacific folded the sky down to itself at a black horizon.

Under the night-light of the sentinel moon, ruffled hems of surf and a decorative stitching that fringed the incoming waves suggested billows of fancy bedding under which the sea turned restlessly in sleep.

After a silence, Linda said, "The thing is, I don't much like cops."

She stared forward at the highway, but in the wash of headlights from approaching traffic, her unblinking eyes seemed to be focused on some other scene.

He waited for her to continue, but when she lapsed into silence again, he said, "Is there something I should know? Have you been in trouble sometime?"

She blinked. "Not me. I'm as straight as a new nail that never met a hammer."

"Why does that sound to me like there was a hammer, maybe a lot of hammers, but you didn't bend?"

"I don't know. I don't know why it sounds that way to you. Maybe you're always inferring hidden meaning when none is implied."

"I'm just a bricklayer."

"Most car mechanics I know—they think deeper than any college professor I've ever met.

They have to. They live in the real world. A lot of masons must be the same."

"There's a reason we call ourselves **stoneheads.**"

She smiled. "Nice try."

At Newport Coast Road, he turned right and headed inland. The land rose ahead, and behind them the sea was pressed down under a growing weight of night.

"I know this carpenter," she said, "who loves metaphors because he thinks life itself is a metaphor, with mystery and hidden meaning in every moment. You know what a metaphor is?"

He said, "'My heart is a lonely hunter that hunts on a lonely hill.'"

"Not bad for a stonehead."

"It's not mine. I heard it somewhere."

"You remember where. The way you said it, you remember. Anyway, if this Santo is sharp, he'll know I don't like cops."

"He's sharp. But there's nothing not to like about him."

"I'm sure he's a great guy. It's not his fault if sometimes the law has no humility."

Tim sifted those words a few times but was left with no meaning in his net.

"Maybe your friend is a boy scout with a

badge," she said, "but cops spook me. And not just cops."

"Want to tell me what this is about?"

"It's not about anything. It's just the way I am."

"We need help, and Pete Santo can give it."

"I know. I'm just saying."

When they topped the last of a series of hills, inland Orange County shimmered below them, a great panoply of millions of lights, a challenge to the stars, which were dimmed by this dazzle.

She said, "It seems so formidable, so solid, so enduring."

"What does?"

"Civilization. But it's as fragile as glass." She glanced at him. "I better shut up. You're starting to think I'm a nut case."

"No," Tim said. "Glass makes sense to me. Glass makes perfect sense."

They traveled miles without speaking, and after a while he realized that theirs had become a comfortable silence. The night beyond the windows was an oblivion machine waiting to be triggered, but here in the Explorer, a kind of peace took temporary residence in his heart, and he felt that something good could happen, even something fine.

Seven

After walking through the entire bungalow, boldly turning on lights as he went, Krait returned to the bedroom.

The inexpensive white chenille bedspread was as smooth as the bedding of a military man. Not one tangle spoiled the fringed hem.

Krait had been in houses where the beds were unmade and the sheets were too seldom changed. Sloppiness offended him.

If a gun were allowed, an untidy person could be killed from a distance of at least a few feet. Then it mattered less that the target didn't change underwear every day.

Often, however, the contract specified strangulation, stabbing, bludgeoning, or another more intimate method of execution. If the victim turned out to be a slob, a potentially enjoyable task could become a distasteful chore.

When a person was being garroted from behind, for instance, he would in desperation attempt to reach back and blind his assailant. You could easily keep your eyes safe, but the victim might pull at your cheek, grip your chin, brush fingers across your lips, and if you suspected he was the type who didn't always wash his hands after using the men's room, you sometimes wondered if the good pay and the many benefits of your job really outweighed the negatives.

Linda Paquette's closet was small and orderly. She didn't have a lot of clothes.

Krait liked the simplicity of her wardrobe. He himself had always been a person of simple tastes.

From the shelf above the hanging garments, he took down a few boxes. None of them contained anything enlightening.

Curiosity about his target was forbidden. He wasn't supposed to know any more about her than her name, address, and appearance.

Usually he would respect such a criterion in an assignment. The events at the tavern, however, required new rules for this project.

He hoped to find snapshots of family and friends, high-school yearbooks, mementos of holiday travels and of faded romances. No photographs stood on the dust-free dresser or on the nicely polished nightstands, either.

She seemed to have cut herself loose from her past. Krait did not know why she had done so, but he approved. He could deal more easily with people who were adrift, and alone.

He had been expected to stage the incident to look like a break-in, rape her, then kill her in some fashion that would encourage the police to believe he had been nothing more than a sexual psychopath and that she had been a randomly chosen victim.

The details of such a killing were invariably left to him. He had a genius for creating tableaus that convinced the best police profilers.

At the dresser, he opened drawers, searching for the photos and the revealing personal items that he had not discovered in the closet.

In spite of being forbidden, curiosity had infected Krait. He wanted to know why the big guy in the bar had played spoiler. What about the woman had encouraged the barfly to take such risks?

Krait's work was usually cut-and-dried. A lesser man, incapable of enjoying the subtle nuances of this profession, would have been bored after a few years. Krait found his work satisfying, in part because of the comforting sameness of his assignments.

After cleanliness, familiarity was the quality that Krait valued most highly in any experience. When he found a film that he enjoyed, he would watch it once or twice a month, sometimes twice in an evening. Often he ate the same dinner every night for a week or two.

For all their variety of appearance, people were as predictable as the plot turns in a film that he had committed to heart. A man whom Krait admired had once said that human beings were sheep, and in most matters, that was true.

In Krait's experience, however, as regarded his most intimate work with the species, human beings were inferior to sheep. Sheep were docile, yes, but vigilant. Unlike many people, sheep were always aware that predators existed and were alert for the scent and the schemes of wolves.

Contemporary Americans were so prosperous, so happily distracted by such a richness of vivid entertainments, they were reluctant to have their fun diminished by acknowledging that anything existed with fangs and fierce appetites. If now and then they recognized a wolf, they threw a bone to it and convinced themselves that it was a dog.

They denied real threats by focusing their fear on the least likely of armageddons: a massive asteroid striking the earth, superhurricanes twice as big as Texas, the Y2K implosion of civilization, nuclear power plants melting holes all the way through the planet, a new Hitler suddenly rising from the ranks of hapless televangelists with bad hair.

Krait found people to be less like sheep than like cattle. He moved among them as if invisible. They grazed dreamily, confident in the security of the herd, even as he butchered them one by one.

His work was his pleasure, and he would have both in abundance until such a day as some more flamboyant murderer hurled fire at the herd, stampeding them by the tens of thousands over a cliff. Then the cattle might be wary, and for a while Krait would find his job more difficult.

He wanted to know more about the woman, Linda Paquette, because he hoped that through her he might learn about the man who had intervened to spare her from execution. Soon he would receive a name for that interloper, but he didn't have one yet.

In her dresser drawers he found only clothes, but they told him things about her. She had many socks in various colors but only two pairs of nylons. Her underwear were simple cotton, much like men's briefs, without lace or other frills.

The simplicity of these garments charmed him.

And they smelled so fresh. He wondered what detergent she used, and hoped it was a brand friendly to the environment.

After closing the last of the drawers, he regarded his face in the mirror above the dresser, and he liked what he saw. No flush had risen to his cheeks. His mouth was neither tight with tension nor loose with desire.

The reflection of a framed painting drew his attention from his face before he finished admiring himself. Smile faltering, he turned away from the mirror and toward the true image.

He should have noticed the painting immediately on entering the room. No other art adorned the walls, and the only decorative items on the pair of nightstands were a luminous clock and an old Motorola radio, both from the 1930s and made out of Bakelite.

He took no offense at the clock or the radio, but the painting—a cheap print—vexed him. He took it off the wall, smashed the glass on the footboard of the bed, and peeled the artwork from the frame.

After folding the print three times, he slipped it into an inner pocket of his sports coat. He would save it until he found the woman.

When he had stripped away her clothes and her defenses, he would shove the wadded poster down her throat, clamp her mouth shut, and insist that she swallow it, and when it proved too much to swallow, he would let her gag it up, only so that he could shove it somewhere else, and then somewhere else again, and shove other things, too, shove in anything he wanted, until she pleaded with him to kill her.

Unfortunately, he lived in an age when such measures were sometimes necessary.

Returning to the mirror, he liked what he saw, as before. Judging by his reflection, he possessed a blameless heart, and his thoughts were full of charity.

Appearances were important. Appearances were all that really mattered. And his work.

In her well-ordered bathroom vanity, he didn't find anything of interest except a brand of lip balm that he had never used.

Lately, humidity had been low, and his lips had been constantly chapped. The product that he usually relied upon had not helped much.

He smelled the balm and detected no offensive perfume, licked it and tasted an acceptably bland orange-cream flavor. He greased his lips, which at once felt cooler, and pocketed the tube.

In the living room, Krait pulled from the shelves some of the old hardcover books in the woman's collection. They had quaint but colorful jackets, and were all fiction by popular novelists of the 1920s and '30s: Earl Derr Biggers, Mary Roberts Rinehart, E. Phillips Oppenheim, J. B. Priestley, Frank Swinnerton. . . . With the exceptions of Somerset Maugham and P. G. Wodehouse, most were forgotten.

Krait might have taken a book that looked interesting, except that these authors were all dead. When he read a book that expressed inappropriate views, Krait sometimes felt obliged to search out the author and correct him. He never read books by dead authors because the satisfaction of a face-to-face discussion with a living wordsmith could not be equaled by exhumation and desecration of an author's corpse.

In the kitchen, he found two dirty coffee mugs in the sink. He stood for a while, considering them.

As neat as she was, Linda would not have left this mess unless she had an urgent reason to get out of the house. A companion had joined her for coffee. Perhaps the companion had convinced her that she dared not delay long enough to wash the mugs.

In addition to what the mugs suggested, Krait was interested in the one with the parrot handle. He found it charming. He washed it, dried it, and wrapped it in a dishtowel to take it with him.

A knife was missing from the rack of fine cutlery, and that was interesting, too.

From the refrigerator, he withdrew the remaining half of a cinnamon-dusted homemade egg-custard pie. He cut a generous slice for himself and put it on a plate. He put the plate on the kitchen table, with a fork.

He poured a cup of coffee from the pot that stood on the warming plate. The brew had not yet turned bitter. He laced it with milk.

Sitting at the table, he studied the '39 Ford while he ate the pie and drank the coffee. The egg custard was excellent. He would have to remember to compliment her on it.

As he finished the coffee, his cell phone vibrated. When he checked, he had received a text message.

Earlier, when Krait had returned to the Lamplighter Tavern, seeking the name of the big man on the end stool, the bartender had pleaded ignorance.

Five minutes after Krait left the joint, however, Liam Rooney had phoned someone. In this text message were the number that had been called and the name of the person to whom that telephone was registered—TIMOTHY CARRIER.

On screen appeared an address for Carrier, too, although Krait doubted that it would be of immediate use to him. If Carrier was the barfly and if he had hurried to Laguna Beach to warn the woman, he would not be witless enough to return home.

In addition to a name and address, Krait had wanted to know the occupation of this guy. Carrier was a licensed masonry contractor.

Krait stored the data, and the phone vibrated again. A photo of the mason appeared with megapixel clarity, and he was without doubt the man in the tavern.

In the wet of business, Krait worked alone, but he had awesome data and technical support.

He pocketed the phone without saving the photo. He might need to know more about Carrier, but not yet.

A final cup of coffee remained in the pot, and he sweetened the brew with a generous slug of milk. He drank it at the table.

In spite of the boldness with which the

kitchen and garage had been combined, the space was cozy.

He liked the entire bungalow, the clean simplicity of it. Anyone could live here, and you wouldn't know who he really was.

Sooner or later, it would come on the market. Acquiring the property of a person he had murdered would be too risky, but the thought pleased him.

Krait washed his cup, his plate, his fork, the coffeepot, and the FDR mug that had been used by either Linda or her guest. He dried them and put them away. He rinsed the stainless-steel sink, then wiped it dry with paper towels.

Just before he left, he went to the Ford, opened the driver's door, stepped back just far enough to avoid being splashed, unzipped his pants and urinated in the vehicle. This didn't please him, but it was necessary.

Eight

Pete Santo lived in a modest stucco house with a shy dog named Zoey and a dead fish named Lucille.

Handsomely stuffed and mounted, Lucille, a marlin, hung above the desk in the study.

Pete wasn't a fisherman. The marlin had come with the house when he bought it.

He had named it after his ex-wife, who had divorced him when, after two years of marriage, she realized that she couldn't change him. She wanted him to leave the police department, to become a real-estate agent, to dress with more style, and to have his scar fixed.

The marriage collapsed when she bought him a pair of tasseled loafers. He wouldn't wear them. She wouldn't return them to the store. He wouldn't allow them in his closet. She tried to put one of them down the garbage disposal. The Roto-Rooter bill was huge.

Now, as sharp-toothed Lucille peered down at him with one glaring gimlet eye, Pete Santo stood at his desk, watching as the Department of Motor Vehicles home page appeared on the computer screen. "If you can't tell **me** what it's about, who could you tell?"

Tim said, "Nobody. Not yet. Maybe in a day, two days, when things . . . clarify."

"What things?"

"The unclarified things."

"Oh. That's clear now. When the unclarified things clarify, then you can tell me."

"Maybe. Look, I know this might get your ass in a sling."

"That doesn't matter."

"Of course it matters," Tim said.

"Don't insult me. It doesn't matter." Pete sat at the computer. "If they bust me out of the department, I'll be a real-estate agent."

He entered his name, badge number, and access code, whereupon the Department of Motor Vehicles records surrendered to him as a nubile maiden to a lover.

Bashful Zoey, a black Lab, watched from

behind an armchair, while Linda dropped to one knee and, with cooing sounds and declarations of adoration, tried to coax the dog into the open.

Pete typed the license number that Tim had given him, and the DMV database revealed that the plates had been issued for a white Chevrolet registered not to any law-enforcement agency but to one Richard Lee Kravet.

"You know him?" Pete asked.

Tim shook his head. "Never heard of him. I thought the car would turn out to be a plain-wrap department sedan."

Surprised, Pete said, "This guy you want to know about—he's a cop? I'm scoping out a cop for you?"

"If he's a cop, he's a bad cop."

"Look at me here, what I'm doing for you, using police power for a private inquiry. **I'm** a bad cop."

"This guy, if he's a cop, he's seriously bad. At worst, Petey, by comparison, you're a naughty cop."

"Richard Lee Kravet. Don't know him. If he has a shield, I don't think it's one of ours."

Pete worked for the Newport Beach Police Department, but he lived in an unincorporated part of the county, nearer to Irvine than to Newport Beach, because even pre-divorce, he couldn't afford a house in the city that he served.

"Can you get me this guy's driver's license?" Tim asked.

"Yeah, why not, but when I'm a real-estate agent, I'm going to wear whatever shoes I want."

On her belly, Zoey had crawled halfway around the armchair. Her tail thumped the floor in response to Linda's coaxing.

The one small lamp left most of the room dusted with shadows, and the alchemic light from the monitor gave Pete a tin man's face, his smooth scar shining like a bad weld.

He was handsome enough that a half-inch-wide slash of pale tissue, curving from ear to chin, did not make him ugly. Plastic surgery would reduce or even eliminate his disfigurement, but he chose not to submit to the healing scalpel.

A scar is not always a flaw. Sometimes a scar may be redemption inscribed in the flesh, a memorial to something endured, to something lost.

The driver's license appeared on the screen. The photo was of the killer with the Mona Lisa smile.

When the printer produced a copy, Pete handed it to Tim.

According to the license, Kravet was thirty-six years old. His street address was in Anaheim.

Having rolled onto her back and put all four paws in the air, Zoey purred like a cat as she received a gentle tummy rub.

Tim still had no evidence of a murder-for-hire plot. Richard Kravet would deny every detail of their meeting in the tavern.

"Now what?" Pete asked.

As she charmed the dog, Linda looked up at Tim. Her green eyes, though remaining wells of mystery, floated to him the clear desire to keep the nature of their dilemma strictly between them, at least for the time being.

He had known Pete for more than eleven years, this woman for less than two hours, yet he chose the discretion for which she wordlessly pleaded.

"Thanks, Pete. You didn't need to climb out on this limb."

"That's where I'm most comfortable."

This was true. Pete Santo had always been a risk-taker, though never reckless.

As Linda rose from the dog, Pete said to her, "You and Tim known each other long?"

"Not long," she said.

"How'd you meet?"

"Over coffee."

"Like at Starbucks?"

"No, not there," she said.

"Paquette. That's an unusual name."

"Not in my family."

"It's lovely. P-a-c-k-e-t-t-e?"

She didn't confirm the spelling.

"So you're the strong silent type."

She smiled. "And you're always a detective."

Shy Zoey stayed close to Linda all the way to the front door.

From various points in the night yard, a hidden choir of toads harmonized.

Linda rubbed the dog gently behind the ears, kissed it on the head, and walked across the lawn to the Explorer in the driveway.

"She doesn't like me," Pete said.

"She likes you. She just doesn't like cops."

"If you marry her, do I have to change jobs?"

"I'm not going to marry her."

"I think she's the kind, you don't get a thing without a ring."

"I don't want a thing. There's nothing between us."

"There will be," Pete predicted. "She's got something."

"Something what?"

"I don't know. But it sure is something."

Tim watched Linda get into the Explorer. As she pulled the door shut behind her, he said, "She makes good coffee."

"I'll bet she does."

Although the secreted toads had continued singing when Linda had walked among them, they fell silent when Tim set foot on the grass.

"Class," Pete said. "That's part of the something." And when Tim had taken two further steps, Pete added, "Sangfroid."

Tim stopped, looked back at the detective. "Sang what?"

"Sangfroid. It's French. Self-possession, poise, steadiness."

"Since when do you know French?"

"This college professor, taught French literature, killed a girl with a chisel. Dismembered her with a stone-cutter."

"Stone-cutter?"

"He was also a sculptor. He almost got away with it 'cause he had such sangfroid. But I nailed him."

"I'm pretty sure Linda hasn't dismembered anyone."

"I'm just saying she's self-possessed. But if she ever wants to dismember **me**, I'm okay with that."

"Compadre, you disappoint me."

Pete grinned. "I knew there was something between you."

"There's nothing," Tim assured him, and went to the Explorer in a silence of toads.

Nine

As Tim reversed out of the driveway, Linda said, "He seems all right for a cop. He has a sweet pooch."

"He's also got a dead fish named for his ex-wife."

"Well, maybe she **was** a cold fish."

"He says he won't mind if you want to dismember him."

"What does that mean?"

Shifting into drive, Tim said, "It's sand-dog humor."

"Sand dog?"

Surprised that he had opened this door, he at once closed it. "Never mind."

"What's a sand dog?"

His cell phone rang, sparing him the need to respond to her. Thinking this might be Rooney with some additional news, Tim had it on the third ring. The screen didn't reveal the caller's ID.

"Hello?"

"Tim?"

"Yeah?"

"Is she there with you?"

Tim said nothing.

"Tell her she makes an excellent egg-custard pie."

Conjured by the voice, into memory rose those impossibly dilated eyes, greedy for light.

"Her coffee isn't bad, either," said Richard Lee Kravet. "And I liked the mug with the parrot handle so much that I took it with me."

This residential neighborhood had little traffic; at the moment, none. Tim came to a stop in the middle of the street, half a block from Pete Santo's house.

The killer had gotten Tim's name from someone other than Rooney. How he had obtained the unlisted cell-phone number was a mystery.

Although she couldn't hear the killer, Linda clearly knew who had called.

"I'm back on track, Tim, no thanks to you. I've been given another picture of her, to replace the one you kept."

Linda picked up the printout of Kravet's

driver's license and held it to the window, studying his face in the glow of a nearby streetlamp.

"Before the coup de grâce," said Kravet, "I'm supposed to rape her. She looks sweet. Is that why you sent me away with half my money? Did you see this skank's picture, want to rape her yourself?"

"This is over," Tim said. "You can't put it together again."

"What—you'll never go home, she'll never go home, you'll both run forever?"

"We're going to the police."

"I have no problem with that, Tim. You should go to the police at once. It's the responsible thing to do."

Tim considered saying **I know you're a cop, I saw you drive away from the tavern, now I know your name,** but revealing this knowledge to Kravet would diminish its value.

"Why are you doing this, Tim? What is she to you?"

"I admire her sangfroid."

"Don't be silly now."

"It's a French word."

"Spend the night with her if you want. Do her a couple of times. Enjoy yourself. Then drop her off at her place in the morning. I'll take it from there, and I'll forget you ever interfered."

"I'll consider your suggestion."

"You better do more than that, Tim. You better make a deal with me, and convince me you mean it. Because I'm still coming, you know."

"Have fun combing through the haystack."

"The haystack isn't as large as you think, Tim. And you're a lot bigger than a needle. I'll find you soon. Sooner than you can imagine—and then no deal is possible."

Kravet terminated the call.

At once, Tim pressed *69, but Kravet's cell was shielded against a call-back.

Ahead, a car ran the stop sign, roared through the intersection. As it bounced through a drainage swale, its headlights swept up across the Explorer's windshield, then down.

Tim shifted his foot from brake to accelerator, and swung away from the center line, expecting the oncoming vehicle to angle into his lane and attempt to block him.

The car shot past, taillights dwindling in the rearview mirror.

Having swerved into the parking lane, Tim braked hard to a halt just short of the intersection.

"What was that about?" she asked.

"I thought maybe it was him."

"That car? How could it be him?"

"I don't know. It couldn't be, I guess."

"Are you all right?"

"Yeah. Sure." A sudden breeze shook the ficus tree that overhung the streetlamp, and leaf shadows swarmed like black butterflies across the windshield. "If they sell sangfroid at 7-Eleven, I should stop and buy a six-pack."

Ten

The residence in Anaheim proved to be a single-story structure dating to the 1950s. Pierced and scalloped eave boards, rococo carved shutters, and patterned Alpine door surrounds failed to convince that this California ranch house belonged in Switzerland, or anywhere.

Penetrating the branches of two huge stone pines, moonlight painted scattered patches of faux ice on the age-silvered cedar-shingle roof, but not a single lamp brightened any window.

Flanking Kravet's house were a Spanish casita and a New England cottage. Lights were on in the cottage, but the casita appeared to be uninhabited, the windows dark, the yard in need of mowing.

Tim twice drove past the Kravet house, then parked around the corner, on a side street.

He compared his wristwatch to the SUV's clock. Both read 9:32.

"I'll need maybe fifteen minutes," he said.

"What if he's in there?"

"Just sitting in the dark? No. If he's anywhere, he's staking out my place—or searching it."

"He might come back. You shouldn't go in without a gun."

"I don't have a gun."

From her open purse, she withdrew a pistol. "I'll go with you."

"Where'd you get that?"

"From my nightstand drawer. It's a Kahr K9 semi-auto."

The thing was coming, all right, the thing that was always coming for him, that could never be escaped.

At the tavern, he had been in a place that had always been right for him, where he was just another guy on a bar stool, where from the perspective of the front door, he was the smallest man in the room. But this evening it had been the right place at the wrong time.

He had found a way of living that was like train wheels on a track, turning on a known path, toward a predictable future. The thing pursuing him, however, was not only his past but also his fate, and the rails that led away from it also led inexorably to it.

"I don't want to kill him," Tim said.

"Me neither. The gun is just insurance. We've got to find something in his place the cops can hang him with."

Leaning closer to see the weapon, he said, "I'm not familiar with that gun." She didn't wear perfume, but she had a faint scent he liked. The scent of clean hair, well-scrubbed skin.

She said, "Eight-shot 9-millimeter. Smooth action."

"You've used it."

"On targets. A shooting range."

"There's nobody you fear, yet you keep a pistol by your bed."

"I said nobody I know would want me dead," she corrected. "But I don't know everybody."

"You have a concealed-carry permit?"

"No. Do you have a permit to break into his house?"

"I don't think you should go in there with me."

"I'm not sitting here alone, with or without the gun."

He sighed. "You don't exactly have attitude. . . ."

"What do I have, exactly?"

"Something," he said, and got out of the Explorer.

He opened the tailgate and retrieved a long-handled flashlight from the shallow well in which the car jack was stored.

Together they walked to Kravet's house. The neighborhood was quiet. A dog barked, but in the distance.

As iridescent as a snake's skin, thin ravels of silvery clouds peeled off the face of a molting moon.

A wall defined the property line between the dark casita and the Alpine house. A gate opened onto a passageway alongside the garage.

Suddenly soughing through the stone pines, the inconstant breeze shook dry needles down onto the concrete path.

At the side door to the garage, Tim switched on the flashlight just long enough to determine that there was no deadbolt.

Linda held the extinguished flashlight while he slipped a credit card between the door and frame. He quickly popped the simple latch.

In the two-car garage, with the door closed behind them, Linda switched on the flashlight again. No vehicles were present.

"Masonry's not your only skill," she whispered.

"Everybody knows how to do that door thing."

"I don't."

Most likely the front and back entrances featured deadbolts, but the door between the garage and the house had only a cheap lockset. Many people think the **appearance** of having defenses is good enough.

"What kind of prison time do you get for burglary?" she asked.

"This is housebreaking, not burglary. Maybe ten years?"

The lock disengaged, and she said, "Let's be quick."

"First, let's be sure there's not a pit bull."

Taking the flashlight from her, he eased the door open. He played the beam through the narrow gap, but saw no animal eyeshine.

The kitchen was not what he expected. The flashlight found chintz curtains. A canister set painted like teddy bears. The wall clock, in the form of a cat, featured a swinging tail for a pendulum.

In the dining room, the linen tablecloth was trimmed with lace. A bowl of ceramic fruit stood in the center of the table.

Colorful afghans protected the living-room sofa. A pair of well-used recliners faced a big-screen TV. The art was reproductions of paintings of big-eyed children popular about the year Tim was born.

Turning to follow the sweep and probe of the light, Linda said, "Would a hit man live at home with his mom and dad?"

The larger bedroom offered a rose-patterned comforter, silk flowers, and a vanity with mother-of-pearl combs and brushes. In the closet were men's and women's clothes.

The second bedroom served as a combination sewing room and home office. In a desk drawer, Tim found a checkbook and several bills—telephone, electrical, TV cable—awaiting payment.

Linda whispered, "Did you hear something?"

He switched off the light. They stood in darkness, listening.

The house wore silence like a coat of armor, with an occasional click or creak of gauntlet and gusset. None of the small noises seemed to be more than the settling pains of an aging structure.

When Tim had convinced himself that nothing in the silence was listening to him, he switched on the flashlight.

In the darkness, Linda had drawn the pistol from her purse.

Examining the checkbook, Tim found that the account was in the name of Doris and Leonard Halberstock. The bills awaiting payment were for the Halberstocks, as well.

"He doesn't live here," Tim said.

"Maybe he used to."

"More likely, he's never seen this place."

"So what're we doing here?"

"Housebreaking."

Eleven

Linda drove while Tim sat with her open purse on his lap, the gun in the purse. He was on the phone with Pete Santo.

Having gone back into the DMV database as they spoke, Pete said, "Actually, the car that's registered to Kravet isn't at the Anaheim address. In that case, it's Santa Ana."

Tim repeated the address aloud as he wrote it on the printout of Kravet's driver's license. "It's no more real than the other one."

"You ready to tell me what this is about?" Pete asked.

"It's not about anything that happened in your jurisdiction."

"I think of myself as a detective to the world."

"Nobody's been killed," Tim said, and mentally added **yet**.

"Remember, I'm in the robbery-homicide division."

"The only thing that's been stolen is a coffee mug with a ceramic parrot for a handle."

Scowling, Linda declared, "I loved that mug."

"What'd she say?" Pete asked.

"She says she loved that mug."

Pete said, "You want me to believe this is all about a stolen coffee mug?"

"And an egg-custard pie."

"There was only half a pie left," she said.

On the phone, Pete said, "What'd she say?"

"She says it was only half a pie."

"But it's still not right," she said.

"She says," Tim reported, "even half a pie, it's not right."

"It's not just the cost of the ingredients," she said.

"It's not the cost of the ingredients," Tim repeated to Pete.

"He's stolen my labor, too, and my sense of security."

"He's stolen her labor, too, and her sense of security."

"So you want me to believe," Pete said, "this is about nothing more than a stolen coffee mug and half an egg-custard pie?"

"No. It's about something else entirely. The mug and the pie are just associated crimes."

"What's the something else entirely?"

"I'm not at liberty to say. Listen, is there any way to find out if Kravet has another driver's license under a different name?"

"What name?"

"I don't know. But if the address in Anaheim was bogus, then maybe the name is, too. Does the DMV have any facial-recognition software that could search its files for a repeat of Kravet's image?"

"This is California, dude. The DMV can't keep its public restrooms clean."

"Sometimes," Tim said, "I wonder if **The Incredible Hulk** had been a bigger hit on TV, ran a few more years—maybe Lou Ferrigno would be governor. Wouldn't that be nice?"

"I think I would trust Lou Ferrigno," Pete said.

To Linda, Tim said, "He says he would trust Lou Ferrigno."

"I would, too," she said. "There's a humility about him."

"She says Lou Ferrigno has humility."

Pete said, "That's probably because he had to overcome deafness and a speech impediment to become an actor."

"If Lou Ferrigno were governor, the state wouldn't be bankrupt, DMV restrooms would be clean, **and** you'd have that facial-recognition software. But since he's not the governor, is there any other way you can search to see if Kravet has a license under a different name?"

"I've been thinking about that while we've been talking about Lou Ferrigno," Pete said.

"I'm impressed."

"I've also been rubbing Zoey's ears the way she likes."

"You're a full-on multitasker."

"There's something I can try. It might work. Keep your cell charged, and I'll get back to you."

"Ten-four, holy one."

As Tim terminated the call, Linda said, "Holy one?"

"**Santo** means 'saint.' Sometimes we call him holy one."

"We?"

Tim shrugged. "Some of us guys."

While Tim had been on the phone, Linda had set out for Santa Ana. They were ten minutes from the address where, according to the DMV, the Chevy sedan registered to Kravet might be found.

"You and Santo," she said, "you've been through something together."

"We've known each other a long time."

"Yeah, but you've been through something, too."

"It wasn't college. Neither of us went to college."

"I didn't think it was college."

"It wasn't an experimental gay relationship, either."

"I'm absolutely sure it wasn't a gay relationship." She stopped at a red traffic light and turned that analytic green gaze on him.

"There you go again with those things," he said.

"What things?"

"Those eyes. That look. When you go carving at somebody with that look, you should have a medic standing by to sew up the wound."

"Have I wounded you?"

"Not mortally."

The traffic light didn't change. She continued to stare at him.

"Okay," he said. "Me and Pete, we went to a Peter, Paul and Mary concert once. It was hell. We got through that hell together."

"If you don't like Peter, Paul and Mary, why did you go?"

He said, "The holy one was dating this girl, Barbara Ellen, she was into retro-folk groups."

"Who were you dating?"

"Her cousin. Just that one night. It was hell. They sang 'Puff, the Magic Dragon' and 'Michael, Row the Boat Ashore,' and 'Lemon Tree' and 'Tom Dooley,' they just wouldn't stop. We're lucky we got out of there with our sanity."

"I didn't know Peter, Paul and Mary performed anymore. I didn't even know they were all still alive."

"These were Peter, Paul and Mary impersonators. You know, like **Beatlemania**." He glanced at the traffic light. "A car could rust waiting for this light to change."

"What was her name?"

"Whose name?"

"The cousin you were dating."

"She wasn't **my** cousin. She was Barbara Ellen's cousin."

"So what was her name?" she persisted.

"Susannah."

"Did she come from Alabama with a banjo on her knee?"

"I'm just telling you what happened, since you wanted to know."

"It must be true. You couldn't make it up."

"It's too weird, isn't it?"

"What I'm saying," she said, "is I don't think you could make anything up."

"All right then. So now you know—me and Pete, our bonding experience, that night of hell. They sang 'If I Had a Hammer' **twice.**" He pointed to the traffic signal. "Light's green."

Crossing the intersection, she said, "You've been through something together, but it wasn't just **PeterPaulandMarymania.**"

He decided to go on the offensive. "So what do you do for a living, besides being self-employed and working at home?"

"I'm a writer."

"What do you write?"

"Books."

"What kind of books?"

"Painful books. Depressing, stupid, gut-wrenching books."

"Just the thing for the beach. Have they been published?"

"Unfortunately. And the critics love them."

"Would I know any titles?"

"No."

"You want to try me?"

"No. I'm not going to write them anymore, especially not if I end up dead, but even if I don't end up dead, I'm going to write something else."

"What're you going to write?"

"Something that isn't full of anger. Something in which the sentences don't drip with bitterness."

"Put that quote on the cover. 'The sentences don't drip with
bitterness.' I'd buy a book like that in a minute. Do you write under the name Linda Paquette, or do you use a pen name?"

"I don't want to talk about this anymore."

"What do you want to talk about?"

"Nothing."

"**I** didn't clam up on **you**."

She glanced sideways at him, cocking one eyebrow.

For a while they rode in silence through an area where the prostitutes dressed only slightly less brazenly than Britney Spears, where the winos sat with their backs against the building walls instead of sprawling full-length on the pavement. Then they came into a less-nice precinct, where even the young gangsters didn't venture in their low-rider street rods and glitterized Cadillac Escalades.

They passed grungy one-story buildings and fenced storage yards, scrap-metal dealers that were probably chop-shop operators, a sports bar with windows painted black and the air of a place that included cockfights in its definition of **sports,** before Linda pulled to the curb in front of a vacant lot.

"According to the numbers on the flanking buildings," she said, "this is the address on the registration for that Chevy."

A chain-link fence surrounded a weed-filled empty lot.

"Now what?" she asked.

"Let's get something to eat."

"He said he'd find us sooner than you think," she reminded Tim.

"Hired killers," he said, "are so full of big talk."

"You know about hired killers, do you?"

"They act so tough, so big-bad-wolf-here-I-come. You said you hadn't eaten. Neither have I. Let's have dinner."

She drove to a middle-class area of Tustin. Here, the winos sucked down their poison in barrooms, where they belonged, and the prostitutes were not encouraged to strut half-naked in public as if they were pop-music divas.

The coffee shop was open all night. The air smelled of bacon and French fries, and good coffee.

They sat in a window booth with a view of the Explorer in the parking lot, the traffic passing in the street beyond, and the moon silently drowning in a sudden sea of clouds.

She ordered a bacon cheeseburger and fries—plus a buttered muffin to eat while she was waiting for the rest of it.

After Tim ordered his bacon cheeseburger with mayonnaise and requested that the fries be well done, he said to Linda, "Trim as you are, I was sure you'd order a salad."

"Right. I'm going to graze on arugula so I'll feel good about myself when some terrorist vaporizes me tomorrow with a nuke."

"Does a coffee shop like this have arugula?"

"These days, arugula is everywhere. It's even easier to get than a venereal disease."

The waitress returned with a root beer for Linda and a cherry Coke for Tim.

Outside, a car pulled off the street, drove past the Explorer, and parked in the farther end of the lot.

"You must exercise," Tim said. "What do you do for exercise?"

"I brood."

"That burns up calories, does it?"

"If you think about how the world's coming apart, you can easily get the ticker above a hundred thirty and keep it there for hours."

The headlights of the recently arrived car switched off. Nobody got out of the vehicle.

The buttered muffin was served, and Tim watched her eat it while he sipped his cherry Coke. He wished he were a buttered muffin.

He said, "This sort of feels like a date, doesn't it?"

"If this feels like a date to you," she said, "your social life is even more pathetic than mine."

"I'm not proud. This feels nice, having dinner with a girl."

"Don't tell me this is how you get dates. The old a-hit-man-is-after-you-come-with-me-at-once gambit."

Even by the time the burgers and fries arrived, no one had gotten out of the car at the farther end of the parking lot.

"Dating isn't easy anymore," Tim said. "Finding someone, I mean. Everybody wants to talk about **American Idol** and Pilates."

She said, "And I don't want to listen to a guy talk about his designer socks and what he's thinking of doing with his hair."

"Guys talk about that?" he asked dubiously.

"And about where he gets his chest waxed. When they finally make a move on you, it's like fighting off your girlfriend."

The distance and the shadows prevented Tim from seeing who was in the car. Maybe it was just some unhappy couple having an argument before a late dinner.

After an enjoyable conversation and a satisfying meal, Tim said, “I’m going to need your gun.”

“If you don’t have money, I’ll pay. There’s no reason to shoot our way out of here.”

“Well, there might be,” he said.

“You mean the white Chevy sedan in the parking lot.”

Surprised, he said, “I guess writers are pretty observant.”

“Not in my experience. How did he find us? Was the sonofabitch there somewhere when we stopped at that vacant lot? He must have followed us from there.”

“I can’t see the license plate. Maybe this isn’t him. Just a similar car.”

“Yeah, right. Maybe it’s Peter, Paul and Mary.”

Tim said, “I’d like you to leave ahead of me, but by the back door, through the kitchen.”

“That’s what I usually say to a date.”

“There’s an alley behind this place. Turn right, run to the end of the block. I’ll pick you up there.”

"Why don't we both go out the back way, leave your SUV?"

"We're dead on foot. And stealing a car doubles our trouble."

"So you're just going to go shoot it out with him?"

"He doesn't know I've seen his car. He thinks he's anonymous. When you don't come out with me, he'll think you're in the restroom, you'll be along any moment."

"What's he going to do when you drive off without me?"

"Maybe he'll come in here looking for you. Maybe he'll follow me. I don't know. What I **do** know is if we go out the front door together, he'll shoot us both."

As she considered the situation, she chewed her lower lip.

Tim realized that he was staring too intently at her lip. When he raised his eyes, he saw that she had been watching him stare, so he said, "If you want, I could chew that for you."

"If you're not going to shoot him," she said, "why can't I take the pistol with me?"

"I'm not going to **start** the shooting. But if he opens fire on me, I'd like to have some option besides throwing my shoes at him."

"I really like this little gun."

"I promise I won't break it."

"Do you know how to use a pistol?"

"I'm not one of those guys who waxes his chest."

Reluctantly, she passed her purse across the table.

Tim put the purse on the booth beside him, glanced around to be certain that he wasn't watched by one of the few other customers or a waitress, fished out the pistol, and slipped it under his Hawaiian shirt, under his belt.

Her stare was not sharp any longer, but as solemn and knowing as the sea, and it seemed to him that right then she took down into her depths a new understanding of him.

"They're open twenty-four hours," she said. "We could just sit here until he goes away."

"We could tell ourselves he isn't really out there, it's someone else, nothing to do with us. We could tell ourselves all the way out the door, just walk into it and get it over with. A lot of people would."

She said, "Not a lot would have in 1939."

"Too bad your Ford isn't a real time machine."

"I'd go back there. I'd go back all the way. Jack Benny on the radio, Benny Goodman from the Empire Room of the Waldorf-Astoria . . ."

He reminded her: "Hitler in Czechoslovakia, in Poland . . ."

"I'd go back to it all."

The waitress asked if they wanted anything more. Tim requested the check.

Still no one had gotten out of the white Chevy. Traffic on the street had diminished. The incoming tide of clouds had extinguished the moon.

When the waitress brought the check, Tim had the money ready to pay it and to tip her.

"Turn right in the alley," he reminded Linda. "Run to the end of the block. Look for me coming west on the main street."

They slid out of the booth. She put a hand on his arm, and for a moment he thought she was going to kiss him on the cheek, but then she turned away.

Under his belt, the gun felt cold against his abdomen.

Twelve

When Tim Carrier pushed through the glass door and exited the coffee shop, all the air seemed to have escaped the night, leaving a vacuum that could not sustain him.

Along the street, with swish and clatter, queen palms shuddered in a freshening breeze that belied the impression of airlessness.

After a shallow breath gave way to a deeper one, he was all right, and he was ready.

His paralysis had not been caused by fear of Kravet, but by dread of what would come after he dealt with Kravet. Over the years, he had successfully sought anonymity. This time it might elude him.

Pretending to be at ease, showing no interest in the distant Chevy, he walked directly to the Explorer. Behind the wheel, when the interior lights went off, he glanced once toward the suspect vehicle.

From this better vantage point, he could see a man in the car, the gray smear of a face. He was not close enough to discern any details, and couldn't tell if this might be the man to whom he had given ten thousand dollars in the tavern.

Tim withdrew the pistol from under his belt and put it on the passenger's seat.

He started the engine but didn't switch on the headlights. At little more than an idle, he coasted toward the restaurant, as though intending to pick up Linda near the entrance.

In the rearview mirror, he saw the driver's door of the Chevy open. A tall man got out.

As the Explorer neared the restaurant and began to pull parallel to it, the man from the Chevy approached. He kept his head down, as if in thought.

When the guy came out of the shadows and into the parking-lot lights, he proved to be of a size and a physical type that matched the killer.

Tim braked to a stop, apparently waiting for Linda, but in fact luring his adversary as far from the Chevrolet as he dared. If he delayed too long, the gunman might suddenly sprint to the Explorer and shoot him dead in the driver's seat.

About forty yards directly ahead was an exit from the parking lot. Tim waited perhaps a beat longer than he should have, then switched on the headlights, tramped the accelerator, and raced toward the street.

Fate plays with loaded dice, so of course the light traffic abruptly became heavier. An east-bound trio of vehicles brightened toward him in excess of the speed limit.

Expecting a gunshot, glittering glass, and a bullet to the brain, Tim remained committed to flight. As the Explorer shot into the street, however, he realized that the momentum lost in a right turn would ensure that one or all of the approaching vehicles would tail-end him.

Brakes shrieked, horns blared, headlights seemed to sear him. Instead of turning right, he highballed straight across the two east-bound lanes.

Without a further scream of brakes, although with a vigorous condemnation of horns, two cars and a panel truck sailed past behind him. Not one vehicle so much as kissed the Explorer's bumper, but their turbulent breath buffeted it.

When he barreled into the westbound lanes, oncoming traffic was at a safe distance but closing fast. Turning west, he glanced south, and saw that Kravet had sprinted back to the Chevrolet. The killer was in the driver's seat, pulling the door shut.

Tim continued turning, out of the westbound lanes, crossing the yellow median lines. He drove east, into the wake of the traffic with which he had almost collided.

As he drew near the next major intersection, he checked the rearview mirror, then a side mirror, and saw the Chevy exiting the coffee-shop parking lot.

With no respect for the stop sign, Tim hung a hard left turn, drove only fifteen yards north on a quiet cross street of older two-story homes, executed a U-turn, and pulled to the curb. He came to a stop facing the broader avenue that he had just departed, left the engine running, and killed the headlights.

He snatched up the pistol, threw open the door, got out of the SUV, stepped into the street, and assumed a shooting stance, both hands on the weapon.

The Chevy, out of sight but on its way, sounded like it had a much bigger engine than an ordinary sedan, confirming that it had been upgraded for pursuits and, regardless of what the DMV claimed, might be a supercharged police bucket.

The glow of headlights bloomed, and a moment later the Chevy cut the corner.

Point-blank, at risk of being run down, Tim squeezed off three shots, aiming not at the windshield, not at the driver's-side window, but at the front tire as the car swept past him, fired two more rounds at the rear tire. He saw the front rubber deflate and peel, and maybe he got the back tire, too.

Surprised, no doubt expecting to be shot himself, the driver lost control. The sedan jumped the curb, sheered off a fire hydrant, and slammed through a wooden fence in a shower of splintered pickets and a flailing mass of climbing-rose vines.

A geyser erupted from the stump of the standpipe where the hydrant had been, a thick column of water that surged thirty feet into the night.

As the Chevy rocked to a stop on the lawn, Tim considered going to it and pulling open the driver's door. Kravet might be stunned, briefly disoriented. Perhaps he could be dragged out of the car and relieved of whatever weapons he might have before he was able to use one of them.

Tim didn't want to kill Kravet. He needed to know who had hired him. Linda would never be safe until they knew the identity of the man who had put the money on the bar.

A bent cop who carried out contract killings on the side would be too tough to be cracked by a threat alone. But if the hot muzzle of a pistol was stretching one of his nostrils to the tearing point, and if, eye to eye, he had sufficient instinct to read correctly his adversary's capacity for violence, he might spill the name. He was not, after all, a man of honor.

Even as the Chevy sagged to a halt, porch lights came on at the house in front of which the car had landed, and a bearded man with a beer belly stepped out of the front door.

The water gushed skyward under great pressure and crashed back to the pavement in such noisy cascades that a police siren might not be audible until the squad car had closed to within half a block of the scene.

Splashing through torrents of foaming water, Tim hurried to the Explorer.

He put the pistol on the passenger's seat. According to Linda, it held an eight-round magazine. He had fired five.

Not only boldness is required for the successful implementation of any strategy, but also calculated and economical action.

As Tim drove to the nearby intersection, he

saw the Chevy trying to reverse off the lawn. The rear wheels spit out a spray of sod and mud and white rose petals, and the car seemed to have trouble gaining traction.

With at least one blown tire and untold other damage, the Chevy was in no condition to mount an effective pursuit.

In addition to calculated and economical action, however, a wise man expects the unexpected.

Instead of crossing the intersection in full sight of Kravet and heading south, where Linda waited, Tim swung left. He switched on the headlights and sped east two blocks, rounded a gradual curve that put him beyond Kravet's view, and only then turned right on a cross street.

He kept glancing at the rearview mirror, and he was alert, but his mind repeatedly went back to the gunfire, to the five crisp shots.

The pistol had a slick double-action trigger pull that felt like it broke at just about seven pounds.

The recoil-spring weight seemed to be about sixteen pounds, good enough for standard-pressure ammo.

The piece had felt remarkably comfortable in his grip.

He didn't know what to think about that.

He told himself that not just any gun would have served him so agreeably, that the credit belonged entirely to this fine compact weapon, but he knew that he was lying to himself.

Thirteen

Walking to the rear of the coffee shop, Linda glanced back just once and saw the front door closing behind Tim after he had stepped out into the night.

Although she had known him only a few hours, the thought of never seeing him again pinched off her breath.

He had chosen to help her when he could have left her to the wolves. She had no reason to expect that he would choose to leave her life as unexpectedly as he had entered.

No reason except experience. Sooner or later, everyone walked out. Or they fell through a crack in the floor. Or they were pulled screaming down into the crack, unable to hold fast, gone.

Given enough time, you could convince yourself that loneliness was something better, that it was solitude, the ideal condition for reflection, even a kind of freedom.

Once you were thus convinced, you were foolish to open the door and let anyone in, not all the way in. You risked the hard-won equilibrium, the tranquility that you called **peace**.

She didn't think he would get himself shot, not here tonight, not when his guard was up. He had a way about him that suggested he knew things, that he was not a man who would be killed easily.

Nevertheless, she was prepared to walk to the end of the alley and wait, and wait, and never see him again.

As she reached the door to the kitchen, it opened toward her. A waitress came out, balancing on one arm a tray of food-laden dishes.

"Kitchen, honey," she advised Linda. "Employees only."

"Sorry. I was looking for the restroom."

"There you go," said the waitress, indicating a door to the right.

Linda stepped into a lavatory that smelled of pine disinfectant and wet paper towels. She waited a moment, left the room, and went into the kitchen, where the smells were markedly better.

Past ovens, past a long cooktop, past deep

fryers full of hot oil, smiling at a short-order cook, nodding at another, she traversed two-thirds of the kitchen before a man with large ear lobes rounded a tall storage rack and almost collided with her.

She would not have noticed the size of his lobes if he had not worn studs: a tiny silver rose in the left, a ruby in the right.

Otherwise, he looked like a bodybuilder with a soap obsession and exhaustive knowledge of every detail of every Quentin Tarantino movie: pumped, scrubbed, and nerdy. Pinned to his white shirt, a name tag declared DENNIS JOLLY/NIGHT MANAGER.

"What're you doing here?" he asked.

Because he blocked the narrow aisle and she could not slip past him, she said, "I'm looking for the back door."

"Only employees are allowed here."

"Yes, I understand. Sorry for the intrusion. I'll just use the back door and be gone."

"I can't allow you to do that, ma'am. You'll have to leave the kitchen."

In spite of the earrings and his red necktie, he managed to appear solemn and mantled in authority.

She said, "That's what I want to do. I want to leave the kitchen by the back door."

"Ma'am, you'll have to leave the way you came in."

"But the back door is closer. If I go out the way I came in, I'll be in the kitchen longer than if I just use the back door."

By now, Tim might have driven out of the parking lot. If Kravet didn't follow the Explorer, if he came into the coffee shop looking for Linda, she needed to be gone.

The manager said, "If you don't have money to pay your check, we won't make an issue of it."

"My date is paying the check. He thinks I'm in the ladies' room. I don't want to leave with him. I want to leave on my own."

Dennis Jolly's scrubbed-pink face paled, and his dishwater eyes widened with alarm. "Is he violent? I don't want him back here, angry and looking for you."

"Look at you. You're way pumped. You could handle anyone."

"Count me out. What do I need to handle anyone for?"

She changed tack. "Anyway, he's not violent. He's just a creep. He's all hands. I don't want to get in his car again. Just let me out the back door."

"If he comes back here and you're not here,

then he's going to be pissed at us. You have to leave the way you came in."

"What is **wrong** with you?" she demanded.

"So he's all hands," said Dennis Jolly. "If he's not violent, he's just all hands, you let him drive you home, he cops a few feels, gets some boob, it's nothing."

"It's not nothing."

She glanced back through the kitchen. No sign of Kravet.

If she didn't get out of here soon, she would not be waiting for Tim when he drove up at the end of the alley.

"It's not nothing," she repeated.

"When he gets you home, you can cut him off at the knees there, then he's not pissed at **us**."

She closed the one step between them, shoved her face close to his, seized him by the belt, and in maybe one second flat, slipped the tip out of the keeper loop—

"Hey!"

—yanked the prong out of the punch hole, and freed the belt from the buckle.

Slapping ineffectively at her hands, he said, "Stop, what the hell you doing, hey!"

He backed off, but she stepped aggressively into him, found the tab on his zipper and yanked his fly open.

"No, hey, hey."

Linda stayed in his face as he stumbled backward, pressing him along the narrow aisle, clawing at his hand as he tried to close his zipper.

"So what's the problem?" she demanded, spraying spittle with the **p** in **problem**. "All I want to do is cop a little feel. You shy, Denny? It's just a little feel. It's nothing. I'm sure it's nothing. I'm sure it'll be a very **little** feel. Are you afraid I won't even be able to find it, Denny?"

The night manager knocked against a prep table, and a stack of dishes slid to the floor, shattering with the hard clatter of thick cheap china.

Prying at his protecting hand, trying to get in his pants, she said, "Has anyone ever tied it in a knot for you, Denny? You'll like that. Let me tie it in a knot for you."

Red-faced, sputtering, frantically backpedaling, his superbuffed physique working against him—too much bull wedged in the confines of a rodeo corral—he tripped himself and fell.

Resisting the urge to give Mr. Jolly a cheerful kick, Linda stepped between his splayed legs, then over him, and hurried toward the end of the kitchen.

"You crazy bitch!" he shouted in the breaking voice of a squeaky adolescent.

Three doors faced a vestibule, and logic suggested the one in the back wall would be the exit. Instead, beyond lay a refrigerated food locker.

The door to the left revealed a small, cluttered office. The one to the right opened onto a janitorial closet with sink.

Realizing her mistake, she returned to the first door, yanked it open, and entered the food locker, which proved to be a refrigerated receiving room. A door at the farther end gave access to the alley.

A pair of big Dumpsters flanked the back entrance. They didn't smell as good as the bacon, burgers, and buttered muffins.

Here and there, a caged security light above a door poured a puddle of light on the pavement, but for most of its length, the alleyway funneled through deep shadows and seemed to be a gauntlet of threats.

Rattled by the encounter in the kitchen, she hurried half a dozen steps before she realized that she had gone left instead of right. She turned toward the farther end of the alley.

As she was passing the door to the coffeeshop kitchen, she heard a car pull in from the nearer street, behind her.

Cluttered with Dumpsters, the service passage could accommodate only one vehicle.

She stepped out of the way, figuring to let the car pass.

The engine didn't sound right, riddled with knocks and pings, and the engine wasn't the worst of it.

She looked back and saw a car with a single headlight, canted to port because one or both of the driver's-side tires were blown. Shredded rubber flapped, a steel wheel rim rasped on blacktop, the chassis bounced on shot springs, and something—maybe a muffler—dragged on the pavement, spawning flurries of sparks that flew like fireflies from under the vehicle.

In the fall of light from a security lamp, she recognized the white Chevrolet sedan.

How Tim had done this, she didn't know, but she knew that he had done it. He thought that he had left the Chevy totally disabled, but lame and spavined life remained in the old plug.

Kravet had tumbled to the trick. He knew she had gone out the back of the coffee shop. He had come for her.

As she turned toward the kitchen entrance, Dennis Jolly flung the door open, his thick neck swollen thicker with indignation, tiny jewelry gleaming in his big ear lobes.

If she tried to return to the restaurant, he would block her, and he might even hamper her here with the intention of giving her a piece of his mind.

"If he sees you," she warned, "he'll blow your brains out."

Her tone of voice, Jolly's high regard for his own skin, and the hellish clatter of the Chevrolet convinced the night manager to retreat an instant after he appeared.

Like the pale horse of the Apocalypse, the sedan roared and lunged, spitting sparks, and Linda ran.

Fourteen

Shoulder-slung purse pinned to her side with her right arm, left arm pumping rhythmically as if to pull her forward, Linda ran.

Couldn't have outrun a car in good repair. Might have a chance against the crippled Chevy. Anyway, no option.

Try the back door at one of the businesses along the alleyway? Most were shops. Offices. Here a dry cleaner. There a nail salon. Closed at this hour. But a restaurant and a couple of bars were still open at ten till eleven.

If she dodged into a place where people were gathered, Kravet wouldn't come in after her, wouldn't kill everyone in a barroom just to get her. Too risky. Bartender might have a gun. A customer might be armed. Security video might record the whole thing. Kravet would back off, wait.

Should she stop, however, and find a door locked, she'd be dead. The sedan so close behind. No margin for error. She'd be run down, smeared along a building wall.

Judging by the sound of it, the Chevy was gaining on her. She'd had a thirty-foot lead, now twenty at most.

The south end of the alley remained a perilous sprint away, and her legs felt heavy, clumsy. She regretted the bacon cheeseburger.

Crushed underfoot, an empty soda can clamped to her shoe for one step, two, three, breaking her gait, then scraped loose and clattered away.

A cacophony of self-dismantling Chevrolet swelled behind her, and she expected to feel the twisted front bumper nudge the backs of her legs. When the noise seemed as loud as it could possibly get, the tumult abruptly cranked tremendously louder with a ripping shriek of metal clawing metal. Maybe the car sideswiped one of the Dumpsters.

As if the blast of sound blew her forward, her pumping legs felt lighter, and her feet seemed to be winged.

Even as the noise soared in volume, its proximity declined, and she realized that she had smelled the overheated engine for a moment, smoking oil like dragon's breath at her back, but smelled it no longer.

Daring to glance over her shoulder as she ran, she saw the sedan had sideswiped a Dumpster, had become locked to it. Kravet tried to accelerate out of the hang-up, but the metal wheels of the big trash bin gouged the blacktop. Dragged along a building, hinged lid banging up and down like a crocodile's mouth, the Dumpster cast out a jetsam of half-digested trash, shaved off showers of stucco, ripped loose a door frame.

Racing ahead, leaving the car behind, she was safer with every step, or so she told herself. Out of the alley, into a new street, she almost blundered in front of a hurtling car in the nearest of the two westbound lanes.

She looked east, desperate to spot the Explorer, but it didn't appear in the sparse flow of oncoming traffic.

Behind her, in the alley, the boom-bang-shriek of destruction fell suddenly silent. Kravet had given up on the sedan.

He would be coming now on foot. He would have a weapon. He would shoot her in the back.

Staying close to the curb, Linda ran east in the street, hoping to see the Explorer appear ahead of her.

Fifteen

Krait almost drove her down, but then the Dumpster.

A lesser man, whose emotions were not exquisitely balanced by his intellect, might have succumbed to rage. In fury, he might have shot at the woman through the windshield, although angle of fire and distance allowed little hope of a mortal hit.

If Krait had not been made for this work, he had nonetheless fallen to it as naturally as an acorn falls from branch to forest floor. No lesser man could have been as successful at the job as Krait had long proved to be, and he did not believe that any man existed who was his equal at it.

Indeed, moments arose when he wondered if he was a man at all, for he could honestly say, based strictly on rational analysis and logic, applying fair and sincere standards of judgment, that he was apart from humanity and superior to it.

This was not one of those moments.

When the car came to a stop, he twisted the key in the ignition, but the engine did not shut off. Freakishly, the damage had disrupted this one function of the electrical system.

From under the car rose the astringent odor of spilled gasoline. No doubt the idling engine or a shorting wire would conspire in some fashion to set the Chevrolet afire.

He sighed, annoyed that the universe had been organized in such a way that his will was sometimes thwarted. Well, no one had promised him a rose garden; in fact, quite the opposite.

Because of the Dumpster hung up on the car, Krait could not get out through the driver's side. When he slid across the seat and tried the passenger's door, he discovered that it was firmly jammed, maybe because the frame had torqued.

He could have clambered into the backseat and tried that door; however, he had sufficient experience to know when the cosmos was dealing him a bum hand. That door, too, would be inoperable, and by then he would be afire, which would be ironic, and amusing to some, but a distinct impediment to the completion of his mission.

Drawing his SIG P245, he fanned three shots at the windshield, which fractured and dissolved like a sheet of ice. The gun was loaded with .45 ACPs, so a round might travel the length of the alley and take the throat out of a passing pimp, young mother, or priest, depending on his luck.

Holstering the weapon, careful of his hands, which were vital to his work, he squirmed across the dashboard, out of the Chevy, and onto the hood with as much dignity as he could muster.

The woman had reached the end of the alleyway and had turned left or right, out of sight.

Taking swift strides, Krait went after her, but he did not run. A pursuit that required running was probably a pursuit already lost.

Besides, a running man did not appear to be a man in control. He might even give the impression of being panicked.

Appearances are not reality, but they often can be a convincing alternative to it. You can control appearances most of the time, but facts are what they are. When the facts are too sharp, you can craft a cheerful version of the situation and cover the facts the way that you can cover a battered old four-slice toaster with a knitted cozy featuring images of kittens.

Appearances were the currency of Krait's profession.

Striding swiftly but not running, with his cultured smile in place, he reached the end of the alley and stepped onto the sidewalk along the main street. He glanced right, looked left, and saw the Explorer angled to the curb, the woman boarding it.

At fifteen yards, with the SIG P245, he could at least shoot the numbers on a range target and usually place a ragged cluster.

The Explorer was maybe thirty yards away, thirty-five, so he strode east along the sidewalk, closing on the target.

The P245 featured a six-round magazine. He had three rounds left, no spare ammo.

Because originally he had been supposed to make the woman's murder look like the aftermath of a violent sexual assault, he had not intended to shoot her. He had seen no reason to pack a lot of fire power.

The situation had changed.

He had closed to within twenty yards when evidently they saw him. The SUV shifted into reverse, arced into the street, and backed eastward at high speed.

If any westbound traffic had been behind Carrier, he would have collided with it or would have been at least fatefully delayed. But on this night, the infinite wheel of the cosmos revolved in harmony with him, and he reversed all the way to the intersection, where he executed a slick fishtail turn and sped south on the cross street, out of sight.

Even this development did not elicit a snarl of rage or a curse from Krait. Frustrated but smiling, he holstered the pistol once more and continued to stride along the sidewalk, though not as swiftly as before.

If he stood apart from humanity and ranked superior to it, as on other days the evidence suggested that he did, he nevertheless had a rightful place in this sorry world. In fact, he occupied an exalted position. He sometimes thought of himself as secret royalty.

As a high prince of the earth, he had an obligation to conduct himself in a fashion suitable to his station, in a manner always decorous and becoming, with style and grace and quiet confidence, radiating at all times an aura of power and unrelenting purpose.

He changed course, heading south, and crossed the intersection. His intention was not to follow the Explorer on foot, but merely to put distance between himself and the alleyway in which the sedan burned like pitch in perdition.

When the police found the car, they might cruise the surrounding blocks, looking for suspicious pedestrians. Although he was immune to their authority, Krait preferred not to complicate his situation by tangling with them.

Sirens rose in the east.

Not running, never running, Krait increased his pace, striding with quiet confidence. Chin raised, shoulders back, chest out, he proceeded in the posture of a prince on an evening constitutional, lacking nothing more than a silver-headed walking stick and a retinue of retainers to complete the image.

He progressed almost a block as the sirens swelled louder and closer, and then another block as they receded into silence.

Eventually he found himself in a neighborhood of respectable two-story homes. In this pleasant southern California night, the Victorian gingerbread, basketweave brick chimneys, and steep gabled roofs made the houses appear to be in the wrong place at the wrong time.

Krait halted under the flowered limbs of a jacaranda, at a driveway in which four issues of the local newspaper were scattered in clear weather-resistant delivery bags.

Usually, if someone went away on vacation without remembering to arrange a hiatus in newspaper deliveries, a neighbor would pick up the accumulating issues to prevent potential burglars from recognizing an easy target. That no one had done so suggested that the people at this residence had not lived here long enough to establish mutually supportive relationships with their neighbors or were not well liked.

In either case, this house offered a sanctuary in which Krait could refresh himself and arrange to be re-equipped. He would need these accommodations only a couple of hours, and the odds were low that the owners would return during that brief window of time.

If they did return, he could deal with them.

He gathered up the newspapers and carried them to the front porch.

Lattice panels twined with night-blooming jasmine shielded the porch from the neighbors. The perfume of these flowers was too rich for a man of his simple tastes, but the screen of greenery served him well.

With a penlight, he examined one of the panels of glass flanking the front door. He found no indication of alarm-system magnetic tape.

From a holster smaller than the one in which he carried the pistol, he withdrew a Lock-Aid lock-release gun, a device restricted for sale to law-enforcement agencies.

If he were forced to choose between going without a pistol or without a LockAid, he would have surrendered his firearm with no hesitation. In less than a minute, often much less, a LockAid could spring all the pins to the shear line in the finest deadbolt ever manufactured.

A gun was not the only tool with which he could fulfill a job assignment. He could kill with a wide array of weapons, with a host of everyday objects that most people would not view as weapons, not least of all with the steel spring inside the roll bar of a toilet-paper dispenser, and of course with his bare hands.

The LockAid, however, not only facilitated Krait's work but also granted him entrée everywhere, a right and a power no less complete than that of any ancient king, before the advent of parliaments, when no door in the kingdom could be barred to His Majesty.

He was as sentimental about his LockAid as a lesser man might have been about his dear old mother or his children.

Krait had no memory of a mother. If he'd ever had one, she must be dead, but he was willing to entertain the notion that, in addition to all the ways he was apart from humanity and superior to it, he might also have come into this world by a route different from the one everybody else had taken.

He did not know what his special route might have been, if not a mother. He had not spent any time thinking about it, for he was not, after all, either a biologist or a theologian.

As for children: He found them incoherent, incomprehensible, boring, and fundamentally inexplicable. A lot of adults' time went to the care of children, and a horrendous amount in social services was spent on them, in spite of the fact that they were small and weak and ignorant and had nothing to give back to society.

Krait had no memories of his childhood. His sincere hope was that he'd never had one, because he was revolted by the thought of a little Krait with head lice and whooping cough, playing in a sandbox with plastic trucks, three teeth missing and snot hanging out of his nose.

After disengaging both the regular lockset and the deadbolt, he stepped into the house, listened to the emptiness for a moment, and then called out, "Yoo-hoo, anybody home?"

He waited for a response, received none, closed the door behind him, and turned on a couple of lamps in the living room.

The decor was too ornate for his taste, and too feminine. His preference for simplicity was so strong that he might have been happy as a monk, in a particularly spartan monastery, except that monks were not permitted to murder people.

Before fully committing himself to this residence, Krait toured the living room, wiping his fingers along the tops of door frames and over the higher surfaces of tall furniture, pleased to discover that these surfaces were as clean as those that could easily be seen.

When he examined the sofa cushions and the armchair upholstery for evidence of discolorations from hair oil and sweat, he found none. He didn't discover a single food or beverage stain.

With his penlight, he looked under a sofa and under a sideboard. No dust bunnies.

Satisfied that the homeowner met his standards of cleanliness, Krait relaxed on the sofa. He propped his feet on the coffee table.

After sending a coded text message that succinctly explained his situation, he requested new transportation, significant new weaponry, and a modest number of high-tech devices that might be useful now that this assignment had become more complex.

He provided the address at which he was currently taking refuge and asked to be given an estimated delivery time when one could be calculated.

Then he stripped down to his underwear and carried his clothes into the kitchen.

Sixteen

Into a night with a lowering sky and a slowly rising wind, Tim drove with no ultimate destination in mind, though as he wove from street to street, avoiding freeways, he gradually proceeded south and toward the coast.

With no trace of anxiety, Linda told him about Dennis Jolly and his big ear lobes, the self-destructing Chevy, and her need to use a bathroom.

They stopped at a service station, filled the tank with gasoline, and visited the lavatories. In the adjacent convenience store, he bought a package of vanilla-flavored Rolaids Softchews.

Tim needed the antacids, but Linda declined an offer of one. Her unflappable calm continued to intrigue him.

On the move once more, he told her about the Chevy, the fire hydrant, the picket fence, and the untimely appearance of the bearded man with the beer belly.

She said, "You shot out the tires?"

"One of the tires, maybe two."

"Right there on a public street?"

"The way it went down, I didn't have time to put up sawhorses and close the block."

"Incredible."

"Not really. Lots of places on the planet, there's more shooting in the streets than driving."

"Where does an ordinary bricklayer suddenly get the grit to walk into the path of a car driven by a hit man, and shoot out the tires?"

"I'm not an ordinary bricklayer. I'm an **excellent** bricklayer."

"You're something, I don't know what," she said, and ejected the magazine from the pistol that he had borrowed.

"So we're in the same club," he said. "Gimme the title of one of the novels you wrote."

"**Despair.**"

"That's one of your titles?"

"Yeah."

"Gimme another one."

"**Relentless Cancer.**"

"Another one."

"**The Hopeless and the Dead.**"

"I'm going to guess—they weren't on the best-seller list."

"No, but they've sold okay. I've got an audience."

"What's their suicide rate? I don't get it. You said you write painful, stupid, gut-wrenching books. But when I look at you, I don't see a chronic depressive."

Replenishing the depleted magazine with spare 9-mm rounds from her purse, she said, "I'm not depressed. I just used to think I ought to be."

"Why did you think you ought to be?"

"Because I was hanging out with university types, they love doom. And because of all the stuff that happened."

"What stuff?"

Instead of answering, she said, "For a long time I was so angry, so bitter, I didn't have room for depression."

"Then it seems like you'd be writing **angry** books."

"There was some anger in them, but mostly anguish, torment, wretchedness, and a festering kind of sorrow."

"I'm glad we weren't dating in those days. Sorrow about what?"

"Just drive," she said.

He drove, but he said, "Now that you won't be writing anguished, wretched, festering books anymore, what **will** you be writing?"

"I don't know. I haven't figured it out yet. Maybe a story about a bricklayer who goes insane at a Peter, Paul and Mary concert."

Tim's cell phone rang. He hesitated, thinking the caller might be Kravet.

Instead, it was Pete Santo. "Hey, Doorman, you've got yourself into something mondo weird."

"Don't call me Doorman. What weird?"

"You know how guys who use a lot of fake ID often keep the same initials for first and last name?"

Pulling to the curb and stopping in a residential neighborhood, Tim said, "All right."

"So I put together a search profile for anyone in DMV records with an **R** first name, **K** surname. Other parameters were from Kravet's license—male, brown hair, brown eyes, six feet, birth date."

"You got some hits?"

"I got twenty-some hits. Nine are what we're looking for. The photo is the same guy, your guy with that creepy little smile. Robert Krane, Reginald Konrad, Russell Kerrington—"

"You think one of them might be his real name?"

"I'm gonna run them all through local, state, and national law-enforcement databases, see if one turns up with some kind of badge. This guy **has** to be connected somewhere."

"Why?"

"This is where the weird starts. According to the DMV, these licenses were applied for in nine different offices up and down the state. But every one has the same photo, not nine different ones."

As Tim processed that news, Linda turned in her seat to stare out the rear window, as though the moment they had come to a stop, they had become easier to find.

Tim said, "So the guy's working with someone inside the DMV."

"Your garden-variety dirtbag," Pete said, "when he wants fake ID, he doesn't go to the DMV. He buys it from a fake-doc shop. It's good for a lot of things, but not all. Say he's stopped for speeding. If the officer ticketing him runs his license for priors, the DMV won't have a record of it. It's just a doc-shop job with no **roots**."

"But these nine licenses have roots. They'll stand up."

"Man, they'll stand up and sing 'God Bless America.' So he's got someone in the DMV or he can funnify their files himself."

"Funnify?"

"Funny them up, insert bogus records."

"I should take one of those vocabulary-enhancement courses."

Pete said, "Save your money and get a personality transplant first. Here's another thing. California has some new DMV-access agreements with a couple of neighboring states. This Kravet Krane Konrad Whoever—he has three licenses in Nevada and two in Arizona, no repeats on the names, but all with the same photo."

"Well, it is a handsome photo," Tim said.

"It is," Pete agreed.

"That smile."

"Those eyes. What is this about, compadre?"

"We've been through that. Parrot mug, egg-custard pie."

"These licenses, funnifying DMV records, these are felonies. Now that I know about this, I can't sit on it forever, not even for you."

The name Richard Lee Kravet was almost certainly not the killer's real name, so the burnt-out Chevy in the alleyway might not be easily tied to him under his true identity. Anyway, the wrecked car was not evidence of anything other than of reckless driving.

"Maybe if you can shake out the real ID from all the fake ones, maybe if we get the guy's born name, who he really works for, where he lives, maybe then I can tell you the story."

"Three maybes. I'm just warning you. I've got a hard ass, and I'll sit on this for you, but not all the way till Judgment Day."

Tim said, "Thanks, Pete. Call when you have something."

"I suspect I'll be working on this into the wee hours. I've already phoned in sick for tomorrow."

"No matter what time it is, if you get something, call."

"She still with you?"

"Yeah. She eats bacon cheeseburgers and hates arugula."

"**American Idol**—does she like it?"

"Doesn't watch it."

"I told you she was something. Didn't I tell you? Ask her what is her favorite chick flick of all time."

To Linda, he said, "Pete wants to know what is your favorite chick flick of all time."

"It's a tossup between **Die Hard** and **Man on Fire**, the Denzel Washington version."

Tim repeated her answer, and Pete said, "You lucky sonofabitch."

Seventeen

In the laundry room, Krait located spare hangers for his pants, shirt, and sports coat. He hung these clothes from handles on the kitchen cabinetry.

Attired only in underwear, socks, and shoes, he closed the blinds at the kitchen windows. He did not approve of people who made spectacles of themselves.

He found a clothes brush with stiff bristles and another with soft bristles. The discovery of a clothes sponge delighted him.

The homeowners seemed to be as fastidious about the condition of their garments as they were about their housecleaning.

Before departing, he would be tempted to leave them a note of approval, but also some advice. Currently on the market were nontoxic, biodegradable dry-cleaning fluids for home use, of which they had none. He felt certain they would be pleased with the products he recommended.

Using the lightly dampened sponge only where necessary, and then each brush as the nature and the condition of the different fabrics required, he had soon completed refreshing the garments.

Because the laundry room was small, he set up the ironing board in the kitchen. The homeowners possessed a high-quality, versatile steam iron.

He had once employed this same brand of steam iron to torture a young man before killing him. Unfortunately, the superb appliance had been ruined by the end of the session.

When he had finished pressing his clothes, he went in search of black shoe polish, a suitable brush, and a buffing cloth. He found a shoeshine kit under the kitchen sink.

After returning everything he had used to its proper place, he dressed and went upstairs in search of a full-length mirror. He found one in the master bathroom.

His appearance pleased him. He might have been a schoolteacher or a salesman, or anyone at all.

Mirrors intrigued him. Everything was reversed in a mirror, which suggested to him some mysterious truth about life that he had not yet been able to grasp.

He had once read an interview with a woman writer who said the fictional character with whom she most intensely identified was Lewis Carroll's young Alice. She claimed that in spirit she **was** Alice.

Because she had many lamentable opinions, Krait visited the writer one evening. She proved to be quite petite. He easily picked her up and threw her at a full-length mirror to see if she would magically pass through and vanish into Wonderland.

In fact, she was not Alice. The mirror shattered. When she failed to pass through the mirror, he spent some time passing the fragments of the mirror through **her**.

Only when his phone vibrated did Krait become aware that he had been standing in front of this particular looking glass for more than a minute or two.

A text message informed him that the order he had placed would be delivered by 2:00 A.M.

According to his wristwatch, he had one hour and fifty-five minutes to wait.

Impatience did not trouble him. He viewed this as an opportunity to visit with the family who, unknowingly, had provided his refuge.

He began by looking through the cabinets in the master bathroom. There he learned, to his satisfaction, that he shared a number of brand preferences with these people: toothpaste, antacids, a headache remedy. . . .

Each time he encountered a brand choice that he believed to be misguided, he dropped the item in a nearby wastebasket.

In two dresser drawers in the master bedroom, Krait found a collection of sexy lingerie. With interest, he unfolded each item, examined it, and then refolded it.

He did not disapprove of this discovery. If the average person was entitled to anything, it was the unrestrained expression of his or her sexuality.

Krait briefly considered expressing his sexuality directly into one of the most provocative pieces of lingerie and returning it to the drawer, but he decided to save himself for the Paquette woman.

At the farther end of the second-floor hall from the parents' room lay the bedroom of their daughter. The immediate evidence suggested that she was a teenager.

The girl's clothes, the manner in which she decorated her room, and her taste in music as embodied in her small collection of CDs suggested that she was not in rebellion against her parents.

Krait did not approve of her apparent complete submission to her mother and father.

As inscrutable and annoying as children were, he could nevertheless see one purpose for them. Contempt and animosity between generations provided tools with which a society could be shaped and controlled.

A nightstand drawer contained, among other things, a locked, leather-bound diary. Krait broke the lock.

The girl's name was Emily Pelletrino. She had clear, graceful handwriting.

Krait read a few pages, then a paragraph here and there, but he encountered no revelations that needed to be kept under lock and key. Emily thought her parents were unintentionally amusing, but she loved and respected them. She wasn't taking drugs. At fourteen, she still seemed to be a virgin. She sounded intent about earning high grades in school.

Until this prissy Emily person, Krait had found nothing in this house to dislike with intensity. Something about her struck him as smug.

Once the current assignment had been fulfilled, if his schedule permitted, he might return for Emily. He would like to take her away somewhere private for a week or two.

After he introduced the girl to a regimen of new experiences, mind-altering substances, and ideas, he would be able to return her home with confidence that she would no longer have such a high opinion of herself. She would also have a new attitude toward her mother and father, and the current unnatural dynamics of this family would have been repaired.

Later, in the living room, as Krait continued visiting the Pelletrino clan, he heard a car in the driveway. When he consulted his watch, he saw that the delivery had arrived right on time—2:00.

He did not go outside to greet the couriers. That would have been a breach of protocol.

Neither did he go to a window to peer between draperies. He had no interest in the couriers. They were mere footmen, walk-ons in the drama.

In the kitchen once more, Krait explored the contents of the freezer and found an ideal portion of homemade lasagna. He heated it in the microwave and accompanied it with a bottle of beer.

The lasagna was delectable. Whenever possible, he preferred to eat homemade food.

After cleaning up after himself, switching off the lights, and locking the front door, he went out to the driveway.

The Chevrolet that waited for him was dark blue, not white, but otherwise it appeared all but identical to the car that he had been forced to abandon in the alleyway.

No conditions of light or environment could have made the plain sedan look sporty. Under the low fast-moving clouds, however, and in the dream-strange lamplight of the sleeping street, and in the wind that chased thrashing jacaranda shadows across the night, the dark-blue Chevrolet appeared more powerful than the white version, a difference that appealed to Krait.

The keys were in the ignition. An attaché case lay on the passenger's seat.

He didn't have to look in the trunk to know that it contained a small suitcase.

At 2:32 A.M., he felt not in the least weary. In anticipation of a long night with the Paquette woman, he had slept until four o'clock the previous afternoon.

In a few minutes, he would know where to find her and her self-knighted champion. Long before dawn, Timothy Carrier would be as intimate with the earth as every man who had sat at King Arthur's Round Table.

Carrier's boldness and expertise with firearms intrigued but did not intimidate Krait. His confidence had not been cracked by recent events, not even dented, and he would not at this time seek to find out more about the man.

The more he knew about his targets, the more likely he might learn the reasons they were wanted dead. If he knew too much about why they were wanted dead, the day would come when people would want him dead, too.

Carrier was a target by association, but Krait still thought it wise to operate by the usual don't-ask rule.

If the woman was not dead long before dawn, as well, she would be in Krait's custody. He would not be as lenient with her as he might have been if she had stayed home and had taken what was coming to her.

After all, because of her and the lummox mason, Krait had lost the parrot-handled mug, which had been so special to him.

At least he still had the tube of effective lip balm.

He started the engine. The dashboard brightened.

Part Two

The Wrong Place at the Right Time

Eighteen

Long ago, the small five-story hotel had been built into a bluff along the coast. Bougainvillea vines with trunks as thick as trees draped purple and red capes across the entry-walk trellis, and the wind stirred a confetti of petals across the pavement.

At a quarter past midnight, when Tim signed the hotel registry, he wrote **Mr. and Mrs. Timothy Carrier,** while the clerk ran his Visa card through the verification machine.

In their third-floor room, sliding glass doors served a balcony with two wrought-iron chairs and a cocktail table. A three-foot gap separated their balcony from the adjacent one.

Under a charcoal sky lay a soot-black sea. Like gray smoke, the froth on the low waves drifted ashore, dissipating on an ashen beach.

To the north and below them, wind shook

more noise from massive phoenix palms than was made by the gently breaking surf.

Standing at the railing, staring toward a western horizon that could not be discerned, Linda said, "They don't care these days."

Beside her, he said, "Who doesn't care about what?"

"Hotel clerks about whether a couple is married."

"Oh, I know. But it didn't seem right."

"Guarding my honor, were you?"

"I think you've got that handled yourself."

She shifted her attention from the lost horizon to him. "I like the way you talk."

"What way is that?"

"I can't quite find the best word for it."

"And you're a writer."

Leaving the balcony to the wind, they went inside and closed the sliding door.

"Which bed do you want?" he asked.

Pulling back the spread, she said, "This one will do."

"I'm pretty sure we're safe here."

She frowned. "Why wouldn't we be?"

"I keep wondering how he found us at the coffee shop."

"He must really have a place near the vacant lot that was on his car registration. So he just happened to see us checking it out."

"'Just happened' doesn't just happen."

"Sometimes it does. There's such a thing as bad luck."

"Anyway," he said, "maybe we should be ready for anything. Maybe we should sleep with our clothes on."

"I already had every intention of sleeping with my clothes on."

"Oh. Yes. Well, of course you did."

"Don't look so disappointed."

"I'm not disappointed. I'm devastated."

While Linda was in the bathroom, Tim turned off the overhead lights. On the nightstand between the beds, the lamp had a three-way switch, and he clicked it to the softest setting.

He perched on the edge of his bed and speed-dialed the tavern, where Rooney remained at work behind the bar.

"Where are you?" Rooney asked.

"Just this side of paradise."

"You're never getting any closer."

"That's what I'm afraid of. Listen, Liam, did he talk to anyone besides you?"

"The shark in shoes?"

"Yeah, him. Did he talk to any customers?"

"No. Just to me."

"Maybe he went upstairs to talk to Michelle."

"No. She was here behind the bar with me when he came in."

"Somebody gave him my name. And he got my cell number."

"Not here, he didn't. Isn't your cell unlisted?"

"That's what the phone company tells me."

"Tim, who is that guy?"

"I'd sure like to know. Hey, Liam, I'm out of practice with women, you've got to help me."

Rooney said, "You lost me on the transition. Women?"

"Give me something nice to say to a woman."

"Nice? Nice about what?"

"I don't know. About her hair."

"You could say 'I like your hair.'"

"How did you ever get Michelle to marry you?"

"I told her, if she didn't accept my proposal, I'd kill myself."

"It's a little early in this relationship," Tim said, "to use a suicide threat. Gotta go."

When she came out of the bathroom, with her face freshly washed and her hair held back by a barrette, she was radiant. She had also been radiant when she went into the bathroom.

He said, "I like your hair."

"My hair? I'm thinking of cutting it."

"It's so glossy and so dark, it's almost black."

"I don't dye it."

"No, of course you don't. I didn't mean you did or that it was a wig or anything."

"Wig? Does it look like a wig?"

"No, no. The last thing it looks like is a wig."

He decided to flee the room. On the threshold of the bathroom, he made the mistake of turning to her again and saying, "I want you to know, I won't use your toothbrush."

"It never crossed my mind that you would."

"I thought it might have. Crossed your mind, I mean."

"Well, now it has."

"If I could have some of your toothpaste, I'll just use one of my fingers for a brush."

"A forefinger works better than a thumb," she advised.

Minutes later, when he came out of the bathroom, she was lying atop the blankets, eyes closed, hands resting on her abdomen.

In the subdued light, Tim thought that she was asleep. He went to his bed and, as quietly as possible, sat with his back against the headboard.

She said, "What if Pete Santo can't winnow all those names down to the right one?"

"He will."

"What if he doesn't?"

"Then we'll try something different."

"What would that be?"

"I'll have it figured out by morning."

After a silence, she said, "You always know what to do, don't you?"

"You must be joking."

"Don't shine me on."

After a silence of his own, Tim admitted, "Seems like, under enough pressure, I tend to make right choices."

"Are you under enough pressure yet?"

"It's building."

"And when you're not under pressure?"

"Then I'm clueless."

His cell phone rang. He plucked it off the nightstand, where it had been charging.

Pete Santo said, "A funny thing happened."

"Good. I could use a laugh. Let me put this on speakerphone." He set the phone on the nightstand. "All right."

"I'm running all these names through law-enforcement databases, state and national," Pete said, "see if maybe one of his identities is real enough to have some kind of badge and a job. My phone rings. It's Hitch Lombard. My chief of detectives."

"Your boss? When—just now, after midnight?"

"I just got off the phone with him. Hitch heard I'm on sick leave tomorrow, he hopes I'm okay."

"Does he also make chicken soup for his sick detectives?"

"Pretending it makes any sense for him to be calling me, I say it's just a stomach thing, and then he asks what case I'm working on, and I say there's like three at the moment, which I name for him, as if he doesn't know them."

"He would know them?"

"He would definitely. So then he says, being as how I'm always an obsessive about my cases, he bets I'm probably working on one of them right now, at home, on my computer, even though I'm sick."

"That freaks," Tim said.

"It freaked me right up out of my office chair."

"How would anyone know you're cruising

databases for Kravet and his multiple personalities?"

"Something in their software. Interest in Kravet and his other names trips an alarm. Somebody gets notified."

Having sat up in bed, Linda said, "Somebody who?"

"Somebody a lot higher up the food chain than me," Pete said. "Somebody higher than Hitch Lombard, high enough they could tell Hitch to shut me down, and he'd say **Yes, sir, I'll do it right away, but could I kiss your ass first?** "

"What kind of a guy is Lombard?" Linda asked.

"He's not as bad as it gets. But if you're on the street, you're happy he's an office guy, not on the street with you. He says when I feel better and I'm back at work, he has an important investigation for me, he wants me to put all my time to it."

"So he's taking you off your current cases?" Tim asked.

"As of now, tonight," Pete confirmed.

"He thinks something in one of those cases must have led you to Kravet."

"Not that he ever said so, but yeah. He never mentioned Kravet, but yeah."

Linda said, "Maybe he doesn't even know

Kravet's name or any of the guy's other names, or what this is about."

Pete agreed. "Somebody somewhere has Lombard in a nutcracker and they'll use it if he doesn't back me off. Hitch doesn't have to be told why they want me shut down. He just has to believe they'll crack him."

In the low lamplight, as he spoke and listened, Tim had been studying his hands. They were rough and callused.

When this business was finished, perhaps his hands would be even rougher, and too hard to be capable of a tender touch.

He said, "You've been a lot of help, Pete. I appreciate it."

"I'm not done with this."

"You're done, all right. They're on to you."

"I just gotta change tactics," Pete said.

"I'm serious. You're done. Don't you go off a cliff."

"What're cliffs for? Anyway, this is as much for me as you."

"How does that make any sense? It doesn't."

"Don't you remember when we grew up together?" Pete asked.

"It happened so fast, there's not much to forget."

"Did we come from there to here for nothing?"

"I wouldn't like to think so."

"We sure didn't come from there to here just to let the usual sonsofbitches have their way."

"They're always going to have their way," Tim said.

"All right. Mostly. But once in a while, they have to see one of their own get his package cut off just so they'll stop and wonder if maybe there **is** a god."

"I've heard that somewhere."

"You **said** it somewhere."

"Well, I'm not going to argue with myself. Okay, we're gonna get some rest."

"Maybe tomorrow you can tell me what this is all about."

"Maybe," Tim said, and terminated the call.

Linda had stretched out on her bed again, her head on a pillow, eyes closed, hands at rest on her abdomen. She said, "Poetry."

"What poetry?" When she didn't answer, he said, "The stuff that happened, the stuff that made you write festering books—"

"Books full of festering sorrow."

"That stuff, whatever it was—you're absolutely sure something from then isn't behind this thing now."

"I'm positive. I've thought it through from a dozen directions."

"Think it through from thirteen."

He removed the pistol from her purse on the nightstand, and he put it within easy reach.

Without opening her eyes, she asked, "Are we going to die here?"

He said, "We'll try not to."

Nineteen

The third-floor hotel room began to feel like a box canyon in an old Western movie. With a single exit, if the wrong people showed up, you had no way out except **through** them.

The average hired killer, if there was such a thing, probably wouldn't try to execute a hit in a hotel. He would prefer to nail his target in the street, where his escape routes would be more numerous.

Remembering the insatiable hunger in those black voids at the center of the killer's eyes, Tim suspected nothing about the guy was average. Kravet had no limits. He might do anything.

Still sitting up in his bed, Tim watched Linda as she lay with her eyes closed. He liked looking at her, especially when he wasn't being dissected by her stare.

He had seen many women more beautiful than she was. He had never seen one at whom he more enjoyed looking.

Why this should be, he didn't know. He didn't try to analyze it. These days, people spent too much time striving to understand their feelings—and then ended up with none that were genuine.

Although a third-floor hotel room might prove to be a trap rather than a refuge, he could not think of any place to go that might be safer. Currently, the world was nothing **but** box canyons.

Instinct told him that the more they stayed on the move, the safer they would be. But they needed rest. If they returned to the SUV, they couldn't drive anywhere except to exhaustion.

He got out of his bed as quietly as possible and stood gazing down at her for a minute, and then whispered, "Are you asleep?"

"No," she whispered. "Are you?"

"I'm just going out to the hallway for two minutes."

"Why?"

"To look around."

"For what?"

"I'm not sure. The gun is here on the nightstand."

"I won't shoot you when you come back."

"That was my hope."

He left the room and eased the door shut behind him. He checked to be sure that it had locked.

Red EXIT signs, denoting stairwells, glowed at each end of the corridor. The elevators were at the north end.

On the west side of the hallway, six rooms lay to the left of theirs. From the knobs of four doors hung signs reading DO NOT DISTURB.

Four units lay to the right of theirs. Only the nearest two featured the signs.

At the south stairs, the door complained with a thin squeal when he opened it. On the landing, he listened for the murmur of the sea in the nautilus-shell turns of the stairwell, but heard only silence.

He descended two flights to the ground level. A door on the left served the first floor of guest rooms. To the right, a door opened on a lighted exterior pathway leading toward the front of the hotel.

Hibiscus bushes bordered the sidewalk. Shuddering in the wind, the big red blooms seemed to burst toward him with ominous portent.

The walkway passed between the hotel and

its three-story parking structure. He went to his Explorer in the garage.

Everyone arriving at the hotel, regardless of the hour, was required to use valet parking. Tim would no more have given his car keys to an attendant, thus compromising mobility, than he would have traded his feet for a claim check.

Between midnight and six in the morning, only one valet was on duty. During those quiet hours, he doubled as a bellman, and he was not at his usual portico station. Upon arrival, a guest had to ring for valet service.

Tim hadn't rung. He had parked where he wished.

Now, shortly before one o'clock in the morning, at the Explorer, he retrieved the flashlight. From the jack well in the cargo space, he withdrew a small zippered vinyl kit of tools.

Wind thrummed and soughed past the open sides of the parking structure, and from various points throughout the hollow concrete bays came sinister whispers and ghostly voices that were only the same wind playing ventriloquist.

When he returned to their room on the third floor, Tim closed the door and engaged the deadbolt. He put on the security chain, too, though it wouldn't stand up to a single kick in a determined assault. If it delayed entrance only two or three seconds, that could be a life-saving margin.

He went to the foot of Linda's bed. As before, she lay on her back with her eyes closed.

He whispered, "Are you asleep?"

"No," she whispered, "I'm dead."

"I need to turn on more lights."

"Go ahead."

"I need to check out something."

"All right."

"I'll try to be quiet about it."

"You can't bother a dead woman."

He stood looking down at her.

After a moment, without opening her eyes, she said, "Is it my hair again?"

Leaving her with her magnificent hair, Tim switched on the overhead light and went to the balcony doors.

His reflection in the glass dismayed him. He looked like a bear. A big, clumsy, disheveled, clueless bear. No wonder she kept her eyes closed.

Each of the two glass doors was four feet wide. The one on the right had been fixed in place. Only the left one slid, bypassing the right-hand door on the inside.

Because this was a high-end hotel, care had

been taken with details. The metal frame of the door-set had not been mounted over the sheetrock, but instead had been plastered into the wall, allowing the wallpaper to be trimmed out to the glass.

Even flat-head anchoring screws would have spoiled the look, so the fixed door had not been secured from inside.

He slid open the operable door a few inches. A curious wind sniffed at him as he worked the latch lever several times.

The hotel had been built long ago, and these doors had been here since day one. Because that had been a more innocent age and because the balcony hung about fifty feet above the beach, the door had not been fitted with a serious lock.

A simple spring latch did a good job of holding the door closed. As a lock, however, it would fail under moderate stress.

Rising from his crouch, turning to ask for Linda's assistance, Tim discovered her standing behind him, watching.

He said, "You aren't dead after all."

"It's a miracle. What's going on?"

"I want to see if I can do this without waking anyone."

"I'm wide awake. I've been wide awake. Remember?"

"Maybe you have a sleeping disorder."

"I'm looking at it."

"I mean, I want to see can I do this and not wake people in the next room. Will you lock me out on the balcony?"

"Absolutely."

Carrying the flashlight and the tool kit, Tim stepped outside. Less mild than it had been, the night wind nipped him, as though he annoyed it.

Linda slid the glass door shut, and the latch engaged. She stood in there, staring out at him.

He waved at her, and she waved back.

He loved that she waved back. A lot of women would have gestured for him to hurry or would have stood with their fists balled on their hips, glaring. He loved her deadpan expression when she waved.

Although he considered waving again, he restrained himself. Even a woman as exceptional as this one might have limits to her patience.

He decided to start with the fixed door. With luck, he wouldn't have to deal with the latch in the other panel. Using the flashlight, he quickly located two anchoring screws in the header and two in the vertical frame.

From the tool kit, he chose one of three

Phillips screwdrivers. He got the right fit on his first try.

The door-set was less than seven feet high. He could easily get enough torque even though he had to work above his head.

He expected the screws to be frozen by decades of corrosion, and he wasn't disappointed. He persisted, and the head of the screw broke off. The shank dropped with a rattle into the hollow metal header.

The second screw snapped, as well, but the two in the vertical frame turned with rasping resistance. The noise he made extracting them wouldn't have drawn the attention even of an insomniac princess troubled by a hard pea secreted under twenty mattresses.

All sliding doors are lifted into their tracks after the frame is set. Consequently, they can be easily removed. Because these doors had been manufactured in an age of innocence, they featured recessed finger grips in the stiles to facilitate an installer's work.

If these had been six-foot-wide panels, he wouldn't have been able to handle one himself. But they were only four feet, and he was a big disheveled bear.

He lifted the door straight up, and the top rail

receded into the installation gap above it. Scraping softly, the bottom rail rose out of the track.

Had he tilted the bottom of the door toward himself and slowly lowered it, the top rail would have come out of the installation gap. He would have been able to lift the door entirely from the frame, to put it down on the balcony.

This had been only a test, however, to determine his ability to remove the door in relative silence. Muscles straining, he lifted it back into the track and left it in its frame where, no longer fixed, it could be slid aside as easily as its mate.

He gathered up his tools and the flashlight, and indicated to Linda that she should unlock and let him in.

As she was closing the door behind him, he glanced at his watch and said, "Took about four minutes."

"Just imagine how much of the place you'll be able to dismantle in an hour."

"Suppose you'd been sleeping—"

"I can't even imagine it anymore."

"—I might have gotten in from the balcony without waking you. I certainly wouldn't have awakened the people in the next room."

"When Kravet comes up fifty feet from the beach and in through this door, we'll know he's Spider Man's evil twin."

Tim said, "If he finds us as quick as he found us at the coffee shop, I'd rather he came for us one way or the other instead of waiting for us in the parking garage. We'll be most vulnerable going to the Explorer among all those cars, all those support columns."

"He won't find us tonight," she said.

"I'm not so sure."

"He's not magical."

"Yeah, but you heard Pete Santo. Kravet has connections."

"We left him without wheels," she said.

"I wouldn't be surprised if he could fly. Anyway, I feel better. We won't be in a box canyon now."

"You've totally lost me, and I don't care." She yawned. "Come on, let's go to bed."

"Sounds good to me."

"That's not what I meant," she said.

"It's not what I mean, either," he assured her.

Twenty

The draperies were closed over the sliding glass doors. The lamp on the nightstand had been turned to its dimmest setting.

On the floor beside the bed stood Linda's carryall, fully packed and ready to go in case they had to make a quick getaway.

Having pulled the spread aside, she lay on her back, head raised on a pillow. She had not taken off her shoes.

Tim had settled into an armchair. He wanted to sleep sitting up.

He had moved the chair near the entrance door, so any unusual noise in the public corridor would be more likely to wake him. From where he sat, he could see the drapery-covered balcony sliders.

Rather than fall asleep with a loaded pistol

in his hand, he pressed the weapon, muzzle down, between the plush seat cushion and the side of the chair, where he could draw it as quickly as from a holster.

The digital clock over there on the night-stand read 1:32.

At this distance, from this angle, he could not discern whether Linda's eyes were open or closed.

He said, "Are you asleep?"

"Yes."

"What happened to all your anger?"

"When was I angry?"

"Not tonight. You said for years you were bitter, so angry."

She was silent. Then: "They were going to make one of my books into a TV miniseries."

"Who was?"

"The usual psychopaths."

"Which book?"

"**Heartworm.**"

"That's a new one to me."

"I was watching TV—"

"You don't have a TV."

"This was in a reception lounge at one of the networks. They run their own shows on a screen there, all day long."

"How do they stand it?"

"I suspect the average receptionist doesn't last long. I was there for a meeting. This daytime talk show was on."

"And you couldn't change channels."

"Or throw anything at the screen. Everything in those reception lounges is soft, no hard objects. You can guess why."

"I feel right inside the biz."

"All the guests on the show were angry. Even the host, she was angry on their behalf."

"Angry about what?"

"About being victims. People had been unfair to them. Their families, the system, the country, **life** had been so unfair to them."

He said, "I tend to watch really old movies."

"These people were furious about being victims, but they thrived on it. They wouldn't know what to be if they couldn't be victims."

"'I was born under a glass heel, and have always lived there,'" Tim quoted.

"Who said that?"

"Some poet, I can't remember his name. This girl I dated, she said that was her motto."

"You dated a girl who said things like that?"

"Not for long."

"Was she good in bed?"

"I was afraid to find out. So you were watching these angry people on the talk show."

"And suddenly I realized, under a lot of chronic anger is a sewer of self-pity."

"Was there a sewer of self-pity under your anger?" he asked.

"I hadn't thought so. But when I recognized it in those people on the talk show, I saw it in myself, and it sickened me."

"Sounds like a moment."

"It was a moment. Those people loved their anger, they were always going to be angry, and when they died, their last words would be some self-pitying drivel. I was suddenly scared shitless I might end up like them."

"You could never end up like that."

"Oh, yeah, I could've. I was on my way. But I gave up anger cold turkey."

"You can do that?"

"Adults can do that. Perpetual adolescents can't."

"Did they make the miniseries?"

"No. I didn't stay for the meeting."

He watched her from across the room. She hadn't moved whatsoever during their conversation. Her calm plumbed deeper than calm: It was the serenity of a woman who lived above all storm and shadow, or hoped to.

In a voice thick with weariness, she said, "Hear the wind."

Ceaselessly the wind flew across the balcony, not loud and rancorous, but soft and lulling, like an infinite flock on an infinite journey.

In a murmur that he could barely hear, she said, "Sounds like wings that'll carry you home."

For a while he didn't say anything. Then he whispered, "Are you asleep?"

She did not reply.

He wanted to cross the room and stand over her and look down on her, but he was too tired to get up from the chair.

"You're something," he said.

He would watch over her while she slept. He was too tense for sleep. Under one name or another, Richard Lee Kravet was out there. Kravet was coming.

Perhaps some drug explained the dilation of Kravet's eyes. But how could he take in so much light and not be half blinded?

With the gun jammed between the seat cushion and the side of the chair, with silence unbroken in the corridor, with the wind carrying the whole world into darkness, Tim slept.

He dreamed of a flowered meadow in which he had played as a boy, and of a twilit magical forest that he had never seen in life, and of Michelle with shards of something bright in her left eye, her left arm a bleeding stump.

Twenty-One

At 3:16 A.M., Krait parked along the Pacific Coast Highway, half a block south of the hotel.

After sending a text message requesting data on recent credit-card use by Timothy Carrier, especially flagging the name of this hotel, Krait opened the attaché case that had been delivered with the fresh car.

Nestled in the molded-foam interior were a customized Glock 18 machine pistol and four fully loaded magazines. Also included were two state-of-the-art sound suppressors and a shoulder rig.

Krait admired this weapon. He had shot a few thousand practice rounds with one like it. For a 9-mm Parabellum cycling at 1300 rpm, the Glock 18 was exceptionally controllable.

The special magazines held thirty-three

rounds. They maximized the weapon's potential in full-auto mode. He inserted one.

Because the custom barrel had been extended and threaded, he was easily able to screw on one of the sound suppressors.

He felt a kind of kinship with the machine pistol. The gun had no memory of its manufacture, just as Krait had no memory of his mother or of his childhood. They were both clean, relentless, and in the service of death.

For the prince of Earth, the modified Glock 18 made a handsome Excalibur.

On the drive south, at a traffic light, Krait had slipped out of his sports coat. Now he took off his sidearm holster and slid it and the SIG P245 under the driver's seat.

He put on the new shoulder rig, which was suitable for the silencer-fitted Glock with the extended magazine. After adjusting it, he got out of the Chevrolet, shrugged his shoulders, and satisfied himself that the rig fit properly.

From the car, he snared his coat and put it on. He holstered the Glock, and it hung comfortably along his left side.

At this late hour, even the Pacific Coast Highway was traveled only by the wind. He breathed deeply of the night air. Without the malodorous emissions of bustling vehicles, the wind smelled clean.

This was a moment when you could believe that one day no traffic would ever again ply the roads, that no human being would walk the coastal hills or any land, anywhere. When the fallen had failed beyond hope of any rise, wind and rain would in time lick away every trace of what the dumb machine of Nature had not built, and the earth would enfold all the wicked bones to hide them forever from the sun, the moon. Under cold stars would lie a solitude from which had been purged all desire, expectation, and hope. The silence would seem never to have been broken by song or by laughter. The stillness would not be that of prayer or even of contemplation, but of a void. And then the work would be done.

Sitting in the dark car, Krait waited for the information that he had requested. He received a coded text message at 3:37.

Timothy Carrier had used his Visa card twice in the past twelve hours, the first time to buy gasoline. More recently, less than three and a half hours ago, he presented it when registering at the hotel near which Krait was now parked.

Because the hotel belonged to a chain that

had a computerized nationwide reservations system, Krait's sources had been able to discover that Mr. and Mrs. Timothy Carrier were staying the night in Room 308.

The **Mr. and Mrs.** amused him. What a whirlwind romance.

Thinking of them together in a hotel room, Krait remembered that he had been asked to rape the woman.

He wanted to rape her. He had raped women less attractive than she was. He'd never had a problem with that if it was what his contributors asked for when they petitioned him.

He also wanted very much to insert in each of her primary orifices the reproduction art that he had removed from the frame in her bedroom.

Unfortunately, the dynamics of this mission had changed. In his experience, on those rare occasions when you lost the element of surprise, you could assure success only by the ruthless application of overwhelming force.

To get to the woman, he would most likely have to kill Carrier. In the assault, a stray shot might bring her down. And if she screamed, if she resisted, Krait would have no choice but to shoot her dead without raping her.

That was all right, too. Under these circumstances, that was as much as he might hope to achieve. Two more dead was progress toward a day of empty roads, toward the silence of a void.

Krait got out of the car and locked the doors. This was not an honest age.

Instead of directly approaching the hotel, he walked to the associated parking structure.

The Explorer stood where he expected to find it: in the southwest corner of the ground level.

If a guard patrolled the garage, he was currently on another floor. More likely, the hotel relied on security cameras, of which Krait noticed several.

The cameras didn't faze him. Electronic images could be lost; systems could crash.

In a world that daily disconnects further from truth, more and more people accept the virtual in place of the real, and all things virtual are also malleable.

Likewise, he never worried about fingerprints or DNA. They were merely patterns, the first left by skin oils, the second detailed in the structure of a macromolecule.

Experts must read the patterns and judge their usefulness as evidence. Under any of numerous pressures, an expert may wish to misread a pattern or even to alter it. Americans had a touching trust in "experts."

Instead of exiting the parking structure on

the sidewalk that paralleled the main vehicle entrance, he left by a second exit that led him to a lighted walkway along the south side of the hotel.

Wind-shaken red hibiscus bordered the path. The hibiscus was not a poisonous plant.

Occasionally, Krait had need of a poisonous plant to accomplish one of his missions. Jimsonweed, oleander, and lily of the valley had all served him well.

Hibiscus, however, was worthless.

He came to a door. The door opened on a stairwell. He climbed toward the third floor.

Twenty-Two

A sound woke Tim from troubling dreams.

He had long ago learned that survival could depend on throwing sleep off as if it were a blanket. Clearheaded in an instant, he sat up straight in the armchair, and he drew the pistol from the seat cushion.

Although he listened intently, he did not at once hear anything more. Sometimes the sound was in the dream, and it woke you because it was the same sound to which you had seen someone die in real life.

The digital clock presented the time in lighted green numbers—3:44. He had slept perhaps two hours.

He looked toward the balcony doors.

The draperies hung undisturbed.

Now he heard the rushing wind, neither hammering nor prying, but gruff and rhythmic and reassuring.

After a silence, Linda spoke, and Tim realized that her sleep-sodden voice had awakened him. "Molly," she said. "Oh, Molly, no, no."

Her words carried a heavy weight of despondency and longing.

In her sleep, she had turned onto her side. She lay in the fetal position, her arms embracing a pillow, which she held tight against her breast.

"No . . . no . . . oh, no," she murmured, and then her words dissolved into a barely audible keening, a plaint of piercing distress that was not weeping, but worse.

Getting up from his chair, Tim sensed that the woman was not in the thrall of a meaningless dream, that instead sleep had conveyed her into the past, where someone named Molly had been real and, perhaps, had been lost.

Before her sleep talk could reveal some hidden truth about her, another sound disturbed the slumberous hotel, and this one came from the corridor.

At the door, Tim listened with one ear to the crack along the jamb. He thought that he had heard the thin squeal of the door at the south stairwell.

A cool influx of air teased along the turnings in his ear.

The pricked silence resettled itself along the corridor, though now it had a quality of expectation, reluctant to let its hackles smooth down.

If Tim had correctly identified the noise, someone must be on the landing, holding open the stairwell door, surveying the third-floor hallway.

Confirmation came with the signature squeal of the door as it was carefully closed rather than being allowed to fall shut.

Few late-returning guests would be that considerate of others, and, these days, even fewer hotel employees.

Tim put one eye to the security peephole. The wide-angle lens gave him a distorted view of the hallway.

This was not the moment of no return, for Tim had passed that moment earlier in the night. When he had walked out of the street and into her house, when he had seen that she possessed a poster of a TV instead of a TV, he had committed himself to a course as irreversible as the one that Columbus had taken when he weighed anchor in August of 1492.

Where he stood now was at that point in any dangerous enterprise when the mind either sharpens to meet the escalating challenge or proves too dull for the duel, when the heart either becomes a guiding compass or shrinks from the journey, when success becomes a possibility or not.

Into the funhouse-mirror panorama provided by the fisheye lens came a man, only the back of his head visible as he studied the doors on the east side of the corridor. Then he looked this way. Distorted by the convex lens, his face was nonetheless recognizable as that of the killer who embraced a legion of identities.

His smooth pink face. His perpetual smile. His eyes like open drains.

A more powerful weapon than the 9-mm pistol would have been needed to shoot Kravet through the door.

Besides, when this killer was dead, another surely would be hired. And Tim wouldn't have the advantage of knowing what the new man looked like.

He stepped back from the door, turned, and hurried to the bed, where Linda had fallen silent in her sleep.

His plan suddenly seemed less like a strategy than like a roll of the dice.

When he put a hand on Linda's shoulder, she came to full mental clarity in an instant, as if she had matriculated from a survival school equal to the one that he had attended.

She sat up, stood up, as Tim said, "He's here."

Twenty-Three

Krait in the quick of things felt god-like, with neither doubt nor reservations. He knew what he needed to do, and he knew what he liked, and moments such as this were the fulfillment of both need and desire.

After stepping out of the stairwell and easing the door shut behind him, he drew the Glock 18 from his new shoulder rig. He held it down at his side as he moved into the corridor.

Odd-numbered doors lay to his right, the even-numbered to his left, along the west wall. The fifth door from the stairwell was 308.

According to hotel records, Carrier and the woman had registered three and a half hours ago. Unlike Krait, they had not slept until four o'clock Monday afternoon in anticipation of what Monday night would bring. Weary, they would want to believe that they were safe for the time being.

Krait thrived on the fact that humankind could not bear much reality. When they retreated into wishful thinking, he approached, all but invisible because he was the reality that they refused to see.

On his way upstairs, he had stopped at the second floor to ascertain the nature of the door locks. The hotel had replaced the original hardware with electronic card-key locks.

His sweet little lock-release gun would be of no use to him in this instance. He had come prepared for this contingency.

In the stairwell again, he had paused to remove from his wallet what appeared to be a department-store credit card. In fact it was an analytic scanner that could read and repeat the current release code in any electronic lock.

Unlike the LockAid, this item was not for sale even to law-enforcement agencies. No one could buy it. You were presented with it, as a grace.

Now, at the door to 308, Krait at once inserted the card into the key slot. He did not remove it when the indicator light turned from red to green; leaving it in place would freeze the lock open.

The LockAid made little noise when used. The analytic scanner made none whatsoever.

A selector switch on the slide of the pistol allowed it to perform either as a semi-automatic or a full-automatic weapon. Although Krait usually preferred simple tactics and basic weapons, he set the Glock on full-auto fire.

With a two-hand grip on the pistol, assuming that the security chain would be in place, he stepped back and kicked the door as hard as he could, as high as he could.

The retainer plate tore out of the jamb, the door flew open, and Krait went into the room fast, half crouching, arms out straight, a little pressure on the trigger, sweeping the muzzle left, sweeping right, stepping out of the way of the door as it crashed against the wall-mounted stop and rebounded.

Two beds. One lightly mussed. One with the spread turned back. A lamp on a nightstand.

No sign of the Mr. and Mrs. Maybe they had been awake, heard the squeak of the stairwell door.

Only two refuges. The balcony. The bathroom.

Bathroom door half open. Dark in there.

Leaning well into the Glock, compensating

for the downward-bearing forward weight of the sound suppressor, he squeezed off a short burst through the dark gap, shattering a mirror, probably some ceramic tiles, peppering the bathroom with ricochets and shrapnel, one round clipping the door.

Recoil mild. As if the silencer acted as a recoil compensator. Not enough sound to wake a sleeper, if there had been one. Zero muzzle flash.

No screams from the bathroom. No return fire. Nobody in there. Leave it for later.

Draperies shrouding the sliders. Carrier had a gun. So clear the balcony before sweeping the fabric back from the glass.

Regretting the mess he was about to make, Krait squeezed off another short burst, draperies leaped, glass doors dissolved, and something made a **pock-twang** sound. He pulled the draperies aside, stepped outside. A fractured glaze of tempered glass crunched underfoot.

Alone on the balcony, in a wind so fresh off the sea that it smelled faintly of salt, he stepped to the outer railing, looked down. Some rocks directly below, then the beach, the breaking surf. All of it fifty feet down. Too far for them to have jumped without injury.

He did not question the reliability of the

information that he had received from his sources. Never over the years had he been given the slightest reason to doubt them.

Seeking another explanation for the disappearance of his quarry, Krait glanced left and right along the back of the hotel. Balconies. Nothing but identical railed balconies. Deserted balconies.

Deserted **now.**

Less than three feet separated this balcony from the next. If you were not afraid of heights, you could cross quickly from one balcony to another.

With the crunch of glass marking each step, Krait felt as if the sliding door had been a mirror, as if he had crossed into that place where only Alice had gone before.

In Room 308 once more, he registered an important detail that had eluded him previously: the absence of any personal belongings.

When he pushed open the door to the bathroom, he found no dead or wounded. Some towels had been used; but no toiletries stood on the counter surrounding the sink.

Carrier and the woman had not left when the stairwell door had squeaked. Much earlier in the night, they had identified a vacant room and had moved into it without informing the management.

Krait returned to the third-floor corridor, snatching his analytic scanner from the key-card slot and pocketing it.

The kicking-in of the door and the shattering of the glass had awakened guests. Two men—one in his underwear, the other in pajamas—had ventured into the hallway.

Smiling, Krait pointed the Glock at them.

They retreated into their rooms, closed their doors.

By now somebody would have called the front desk to report a disturbance. And one or both of the men whom he had threatened would be dialing 911.

Krait's heartbeat was barely elevated above his usual sixty-four-per-minute resting rate. He appeared calm, and he was calm.

Which had come first in his life, the appearance of calm or the fact, would be no easier to deduce than whether the chicken preceded the egg. The origins of his personality were lost in time, and he had no interest in them.

Like most of California, this town was inadequately policed. Unless a patrol car happened to be in the immediate area, response time would be at least five minutes.

Anyway, there would be only two officers, four at most. With a structure this large as his game board, he could cat-and-mouse his way to the car that he had parked along the highway.

If the cops showed up early, Krait would kill his way out of the hotel. He had no problem with that.

Along the west side of the corridor were eleven rooms. Of the six to the north of 308, DO NOT DISTURB hangers were displayed at four.

He had no reason to believe that the two rooms without signs were vacant or that his quarry had hidden in one of them. Carrier was just as likely to have put out the privacy requests or to have taken them off doors where other guests had earlier hung them, just to further confuse Krait.

To the south of 308 were four rooms, and in front of the last, Room 300, the DO NOT DISTURB hanger lay on the floor. Krait stared down at it. Then he considered the closed door.

He was all but certain that the sign had not been on the floor when he had first arrived here a few minutes ago. Perhaps someone had brushed against it when making a hurried exit.

Room 300 lay only three steps from the south-stairwell door.

Sensing that the clever couple had already descended two flights and had fled the building, choosing not to delay long enough to card open

Room 300 and have a quick look inside, Krait departed the third floor.

They would be racing for the Explorer in the parking structure. Maybe they had already reached it.

Krait did not plunge down the steps, for panic was not in his nature, but he did descend with measured haste.

Twenty-Four

Seconds after the door to Room 308 crashed open, Tim and Linda were out of 300, down the stairs, gone.

Wind scattered red hibiscus at their feet, their footsteps echoed off the low ceiling of the cavernous garage, the Explorer flashed its lights and chirruped when Tim used the remote key, he climbed into the driver's seat, and she accepted the pistol from him as she boarded with her carryall.

Room 300 had indeed been vacant when, earlier in the night, he removed a sliding door and entered from the balcony. He had let Linda into their new quarters through the front door and had hung a DO NOT DISTURB sign on the knob.

Thereafter, he had slept for two hours, although sleep had been a dark road crowded with rough dreams.

Now he started the engine, switched on the headlights, drove out of the parking structure, and went south on the Pacific Coast Highway. At the intersection, he turned left, heading inland.

"All right," she said. "Now I'm freaked."

"You don't seem that freaked."

Turning to look through the rear window, she said, "Trust me. I'm Richard Dreyfuss on the back of the boat and the shark just jumped in my face. How did that guy find us?"

"I'm thinking it was the credit card."

"Just because he's a cop, he wouldn't have people at MasterCard by the **cojones**."

"It was a Visa card." Tim turned right on a residential street. "He's way more than a cop."

"No matter who you are, don't you have to get a court order for that kind of tracking, a warrant, something?"

He said, "Don't thirteen-year-old hackers go into just about any system they want, and nobody gives 'em permission?"

"So this is some supercop with a nerdy nephew who can hack Visa for him twenty-four/seven?"

"Maybe somewhere there's a building full of guys who once were nerdy nephews, used to hack into TV-network computers just to leave obscene messages for Nikki Cox. So they're fifteen years older, and they've gone all the way over to the dark side."

"A building full of them?" she asked. "Who're you saying we're up against?"

"I'm not saying. I don't know."

Hill folded into hill, and he ascended not directly but in a serpentine course, weaving through streets of houses that, in spite of their architectural variety, all seemed to be characterized by a quiet dread.

She said, "Listen, I already have you figured as a guy who knows things."

"Not things like this. I'm out of my league."

"Not that I've noticed."

"So far I've been a little lucky."

"Is that what you call it?"

Wind-harried pepper trees overhung the lampposts, and on the pavement, branch patterns twitched like flayed nerves.

She said, "Who is Nikki Cox?"

"She was in this TV show, **Unhappily Ever After**."

"Good show?"

"Mean-spirited, mostly mediocre, with a talking, floppy-eared, stuffed-toy rabbit."

"Another one of those."

"I was a teenager, hormones squirting out my ears. I watched every episode with my tongue hanging out."

"That must have been one sexy toy rabbit."

In every block, in two or three houses, lights glowed softly behind curtains. Back in the days when Nikki Cox had been on the air with the smartass talking toy rabbit, at this late hour you might have seen fewer than a third as many lamplit windows as there were now. This was the decade of insomnia—or perhaps the century.

"Where are we going?" Linda asked.

"I haven't worked it out yet."

"Wherever we go, let's agree to one thing."

"What's that?"

"Not one more word about this damn Nikki Cox."

"I just remembered the rabbit's name. Mr. Floppy."

"Him you can talk about."

"I think for now we're safer staying on the move. No more hotels."

"I'm glad you didn't fall to your death from a balcony."

"Me, too. We'll keep rolling for a while, try to think this through."

"I thought you were going to fall. If you'd fallen, it would have been my fault."

"How's that figure?"

"You wouldn't be here if somebody didn't want me dead."

"So just stop doing stuff that makes people want you dead."

"I'll work on that."

Block after block, street after street, the conviction grew in Tim that their current safety was a brittle wire over an abyss, strung between rusting eyehooks, unraveling at one end or the other.

Repeatedly he checked the rearview mirror, the side mirrors, expecting sudden pursuit.

Linda said, "I have this friend, Teresa, she lives in Dana Point, but she's out of town for a week. I know where she hides her spare key."

Like agitated rats, fat wind-tumbled magnolia leaves traveled the gutter.

"Tim? Why couldn't we hole up at Teresa's place?"

Although the speedometer showed only thirty miles per hour, intuition told him that he was going too fast, that he would drive into trouble before he recognized it. He let their speed fall to twenty, to fifteen.

"What is it?" she asked, surveying the night.

"Don't you feel it?"

"I feel you feeling it, but I don't know what it is."

"Stone," he said.

"Stone?"

"Think of a very high cliff."

These north-south streets were arranged like the teeth of a comb, all ending in an east-west spine. Once more he turned left, onto the spine—and found that it ended at its intersection with the last north-south street.

"Cliff?" she reminded him.

"A cliff so high you can't see the top, it's lost in mist up there. And not just high, but it overhangs like a wave. We live at the bottom, in its shadow."

He turned left, onto the last street in the neighborhood. Houses on both sides. The headlights swept over a few cars parked at the curb.

"Sometimes big stones come loose from way up in the overhang of the cliff," he said, "come loose without making a sound."

He reduced their speed to ten miles per hour.

"You can't hear it coming, one of these sudden silent stones, but the falling weight . . . maybe it compresses the air under it as it comes, and that's what you feel."

Each of these streets had been three blocks

long, with houses on both sides. In the second and third blocks of this final street, however, houses stood only to the left.

On the right lay a public park with athletic fields, all dark at this hour, and deep.

A silent falling stone, a soundless tsunami outracing the noise that it made, the faulted earth underfoot secretly straining toward a sudden breach . . .

His once-acute sensitivity to threat had returned in recent hours. Now it sharpened to a needle point.

The woolen sky and steadily rising wind should have raised an expectation of a storm. But when blades of lightning sheared the clouds, they startled Tim, and he almost tramped the brake pedal.

The houses and trees and parked cars seemed to flinch from the stabbing light, and flinched again, as brightness insistently cleaved the sky, cutting down a massive weight of thunder.

Although a greater confusion of shadows shuddered across the night than what the wind alone had stirred, the lightning revealed one thing that the widely spaced streetlamps had not touched upon. A man in dark clothes stood in the shelter of an enormous Indian laurel, his back against the trunk.

As he leaned out slightly from concealment to look toward the Explorer, the lightning silvered his face, so that it seemed to be the painted mask of a mime. He was Kravet and Krane and Kerrington and Konrad and unknown others, as ubiquitous as if he were not merely a man with a hundred names but were in fact a hundred men who shared a single mind and mission.

Riveted by the ghostly face as it vanished and reappeared in sympathy with the fulminations of the sky, Linda whispered, "Impossible."

The mystery of this apparition could be puzzled to a resolution later. Before speculation came survival.

Tim pulled the steering wheel to the right and accelerated.

From the cover of the tree, the killer stepped forward, raising a weapon as he moved, like a malevolent spirit long dormant in the earth but now resurrected by a lightning strike.

Twenty-Five

The briefest hesitation would have resulted in a different and bloodier outcome, but the Explorer jumped the curb just as Kravet stepped from cover. Before he could fully raise the gun and open fire, he was forced to leap backward to avoid being run down.

Driving past the killer or reversing away from him would have ensured a barrage through the windshield, another through the passenger's-side windows. Going straight at him was the best hope.

When Kravet scrambled backward, he fell.

Tim swerved, hoping to run over him, break his ankles, knees, break something. The gunman eluded the wheels, and Tim accelerated into the park.

Concrete picnic tables, concrete benches.

Seesaw, junglegym. The wind pushing ghost children in a swing set.

The tailgate window shattered, and Tim felt a bullet punch into the back of the driver's seat.

Before he could warn Linda to get down, she slid low.

Another round rang off metal, and maybe the SUV took a third hit, too, but a cannonade of thunder drowned out the impact of the smaller caliber.

They were out of the pistol's range, vulnerable now only to a lucky shot. The weapon had an extended barrel, probably a silencer that would further reduce its reach.

Kravet wouldn't stand there, trying for a lucky shot. He was a guy who **kept moving.**

Pushing the SUV as hard as he dared on unpredictable terrain, Tim raced in search of the farther end of the park, a way out.

Throbbing storm light revealed empty bleachers, a chain-link backstop, a baseball diamond.

Although the latest explosion of thunder seemed powerful enough to crack the breast of any dam, no rain yet fell.

Linda sat up straight and raised her voice above the wind that quarreled at the broken rear window. "We're out of the hotel ten minutes, he finds us?"

"He's gonna keep finding us."

"How could he be **waiting** there?"

"He's got a dashboard display. And it's not an ordinary one, either."

"Dashboard display? What? My brain's fried. I'm thinking one of those little dogs that its head keeps bobbing."

"Computer display."

"An electronic map?"

"Yeah. He saw the pattern of the streets, figured we might end up on that one, and we did."

As they rocked across a broad grassy drainage swale, she said, "He's tracking us?"

"I just realized. There's a transponder on this bucket. It was an option—a stolen-car tracking service. The cops can follow the thief by satellite."

"They're allowed to do that if the car hasn't been stolen?"

"No more than they're allowed to do murders for hire to maybe get ahead on their mortgage payments."

The swale ended at the base of a long low slope, and Tim drove toward the brow as spasms of storm light bleached the green from the wind-shivered grass.

She said, "The company, the tracking service, they wouldn't just cooperate with some rogue cop. You yourself would have to report it stolen before they'd activate the transponder or whatever they do."

"He probably didn't go through the company."

"Who'd he go through?"

"The building full of grown-up nerdy nephews again. They hacked into the company, they're feeding the satellite tracking to Kravet's car."

"I hate those guys," she said.

At the top of the slope, the land leveled off into a soccer field. Tim saw lampposts on a distant street and sped toward them, and the speedometer needle pricked past sixty.

She said, "So there's no way to shake him off our tail."

"No way."

The first fat raindrops snapped against the windshield, as loud as hard-shelled insects.

"If we stop, he'll know exactly where we are. He'll know and he'll come."

"Or," Tim said, "he'll see something on the map, a way we're likely to go."

"And he'll be waiting ahead again somewhere."

"That worries me more."

"Where's the transponder? Can we stop, tear it out?"

"I don't know where it is."

"Where would they be likely to put it?" she wondered.

"I think they put it all kinds of places, lots of different places, so a thief wouldn't have one easy place to look."

They passed through another area of concrete picnic tables, concrete benches, concrete trash receptacles.

"All the concrete furniture," he said, "it's like a picnic in a gulag."

"When I was a little girl, I remember wood benches in parks."

"People started stealing them."

"Nobody wants concrete."

"They want it," he said. "They just can't carry it."

They reached the end of the park, crossed the sidewalk, jolted off the curb, into the street.

The raindrops were no longer few or fat. He switched on the windshield wipers.

"We've gained some time," Tim said. "If he's in a car like he was before, not an SUV, then he won't risk taking a shortcut through the park. He'll have to come around."

"What now?"

"I want to gain more time."

"Me, too. Like fifty years."

"And I don't want to go downhill to him. We turn a corner, he's got it blocked with his car, he cuts us down. So we go up."

"You know this area well?"

"Wish I did. You?"

"Not well," she said.

At the intersection, he turned right. The wet, rising street glistered when the sky flared.

"I want to go to the top," Tim said, "past the residential streets, over the crest. Maybe there's an old county road we could take fast south."

"It's probably brushland past the crest."

"Then there might be fire roads."

"Why south?" she asked.

"It's the **fast** that's more important to me than the direction. I want to believe we're five minutes ahead of him before we give up our wheels."

"Abandon the Explorer?"

"Have to. If we just drive until somebody runs out of gas, we'd likely go dry first. Then he's still coming behind us, and we don't get to choose the place where we start on foot."

She said, "When we checked into the hotel, I thought we'd have peace to make some kind of plan."

"Won't be any peace till this is over. I see that now. Should've seen it sooner. It's all a razor's edge now until it's finished."

"I don't feel good about this."

"No reason you should."

"Everything's falling away."

"We'll be all right," he said.

"That doesn't smell like bullshit, but it is."

He didn't want to lie to her. "Well, I don't think you'd want me to say we're dead."

"Unless you think we are. Then say it."

"I don't think we are."

"Good. That's something."

Twenty-Six

In the headlights, the silvery rain resem- bled skeins of tinsel, but this didn't feel like Christmas.

On pavement almost slick enough for sledding, Tim ran the stop signs.

Kravet would expect them to have thought of the transponder, the satellite tracking. Because they were desperate to gain a sufficient lead before abandoning the Explorer, he would stay close on their heels to avoid losing them when they went on foot.

"You reloaded your pistol," Tim said.

"Magazine's full."

"More ammo in your purse?"

"Not much. Four rounds. Maybe six."

"I don't want to get in a shoot-out with him. That maybe looked like a machine pistol he was using."

"Machine pistol doesn't sound good."

"Could be thirty-some rounds in the magazine. He could empty it in a fraction of a minute if he wanted, pump a wide spray of lead."

"Definitely no shoot-out."

"Except it might come to that."

She said, "Here's an ugly thought."

"Might as well hear it."

"Are we sure he's freelance?"

"In the bar, he seemed freelance. Guys with a license to kill get a paycheck like anybody else, not envelopes of cash."

"But if he's got all those hacker nerds and God knows who else giving him tech support, why is he the only guy on the street?"

"Somebody hired him to keep distance between them and your murder. They give him support, but they don't put their own gunmen on the ground. They're just puppeteers."

"That's when they thought I'd die easy, it would look like your dime-a-dozen homicidal rapist, but it won't look that way now."

"It's gotten noisy," he agreed.

"So if they think it's out of control, maybe Kravet gets some backup. What then?"

"Then we're screwed."

"Maybe you should lie to me after all."

The ascending street ended at a T intersection. The new street led north and south along the highest ridge line in town.

Tim turned south, right, and accelerated past houses bigger and more ornate than those on lower hills. Two blocks later, he came to a cul-de-sac.

"This blows," he said, circling the coral tree in the island at the center of the turnaround. He raced back the way they had come, acutely aware of the time they were losing.

Three blocks past the intersection, the north portion of the street also ended in a cul-de-sac.

If they left the ridge and went down the street that had brought them up, they would encounter Kravet. And he would see them coming on his map display.

Tim circled another coral tree, drove out of the turnaround, pulled to the curb, doused the headlights, cut the engine, and said, "Give me the gun."

"What're we doing?"

"The spare bullets in your purse. I need those, too. Quick."

She rummaged for the ammo, found five rounds.

Dropping the cartridges in his shirt pocket, he said, "We've got, I don't know, two minutes. Bring the carryall, your purse, the flashlight."

"Why not blow the horn? Wake up the neighborhood."

"No. Come on."

"There'd be too many witnesses. He wouldn't shoot."

"He would," Tim insisted. "And we don't want to get any of these people killed."

He opened the door and got out into the wind-driven rain and walked back into the turnaround that they had just traveled in the Explorer. By the time he had taken half a dozen steps, his clothes were soaked.

In southern California, a major storm in May was rare. The rain wasn't warm, but it didn't chill him, either.

The five houses on the turnaround shared an architectural theme, from sleekly modern with a hint of Tuscany to classic Tuscan style.

Six-foot walls marked the property lines, providing privacy to each backyard. The houses were connected to those walls by gates. Some of the gates might be locked.

No dogs would have been left out in this weather, to bark and betray them. Besides, in a neighborhood of three-million-dollar homes like these, the dogs lived inside; they were part of the family; they weren't penned or chained.

Five backyards. Kravet would go gate to gate. He would search each yard. This was prime ocean-view property, valuable, so the yards were small. He wouldn't need five minutes to search them all.

The cul-de-sac lay at the head of a canyon. Beyond the backyards would be steep slopes difficult to negotiate, wild vines, brush.

These urban canyons were home to rattlesnakes, coyotes, and bobcats. Mountain lions seldom ventured this far out of the true brushland, but the killer cats weren't total strangers to the area, either.

At first, making their way into the canyon, Tim would not want to use the flashlight for fear Kravet would see it. He refused to contemplate let alone undertake a blind descent.

The backyards offered only the illusion of safety, and the canyon was its own kind of dead end.

Linda caught up with him. Drenched. Beautiful.

With a hard crack, the sky broke. Sharp light fell from it. Bright shards danced in the puddles.

Through the back of his wristwatch, against the skin of his wrist, he could have sworn that he felt the motion of the second hand as it swept time away.

In the front yard of a contemporary structure stood a Realtor's FOR SALE sign. Shades were drawn shut over all the windows on both floors, suggesting that the residence might be vacant.

Atop the mailbox, a rectangular frame offered a place to insert a street number and name. The number remained in place. The name had been removed.

No multiple-listing combination lockbox hung on the front door. That didn't prove someone lived here. It might only mean that, even if the house was vacant, the owners preferred that it be shown only to qualified buyers, discreetly, by appointment.

Tim handed the pistol to Linda. She accepted it without comment.

He wrenched loose the Realtor's sign. The two long legs of it were steel staves that had been driven six or eight inches into the ground.

Next door, a curving flagstone walkway—laid in an irregular-fitted pattern with a poured-concrete border—led to a traditional Tuscan home.

Tim worked the pointed staves of the FOR SALE sign into the yard, and the wet soil received them readily enough. It was a little cockeyed, but that was all right.

Two doors from the home that was actually for sale, a kid had left a bicycle on the front lawn. Tim snatched it up and carried it back to where he had removed the sign from the first house, and he put it down there.

Linda watched him without asking a question or making a comment, watched not with a puzzled expression but with the analytical frown of a good student studying equations on a blackboard.

Tim figured that he could easily end up in love with her. Maybe he already was.

Even before he asked for the gun, she held it out to him.

"Come on," he said, and she hurried with him to the house that he believed to be vacant.

The sky, a well-stocked armory, cast down bright spears, and the air smelled seared, and concussions rocked the night.

They went to a gate at the side of the house. It was held shut by only a gravity latch.

A serviceway led between the house and the property wall, and they followed it. At the back, a covered patio gave relief from the rain.

At what might have been the kitchen and

breakfast-room windows, pleated shades were lowered to the sills. Other windows were draped.

Farther along, a pair of French doors lacked coverings of any kind. Linda directed the flashlight inside, revealing an unfurnished family room.

Tim gripped the pistol by the barrel, waited for the storm to bare its white teeth again, and timed the breaking of the glass to the subsequent roar of thunder. He reached inside, found the thumb-turn deadbolt, and opened the door.

She followed him into the house and closed the door, and they stood listening, but the lack of furnishings told the true story. No one lived here.

"A place like this," he said, "there's an alarm system. But because there's nothing in the house and because the alarm would be an annoyance for the real-estate agents, they've left it off."

Looking through the French doors, past the patio, past the dark swimming pool, past the property fence, past the black hole of the canyon, toward the regimented streetlamps on the lower hills and toward the up-coast view of city lights shimmering in the rain, Linda said, "How can this be happening to us here, all these multimillion-dollar houses, that glittering riviera spread out below. . . ."

"Didn't you say civilization is as fragile as glass?"

"Maybe it's worse than that," she said. "Maybe it's a mirage."

"There are always those who'd like to turn out the lights. So far we've been lucky. They've always just been shy of a majority."

She turned from the view as if it pained her. "Are we safe here?"

"No."

"I mean for just a little while?"

"No. Not even for a little while."

Twenty-Seven

Krait drove past the abandoned Explorer. Instead of parking at the curb, he stopped beside the landscaped island in the center of the turnaround, where parking was not permitted.

The rain annoyed him. His clothes would be a mess.

Well, he could do nothing about the storm. Some time ago, he had reluctantly concluded that he had no control over the weather.

For a while, he had suspected that he might be able to influence the elements. His suspicions had been aroused because so frequently he received precisely the weather that he needed in order to set up and commit a murder.

He read several books about psychokinesis, the power of mind over matter. Some people could bend spoons without touching them. Experts in the paranormal said you could move objects from one place to another merely by thinking about transferring them.

Once, Krait had bent a spoon, but not with the power of his mind, just in frustration. He had tied the damn thing in a knot.

He had considered paying a visit to the author who had written the book about how to develop your psychokinetic talent. He wanted to make the guy swallow the knotted spoon.

Krait liked to make people swallow things that no one would want to swallow. He didn't know why this delighted him, but for as long as he could remember, nothing had given him greater pleasure.

Because of the unlikely shapes and sizes of some of the objects, the people to whom he force-fed them often perished while swallowing. Therefore, he found it best not to begin an evening together with this best bit of fun, but instead to save it for later.

Once people were dead, there wasn't anything more you could do with them.

The author who wrote about psychokinesis had also written books about foretelling the future. Maybe they were more helpful than the spoon-bending text, but Krait had no interest in them.

Already he knew the future. He was making it.

Most people were not going to like the future, but Krait was impatient to get there. He knew that he would love the way things were going to be.

He got out of the car and stood in the rain. He thought about clear skies, about stars, and the rain kept falling, as he had known it would, but a little hopeful effort now and then didn't cost him anything.

Human beings, not spoons and the weather, were his subjects. He could do anything to human beings that he wanted, and right now he wanted to kill two of them.

On his electronic-map display, the Explorer had come to a stop about a minute and forty seconds before Krait had turned left at the T intersection, onto this street. They couldn't have gotten far in a minute and forty seconds.

They wouldn't have gone past the houses, into the canyon, not in the rain and the dark.

If they had run south toward the intersection, he would have seen them as he came up the last of the hill.

Krait stood on the turnaround island, under the limbs of the big coral tree, and he surveyed the five houses. Not a single window was brightened by lamplight.

No sane person these days would answer a doorbell and take in two strangers at 4:10 in the morning.

At each house were gates leading to the backyard. He hoped that he wouldn't have to scout all five residences.

With the silencer-fitted Glock machine pistol held at his side, muzzle toward the pavement, he stepped off the island. Walking in the street, he followed the turnaround, studying each property, looking for any telltale irregularity.

Imprisoned light escaped the sky and fled along the glistening blacktop.

Krait had long wanted to see someone struck by lightning, well struck and hard. If he **were** able to control the weather, he would arrange a number of spectacular incinerations.

He had once electrocuted a businessman bathing in a tub, but that was not the same thing at all. The man's eyeballs had not melted, and his hair had not caught on fire, or anything.

The flickering light brought Krait's attention to a FOR SALE sign in the front yard of a Tuscan house that wasn't simple enough for his taste. The sign had not been properly placed. It didn't directly face the street, and it was cocked, one side higher than the other.

The second-floor windows were shielded by draperies, but some of the ground-floor windows were uncovered. In those absolute-black rooms, he saw no pale faces peering out at him.

Next door stood a contemporary house that he liked. He might even spend a weekend there when the owners were out of town, getting to know them, to know their dreams and their hopes and their secrets. Assuming they were clean people.

On the lawn lay a bicycle. This did not bode well for the condition of the interior. If the child had not been taught to pick up after himself, the parents were most likely slobs.

Yet Krait felt strongly that people who appreciated architecture with lines as clean as those of this house could not be disordered in their private lives.

All the windows on both floors were covered by shades.

Beside the front door stood an elegant limestone planter that should have contained perhaps a specimen dwarf tree of some species, with seasonal flowers at the base. The planter stood empty.

Krait regarded the windows, the planter. He lowered his gaze to the bicycle. He looked from the bicycle to the FOR SALE sign in the yard of the neighboring house.

The rain had ruined his wardrobe; but it calmed him and washed the cobwebs from his mind. He felt remarkably clearheaded.

With his left hand, he seized the bicycle by the handlebars and dragged it aside.

On the lawn where the bicycle had rested were two pale spots. When he crouched for a closer look, he saw circles of dead grass three or four inches in diameter.

At the center of each circle lay a darker spot. Probing with his fingers, he discovered holes in the earth. They were approximately as far apart as were the staves on the FOR SALE sign in the neighboring yard.

Timothy Carrier had known that if this house had been obviously vacant, Krait would have gone to it at once. For a bricklayer, he had unusually sharp instincts.

As Krait retreated from the lawn, back to the sidewalk, he stepped on something that tried to roll under his shoe.

The jagged light in the heavens rippled lambently through the film of running water on the sidewalk, caressing a brass object that it briefly turned silver.

When he bent to pick it up, the lightning showed him a second identical item near the first. Two 9-mm cartridges.

Here came upon him one of those moments when he knew that he stood apart from humanity and ranked superior to it. He was a secret prince, indeed, and fate acknowledged his royalty by delivering unto him these unspent cartridges, proof that his quarry had gone to ground here.

He supposed it was even possible that these two dropped rounds might have been the bullets that, once Carrier expended all his other ammunition, would have wounded Krait or even killed him. Fate might not merely be pointing the way to the successful conclusion of this mission but might also be assuring him that, at least for this night, he was invulnerable and possibly even that, in the long run, he would prove to be immortal.

The lightning and thunder seemed to celebrate him.

He put the bullets in a pants pocket.

If everything went smoothly and he had sufficient time, he would make the woman swallow the bullets before he shoved the reproduction art down her throat.

He could not risk trying to take Carrier alive. The mason was too big, and dangerous in unexpected ways.

If he got lucky and severely disabled Carrier with a spine shot, however, he would enjoy forcing him to swallow something, as well. Perhaps a choice piece of the bricklayer's anatomy, severed, could be served to him on a fork.

Twenty-Eight

With little time and no sophisti-cated burglary tools, Carrier and the woman would have gone to the back of the house, out of sight of the street, to break a window or the glass in a door.

Once inside, they might have climbed to the second floor, expecting to defend the staircase from the superior position of the upper hallway.

Or they might be covering the window or door by which they had entered, hoping to shoot him down when he followed in their steps. As if he ever would be that direct.

At the side garage door, Krait quietly employed his beloved lock-release gun.

Inside, he switched on the lights. The garage could accommodate three vehicles, but none was present.

Quality laminate cabinetry made for an orderly space. He opened a few doors. All the shelves were bare.

Proof enough. No one lived here.

The door between the garage and the house probably opened into a laundry room or a service hall. Carrier and the woman were not likely to have taken shelter in either.

Krait used the LockAid. The snaps and clicks were lost in the drums of the storm. He returned the device to its holster.

The in-spill of light from the garage revealed a laundry room so generously proportioned that it included a sewing center and a gift-wrapping station with wall-mounted rolls of fancy wrapping papers.

The farther door was closed.

When he entered the laundry, he discovered a Crestron touch panel embedded in the wall. As befitted a property of this caliber, the house was computerized.

He touched the panel, and the screen brightened, offering him a choice of system controls that included SECURITY, LIGHTING, MUSIC. . . .

He pressed LIGHTING, and the screen listed indoor rooms and outdoor zones. He could control the lights everywhere from this entry point or from any other Crestron panels in the house.

Among the last options were ALL INTERIOR ON and ALL EXTERIOR ON. His quarry would expect him to come in the dark, so they would have a plan to use darkness to their advantage, as well. Because Krait tried never to do what an adversary expected, he pressed ALL INTERIOR ON, at once bringing light to every room in the residence.

The inner laundry-room door opened to a service hall. With the Glock in both hands and his arms locked straight in front of him, he followed the hallway.

Krait entered an unfurnished family room where an immense plasma-screen TV had been crafted into a wall-wide entertainment center. The granite bar was handsome.

A pane had been broken out of one of the French doors. Fragments of glass littered the limestone floor.

Like Krait, Carrier and the woman had been soaked to the skin. They had shed considerable rain on the pale limestone, which had darkened where it absorbed the water.

Tense, sweeping left with the Glock, sweeping right, alert for peripheral movement, Krait proceeded into the big kitchen, which was open to the family room. More limestone, more water.

The dining room also lacked furniture, but it featured wall-to-wall white carpet. Dirt on the carpet drew his attention.

Apparently, two steps inside the dining room, the couple had vigorously wiped their feet on the pristine carpet, staining it. He wondered why they had so aggressively soiled such excellent wool.

By the time he passed through an archway and proceeded to the center of the likewise carpeted living room, he realized that they had cleaned their shoes in order to leave less of a trail. Water alone could not be easily seen on the textured white carpet; and it did not change the color of the fibers. He could no longer discern the route that they had taken through the house.

To the right of the living room, through another archway, lay the entry hall. Rooms waited beyond. Stairs led to the second floor.

Left, at the north end of the living room, double doors served another chamber.

Krait felt certain that his quarry had gone upstairs. Reluctant to leave an unexplored space behind him, however, he eased open one of the doors. He rushed through fast and low, behind the gun, into a library that contained neither books nor intruders.

He went to the entry hall. Drops of water shimmered on the wood floor. They were too widely distributed to indicate an obvious trail.

Another door opened into a home gym large enough to accept an array of exercise machines that would allow circuit training. No machines were present, but three entire walls had been paneled with floor-to-ceiling mirrors.

Such vast mirrored surfaces brought Krait to a halt.

By their subtle reversal of all images, mirrors seemed to be windows to another world in opposition to this one, a world where everything appeared familiar but was in fact profoundly different.

All that was considered evil on this side of the glass might be judged good on the other side. Truth here might be lies there, and the future might precede the past.

This panoramic mirror excited him more than any he had seen before, because the cross-reflections revealed not just one strange world but many, each contained in the others, each promising the absolute power that he yearned to have but could not quite acquire on this side of the looking glass.

He stood before numerous Kraits, each with his own Glock, and they seemed not like reflections but like replications, each as aware as he himself was, separate consciousness in other dimensions. He had become an army, and he felt the **power** of being many, the ferocity of the pack, the viciousness of the stinging swarm, and his heart was lifted, and his mind thrilled.

A sudden awareness of his appearance deflated him. Rain had washed all shape from his clothes. You couldn't see that they had been garments of quality. His hair was plastered to his head.

Anyone might have mistaken him for a homeless person, adrift and penniless. He mortified himself, the way he looked.

This mortification turned his memory back to the embarrassment at the hotel, where he had been outfoxed by Carrier's room switch.

Every Krait in every world within the mirrors spoke as one, but they could be heard only in their separate realms. The single voice of a single Krait spoke aloud the words that the others silently mouthed: "He's done it again."

Krait stepped out of the gym into the entry hall.

He didn't go to the stairs. He didn't care about the stairs. The bricklayer and the bitch weren't on the second floor, ready to defend the staircase from the superior position of the upper hallway. They never had been.

They had left when the lights came on.

The front door was unlocked. No surprise. They didn't have a key with which to lock it from the outside.

He opened the door, and rain blew in.

Leaving the house open behind him, he walked down the front path, into the street.

The Explorer was gone.

The wind drove the rain harder than before. It stung his face.

Although the sky had quieted, a sword of light ripped the night, and Krait flinched. He thought he was going to be struck.

He looked at the bicycle. The FOR SALE sign.

From a pants pocket, he withdrew the two 9-mm cartridges. This one extra detail had been too pat. The bullets had not been dropped. They had been **placed** on the sidewalk.

He returned them to his pocket. He had a use for them.

He went to the island in the center of the turnaround. The dark-blue Chevrolet waited where he had parked it.

After circling the vehicle and finding the tires intact, he got in the driver's seat and shut out the storm.

With the first twist of the key, the engine turned over. He had not expected it to start.

The instrument panel brightened, but not as fully as before. Carrier had shot the electronic-map display.

Krait could send a coded text message explaining his situation, and his tech-support team would track the Explorer for him, allowing him a somewhat delayed pursuit.

Wasted effort. Carrier had used the SUV only to get out of the neighborhood. He would abandon it within minutes, and would switch to whatever vehicle he could find.

This did not mean that Krait had failed in his mission. He had only begun.

A lesser man might have become emotional, surrendering himself to rage or despair, or fear. Krait allowed himself none of that.

Already, he had overcome the twinge of mortification that he had felt when he'd realized what had happened. Anyway, **mortification** was not the correct word. He had felt nothing worse than mild chagrin.

He drove around the island and out of the cul-de-sac.

In truth, the word **chagrin** was too strong to describe what he felt at the moment of realization in the mirrored gym. **Discomfiture** was more accurate. He had been discomfited to think that he had been deceived by the two dropped cartridges.

A psychologically mature person looks for the positive in every situation, for no experience is entirely negative.

These recent events had given him time to reflect on the lessons of the past nine hours. Reflection was a positive thing.

Having turned right at the T intersection, descending now from the ridge line toward the lower hills and the coast, he decided that **discomfiture** was not the word that he needed, either.

He had been disappointed. Indeed, that was the word. He had not been disappointed in himself so much as in the universe that still, from time to time, seemed to orchestrate its energies to thwart him.

In order to engage in some constructive reflection, he needed a place where he could relax, feel at ease. Taverns, coffeehouses, and cafés had never appealed to him.

He was a home-loving man, and pretty much any home would do, as long as it met his standards of cleanliness.

Twenty-Nine

After speaking with Tim on the phone at half past midnight, to inform him about the call from Hitch Lombard, Pete Santo took a two-hour nap before continuing his on-line search for a clue to the hit man's true identity.

Shy Zoey refused to jump on the bed and sleep at his feet. She curled up on her dog bed in the corner.

Her refusal to join him was a reliable predictor that he would have some heavy-duty dreams. Perhaps the capacity to enter a dream state might be preceded by a subtle change in body chemistry that a dog, with a sense of smell thousands of times more powerful than that of a human being, could detect. Or maybe she was psychic.

Half reclining against a pile of feather pillows, Pete said, "Come on. Come up."

She raised her head. Her soulful brown eyes regarded him with what might have been disbelief. Or pity.

"No nightmares. I promise. Has your dad ever lied to you? I'm just taking a nap here."

Zoey lowered her head, resting her chin between her forelegs, and her pendulous upper lips—flews, they were called—bloomed over her paws, and she closed her eyes.

"My feet smell especially fine tonight," he said. "You'd enjoy sleeping with your snout near my feet."

She raised one eyebrow without opening her eyes. She licked her chops. She lowered the eyebrow. She yawned. She sighed. Invitation declined.

Familiar with rejection, Pete matched her sigh and then switched off the lamp.

He went instantly to sleep. He always did. Falling asleep was never a problem. Staying asleep was a bitch.

Of course, he dreamed. Dogs know.

Birds died in flight and fell, and the severed heads of babies sang a sweet and melancholy tune, while the woman pulled out her hair by the roots and made an offering of it because she had nothing else to give.

He woke at 2:48, gasping for light, and turned on the nightstand lamp.

From her bed, Zoey watched him with a sad expression.

He took a quick shower, dressed, and made a pot of coffee almost corrosive enough to test the brewer to destruction.

By 3:22, he had settled at his desk in the study, surfing the Web, drinking the ink-black blend, and eating his mother's walnut brownies.

His mom was a bad cook. She was a worse baker. The brownies tasted all right, but they were hard enough to break teeth.

He ate them anyway. Proud of her imagined kitchen wizardry, she had given him a large plate heaped with the brownies. He couldn't throw them away. She was his mother.

The danger of dreams having passed, Zoey squirmed into the knee space under the desk and slept on his feet. She didn't beg for any of the brownies. A wise dog.

The call from Hitch Lombard had clearly been triggered by Pete's attempt to match Kravet's many aliases to the names of officers in various local, state, and national law-enforcement databases. This time he would stay away from such authorized-access-only resources, where evidently those names triggered embedded security alerts that tagged the inquirer as a potential troublemaker.

Googling each of the names and combing through the hits promised to be an arduous task. A lot of people had the name Robert Krane, for instance.

He needed to string each name to some search words. Considering that the Krane identity and most of the others were supported by a California driver's license and address, even though bogus, Pete added **California**.

Tim had been miserly with information, as though paying out any facts about the woman would only buy her greater trouble than she already had. **Parrot, mug, egg, custard, pie:** They were not words that made a useful search string.

Whoever the many-named man might be, logic suggested that he had been involved with some police agency, on one side of the law or the other. Consequently, Pete added **police** to the list, and began the search.

A few names later, at 4:07 A.M., he made the connection to the brutal Cream & Sugar killings. For forty-eight hours, the police had listed one Roy Kutter, of San Francisco, as a person of interest, which had become the politically correct, tone-deaf way of saying "suspect."

The smiling man's portfolio of identities included Roy Lee Kutter.

As Pete pored through all the news stories that he could find on the Cream & Sugar investigation, his gumshoe intuition raised alarms. He didn't need a dog's superior sense of smell to know this case was rotten.

His bloodhound blood called him to the hunt, and happily he set to work, considering each news story as a series of snapshots, slowly developing a broader picture of the case.

At 4:38, the cable service failed, and he lost his Internet connection.

His cable company was reliable. Often a service interruption proved to be brief.

While he waited to get back on-line, he went to the bathroom and took a whiz.

In the kitchen, he refreshed his coffee.

Turning away from the brewing machine with a full mug, he discovered that Zoey had followed him.

Her intense gaze, raised head, and anxious expression suggested that she might need to visit the backyard. Her tail wasn't wagging, however, and a certain easy wag had always been a component of her I-need-to-pee code.

He put down his mug and got a beach towel from the laundry room. When the dog came in from the rain, Pete would need to rub her dry.

Opening the back door, he said, "Okay. Want to kill some grass, girl?"

She approached the door and stood at the threshold, staring across the porch, into the yard.

"Zoey?"

Her ears lifted. Her black nostrils flared and quivered, testing the air.

The thunder and lightning had stopped. Anyway, storms had never frightened her. Like most retrievers, she loved rain—though not on this occasion.

"Coyote out there?" he asked.

She backed away from the open door.

"Raccoon?" he suggested.

Zoey padded out of the kitchen.

He switched on the outside light and stepped onto the porch. He saw nothing unusual and heard only the rain.

When he went looking for Zoey, he found her in the living room. She stood at the front door.

He opened the door, and again she stared out at the night. She would not cross the threshold.

She made a low sound in her throat. It almost might be mistaken for a growl. Zoey never growled.

The telephone rang. At 4:46 in the morning.

Ears up, head up, tail tucked, Zoey scampered into the study, and he followed her.

The telephone rang again.

He stood looking at it. The caller's ID was blocked.

On the fourth ring, he went into the bedroom. His Galco Jackass rig and service pistol lay on a shelf in the closet. It included an ammo pouch with two spare magazines.

As he rigged up, the phone stopped ringing.

In his study once more, he sat at the desk.

Zoey did not want to return to the knee space, where previously she had been so cozy. She stood by the desk, alert, staring at him. She appeared to be anticipating a nightmare.

The cable service had not been restored.

Pete switched off the computer. He sat for a moment, thinking about the Cream & Sugar case.

The telephone rang.

His wallet and badge case lay on the desk. He put them in his back pockets.

From the study closet, he got a lined and hooded windbreaker, slipped into it.

Zoey followed him into the kitchen, where he snared keys from a pegboard.

The phone stopped ringing.

In the garage, he said, "Dress," and at once the dog came to him to receive her collar. He attached a leash.

When he opened the tailgate of the Mercury Mountaineer, she sprang into the cargo space.

He locked the door between the garage and the house, as he had locked the front and back doors. He intentionally had not turned out the lights.

Action by action, he moved faster, with more economy. He was in gear now. Maybe he would be quick enough.

Thirty

Lumbering south on the coast high-way, the aging Transportation Authority bus perfumed the rainy night with an agri-fuel flatulence. This month it might be running on an ethanol blend, on peanut oil, on reprocessed grease from fast-food restaurants, or on some extract of biologically engineered giant mutant soybeans.

Tim drove around the behemoth, raced five blocks, parked at a restaurant, and abandoned the Explorer, this time perhaps forever.

He had driven past three bus stops. He and Linda ran two long blocks north, returning to the nearest stop, where they waited for their fragrant new transport.

The wind blew rain under the roof of the shelter, dashed it in their faces.

Traffic had increased in the hour before dawn. The **siss** of tires on the storm-sluiced pavement was an icy sound, reminiscent of sled runners slicing across crusted snow.

They boarded the bus, ascertained that it went at least as far as Dana Point, and dripped along the aisle as the driver pulled onto the highway.

This was one of the first buses of the day, and it carried few passengers. Most were women on their way to hard jobs that started early.

Everyone aboard was dry. They had umbrellas. Some regarded Tim and Linda with sympathy. Others couldn't repress smug little smiles.

She led him to seats in the back, at a distance from the nearest other passenger, where they could not be overheard.

"So what was that?"

"What was what?"

"We couldn't park closer to a bus stop?"

"No."

"Because you don't want him to know we got on a bus?"

"I don't want him leaping to the idea right away. He'll get there soon enough."

Her friend Teresa, currently spending a

week in New York with a couple of girlfriends, lived in Dana Point. They were going to use her house briefly.

"You actually think they would track down the bus, interview the driver?"

"I actually do."

"He wouldn't remember us," she said.

"Look at us. Two drowned cats."

"Well, it's raining."

"He'd remember."

"When he leaves us off, we'll be walking several blocks to her house. They won't have any idea where we went, just somewhere in Dana Point."

"Maybe the nerdy nephews have instant access to phone-company computers. When did you last call Teresa?"

She frowned. "Oh. They could get any numbers I regularly call in Dana Point."

"Yeah."

"And from the numbers they could trace addresses."

"Right. And the next time he gets close to us, we won't be able to hoodwink him so easy."

"None of that seemed easy to me."

"It wasn't. So we better not let him get close to us till we're ready."

"We're going to be ready?"

"I don't know."

"I don't see how you get ready for someone like him."

Tim did not reply.

For a while they rode in silence.

She said, "I keep thinking and thinking—what did I do? I didn't do anything."

"This isn't about something you did."

"It can't be."

"It's about something you know," he said.

Those green eyes started working again, trying to open him like a vacuum-packed can.

He said, "You know something that could do serious damage to someone important."

"I've been doing nothing for years but writing navel-gazing novels. I don't know anything about anyone."

"It's something—you don't know that you know it."

"That's for sure."

"Something you heard, something you saw. It didn't seem to be anything at the time."

"When?"

He shrugged. "Last month. A year ago. Anytime."

"That's a lot of territory to walk back through."

"Wouldn't do you any good to walk it. It didn't seem like anything big to you then, it won't seem like anything big now."

"They want to kill me for something so insignificant I can't remember it?"

"Not insignificant. It's something big. Important to them, unremarkable to you. I'm pretty sure that's the way it's got to be. I've been thinking hard about it since he showed up at the hotel."

"You've been thinking hard since I opened the door and first saw you," she replied.

"You said a head as big as mine has to have some brains in it. Are you cold?"

"I've got the chills. But not because I'm wet. The knot's getting tighter, isn't it?"

"Well," he said, "no matter how tight a knot gets, you can always cut the rope."

"If it's something big enough, there might be no way out."

"There's always a way out," he said. "There's just a bunch of ways you don't want to think about."

A small quiet laugh escaped her.

Again, they chose silence for a while.

Tim sat with his fists on his thighs, and after a mile or two, she put her left hand on his right fist.

He opened his hand and turned it palm-up, enfolding her hand.

The bus stopped from time to time, and more people got on than got off. None of the new passengers appeared to be intent on murder.

Thirty-One

Pete Santo slumped behind the wheel of the Mercury Mountaineer, a block from his house.

When he killed the headlights and the engine, Zoey used the console as a bridge to pass from the cargo space to the passenger's seat.

Together, they watched the street and waited. Now and then he rubbed the crest of her neck or behind her ears.

The nearest streetlamp was not close enough to shed any light into the SUV. The spreading boughs of a stone pine, under which he had parked, would cloak them in shadows even for a while after the sun rose.

Only an hour ago, he could not have imagined that he might one day conduct a surveillance of his own home. This was a fine time to be alive if your meat was paranoia and your bread was violence.

Pete expected company to come calling well before sunrise. In fact, they arrived ten minutes after he took up watch from under the pine tree.

The Suburban stopped in front of his house, beside a streetlamp, facing the opposite direction from other parked vehicles on this side of the street. Evidently the visitors saw no need for discretion.

Three men got out of the Suburban. Even seen from a distance and in rain gear, they looked the type.

Pete lost sight of them as they approached his house. From this distance and angle, he could not see his place, only the street in front of it.

He assumed that one of the three would detour to the backyard.

Whatever law-enforcement ID they were carrying, it would trump his PD badge. Maybe FBI or National Security Agency. Maybe the Secret Service or Homeland Security.

In his mind's ear, he could hear his doorbell ring.

Most likely their badges and photo IDs would prove to be no more legitimate than Kravet's many driver's licenses.

If Pete had not fled with Zoey, he would have had to engage these men as though they were who they claimed to be. Because maybe they were.

Whether they were the real deal or not, they came with a message: Lay off the smiley guy with all the identities; lay off the Cream & Sugar murders.

They would claim he was interfering in a major ongoing federal criminal investigation of great delicacy. Or that this was a matter of national security. In either case, the investigation would not be in the jurisdiction of a local cop.

Had Pete remained at home, this delegation would have seriously compromised his ability to assist Tim and Linda.

Now they must be ringing the bell again and discussing their next move.

Zoey began a mild anxiety panting.

"Good girl," he said. "Sweet baby girl."

He doubted that they would ring the bell a third time.

A minute passed. Two. Three.

These were not the kind of guys who would sit in rocking chairs on the porch to jaw about baseball and the weather while they waited for Pete to return.

They had gone into the house. Whoever

they claimed to be, that wasn't who they were. They were renegades.

Maybe they would confiscate the hard drive of his computer to see what else he'd been doing before they had tagged him for chasing the Kravet identities.

They might plant drugs where he wouldn't find them. Then if they needed to control him at a later date, they would conduct a raid and confiscate quantities of cocaine that qualified him as a dealer.

"Sweet baby girl. Sweet, sweet baby girl."

He started the Mountaineer, executed a U-turn, and clicked on the headlights as he drove away.

As if it were oil in a deep fryer, rain sizzled on the pavement.

Two blocks later, his cell phone rang.

Prudence argued that he should ignore it. He flipped it open because Tim might be trying to reach him.

According to the ID line, the caller was Hitch Lombard. This time the chief of detectives would make no pretense of concern about Pete's health.

He closed the phone without taking the call.

Zoey stopped the anxiety panting. She

gazed out the passenger-door window. She enjoyed going for rides.

For her, the night had suddenly taken a turn for the better.

In addition to his computer, maybe the intruders would take his mom's brownies with them, without tasting one first. Even in this age, Pete believed that justice found the guilty one way or another.

Thirty-Two

Krait cruised in search of a home. He did not require luxury or the benefit of a view. A humble domicile would satisfy him.

Some people held jobs in Los Angeles but preferred to live in more benign Orange County. In certain professions, the work day began early, and those with a long commute set out at five o'clock in the morning.

Traveling a charming street of character-rich homes, he spotted a smartly dressed younger couple under sturdy umbrellas. They were making their way from a small but handsome Craftsman-style house to a Lexus parked in the driveway.

Both the man and the woman carried briefcases. They appeared to be determined not to allow the inclement weather to water down their enthusiasm for their business-day adventures.

He imagined them to be aggressive corporate climbers with dreams of corner offices and stock options. Although he did not approve of their materialism and assbackwards priorities, he would grant them the grace of visiting their home.

He followed them for a few blocks. When he determined that they were driving directly to a freeway, he returned to their house and parked in front of it.

In this last darkness of the waning night, they had left no lights on. They were too young to have teenagers, and even greedy beavers of their ilk would probably not have left younger children home alone at this hour. They looked childless to Krait, and of **that** he approved.

He walked directly to the front door and let himself inside. After standing for a minute in the lightless foyer, listening to a stillness relieved only by the white noise of the rain on the roof, he knew that he was alone in the house.

Nevertheless, turning on lights, he investigated every room. Indeed, they had no children. And the bed in the guest room had not been furnished with sheets; no one was staying with them.

Krait stripped naked and deposited his ruined clothes in a trash bag that he found in a master-bath cabinet. He took a shower as hot as he could tolerate, and though he did not consider the bar soap to be satisfactory, he felt refreshed.

He did not need to shave. He'd had his beard permanently removed by electrolysis. Nothing made a man look as disheveled and unclean as did beard stubble.

From the master closet, he selected a man's cashmere bathrobe. It was a good fit.

The house smelled of plug-in lemon-scented air fresheners, but they weren't covering up any underlying malodor that he could detect. Everything appeared orderly, even neat, and clean enough.

Barefoot and decent, he carried the plastic bag of clothes, the Glock machine pistol, the LockAid, and other personal items to the kitchen. Except for his cell phone and the Glock, he put everything on the corner secretary.

He placed the machine pistol on one of the dining chairs, to have it close at hand.

Sitting at the breakfast table, he sent a coded text message requesting a complete change of clothes, including shoes. They knew all his sizes and preferences.

He did not ask for a fresh sedan with a new electronic map. Savvy to the risk of satellite tracking, Carrier would not again allow himself to be pursued by that means.

Krait asked to be informed of the location of the Explorer when it had been at a full stop for longer than five minutes.

After gathering a pile of unopened mail from the secretary, he returned to the table, where he pored through the contents of every envelope, seeking information about his hosts.

They were Bethany and James Valdorado. Apparently, they worked for an investment-banking firm named Leeward Capital. They leased their Lexus, had solid bank balances, and subscribed to **O** magazine.

They had gotten a postcard from friends—Judi and Frankie—who were currently visiting France. Krait didn't approve of a culturally insensitive remark in the postcard, but Judi and Frankie were, for the time being, beyond his reach.

While he finished with the mail, a craving for hot chocolate came over him. He found all the makings, including a can of high-quality dark cocoa.

This was going to be lovely. He felt quite calm now. He needed this respite, a little time for reflection.

Bethany and Jim had a four-slice toaster with

wide slots that would accept English muffins and waffles. But the fresh loaf of cinnamon-raisin bread was irresistible.

He took the butter out of the refrigerator and set it on the counter to soften.

As the delicious aroma of cinnamon-raisin toast began to fill the room, he put a pan on the cooktop and poured fresh milk into it. He set the gas flame just so.

Home. In a world offering limitless adventure and sensation, there was still no place like home.

With his heart gladdened by this domesticity, he began to hum a happy tune when, behind him, a woman said, "Oh, I'm sorry, I didn't know the kids had a houseguest."

Smiling but no longer humming, Krait turned from the stove.

The intruder, an attractive woman in her sixties, had hair as soft and white as the wings of doves. Her eyes were gentian-blue.

She wore black slacks and a blue silk blouse that complemented her eyes. The tailored slacks were lint-free with a meticulously pressed crease. The blouse was tucked into the slacks.

She must have left her umbrella and raincoat on the front porch before letting herself in with a key.

Her smile was less certain than Krait's but no less appealing. "I'm Cynthia Norwood."

"Bethany's mother!" Krait declared, and saw that his guess had been correct. "What a pleasure this is. I've heard so much about you. I'm Romulus Kudlow, and I'm embarrassed. There you are, looking as if you just stepped out of a fashion magazine, and here I am completely"—he indicated the cashmere robe—"dishabille! You must be thinking **What kind of beast have Bethany and Jim let sleep under their roof!** "

"Oh, no, not at all," she hastened to assure him. "I'm the one who should apologize, barging in like this."

"You're incapable of barging, Mrs. Norwood. You came in here as light-footed as a dancer."

"I knew the kids had run off to work, thought they forgot to turn out the lights."

"I'll bet it wouldn't be the first time."

"Or the hundredth," she said. "I wonder what their electric bill would be if I didn't live across the street."

"They're in a high-pressure profession," he said. "They have so much on their minds. I don't know how they do it."

She said, "I worry about them. All work and no play."

"But they love it, you know. They love the challenge."

"Well, they seem to," she agreed.

"And it's a blessing to be doing work you love. So many people spend their lives in jobs they hate, and that's worse."

The toast popped up.

"I didn't mean to interrupt your breakfast," she said.

"Dear," he said, "I'm not sure buttered cinnamon-raisin toast and hot chocolate qualifies as breakfast. A nutritionist would rap my knuckles and call it a wicked indulgence. Will you join me?"

"Oh, I couldn't."

"It's not yet dawn," he said. "You can't have eaten yet."

"No, not yet, but—"

"I am **not** going to miss this opportunity to hear all the very bad things that Bethany did as a little girl. She and Jim have so many stories about **my** foolish behavior, I absolutely must have some ammunition to return fire."

"Well, hot cocoa sounds good on a rainy day, but—"

"Keep me company, dear. Please." He indicated a chair. "Sit there. We'll schmooze."

Relenting, she said, "While you make the cocoa, I'll butter the toast."

If she came around the table, she would see the machine pistol on the chair.

"Sit, sit," he insisted. "I showed up last night with precious little notice, but they were so gracious. They are always gracious. Now I couldn't **stand** myself if, on top of everything else, I allowed Bethany's mother to make my breakfast. Sit, sit. I insist."

Settling into the chair he had indicated, she said, "I love that you call her Bethany. She won't let anyone use her full name."

"And it's a beautiful name," he said, plucking plastic placemats and paper napkins from a drawer.

"It is beautiful. Malcolm and I spent so much time considering names. We must have rejected a thousand."

"I tell her that **Beth** rhymes with **death,**" Krait said, as he went in search of plates and mugs.

"She thinks **Beth** sounds more like a serious businesswoman."

"And I tell her **Beth** rhymes with **bad breath.**"

Cynthia laughed. "You're fun, Mr. Kudlow."

"Call me Romulus or Rommy. Only my mother calls me Mr. Kudlow."

Laughing again, she said, "I'm so glad you're here. The kids need to have some fun once in a while."

"Jim used to be a lot of fun."

"And I love that you call him Jim."

"He can save the pretentious **James** for the investment-banking crowd," said Krait. "I knew him when he was just plain Jim, and he will always be Jim to me."

"We do best in life," she said, "when we remember our roots and keep things simple."

"I have no idea what my roots are," Krait said, "but you are so right about simplicity. I love simplicity. And you know what? I love this place. I feel entirely at home here."

"That's very sweet," she said.

"Home is so important to me, Mrs. Norwood."

"Where is your home, Rommy?"

"Home," Krait said, "is the place that, when you go there, they have to take you in."

Thirty-Three

Through the rain-streaked bus win-dows, the world seemed to be melting, as if all the works of humankind and of Nature would drain through a hole at the bottom of the universe, leaving only an eternal void and the bus traveling through it until the bus also deliquesced around them, taking its light with it, setting them adrift in perfect blackness.

Holding Tim's hand, Linda felt tethered to something that would not melt away.

She had not needed to hold on to anyone in a long time. She had not dared.

Nor had there been, in an even longer time, anyone who offered her a hand with such conviction, with such commitment. In less than ten hours, she had come to trust him as she had trusted no one since childhood.

She knew little about him, yet she felt that

she knew him better than anyone in her life, understood the essentials of him, the shape of the spirit that lived in his heart, the strength of the heart that was the compass of his mind.

At the same time, he remained a mystery to her. And though she wanted to know everything about him, a part of her hoped that no matter what relationship might develop between them, he would always retain some element of mystery.

To do for her what he was doing, surely at the core of him must lie something magical, transcendent. To discover that his Merlin was not a sorcerer but instead a seventh-grade teacher who had mentored him, to discover that his courage came not from having been raised by a pride of lions but from reading superhero comics as a boy would be to render goodness as banal as evil.

Her desire for enduring mystery surprised her. She had thought that the romantic in her had been burned at the stake at least sixteen years ago.

As the bus approached the outskirts of Dana Point, Tim said, "Who is Molly?"

His question inspired in her a frisson of wonder, and she regarded him with astonishment.

"At the hotel," he said. "You talked in your sleep."

"I never talk in my sleep."

"Do you never sleep alone?"

"I always sleep alone."

"Then how would you know?"

"What did I say?"

"Just the name. Molly. And **no**. You said **No, no.**"

"She was a dog. My dog. Beautiful. So sweet."

"And something happened."

"Yes."

"When was this?"

"We got her when I was six. She was sent away when I was eleven. Eighteen years ago, and it still hurts."

"Why was she sent away?"

"We couldn't keep her anymore. Angelina didn't like dogs, said there wasn't money for dog food and vet bills."

"Who's Angelina?"

Linda gazed out at the dissolving world.

"In some ways, it was the worst part of it all. Molly was a dog. She didn't understand. She loved me, and I was sending her away, and I couldn't explain because she was just a dog."

Tim waited. In addition to all the things he

knew, he also knew when to wait, which was a rare grace.

"We couldn't find anyone to take Molly. She was beautiful, but no one would take her because she was not just any dog, she was **our** dog."

Sorrow is not a raven perched persistently above a chamber door. Sorrow is a thing with teeth, and while in time it retreats, it comes back at the whisper of its name.

"I can still see Molly's eyes the way they were when I sent her away. Confused. Afraid. Entreating me. No one would take her, and so she had to go to the pound."

"Someone adopted her from there," he said.

"I don't know. I never knew."

"Someone did."

"So often I thought of her lying in a cage, in a kennel full of sad and anxious dogs, wondering why I'd sent her away, wondering what she'd ever done to lose my love."

Linda looked from the window to her hand in his hand.

This seemed as if it was a weakness, this need to hold on to him, and she had never been weak. She would rather be dead than be fainthearted in a world where the weak were preyed on often just for sport.

Strangely, however, it did not feel like weakness. For some reason, it felt like defiance.

"How lonely Molly must have been," she said. "And if they couldn't adopt her . . . did she think of me when the needle went in?"

"No, Linda. No. It didn't happen."

"It probably did."

"And if it did," he said, "she didn't know what the needle meant, didn't know what was coming."

"She would know. Dogs know. I won't lie to myself about it. That would only make it worse."

The air brakes exhaled, and the bus began to slow.

"Of all the things that happened back then—in a funny way, that's the worst. Because nobody else expected me to save them. I was just a child. But I wasn't just a child to poor Molly. We were best pals. I was the world to her. And I failed her."

"You didn't fail Molly," he assured her. "Sounds to me like the world failed both of you."

For the first time in more than ten years, she felt able to talk about it. She had used up all her anger in her bitter books and might now speak of it with dispassion. She could have told him everything right then.

From the flooded gutter, a wing of water flew up as the bus arrived at their stop in Dana Point. The folding doors clattered open. They got out into the rain.

The wind had followed the thunder and the lightning into the east. Torrents fell straight down, silver in the air and dirty on the pavement. Soon dawn would break behind the clouds, the dawn that she had thought she might never see.

Thirty-Four

"Do you like the hot chocolate, Cynthia?"

"I think it's the best I've ever had."

"That tiny drop of vanilla makes all the difference."

"How very clever."

"May I quarter your toast for you?"

"Thank you, Rommy."

"I like to dunk," he said.

"Me, too."

"James might not approve."

She said, "We won't tell him."

They sat catercorner at the kitchen table. They stirred their hot chocolate with spoons, and a delicious aroma rose from their steaming mugs.

"What an unusual name—Romulus."

"Yes, it even sounds unusual to me. In Roman legend, Romulus was the founder of Rome."

"You've got quite a lot to live up to with a name like that."

"Romulus and his twin brother, Remus, were abandoned at birth, suckled by a she-wolf, raised by a shepherd, and when Romulus founded Rome, he killed Remus."

"What an awful story."

"Well, Cynthia, it's the way of the world, isn't it? Not the she-wolf part, but the rest of it. People can be so horrid to one another. I'm so grateful for my friends."

"How did you meet Bethany and James?"

"Jim," he admonished with a wag of his finger.

She smiled and shook her head. "He's got me quite brainwashed on the issue."

"We met through mutual friends. Do you know Judi and Frankie?"

"Oh," she said, "I adore Judi and Frankie."

"Who wouldn't?"

"They are such a wonderful couple."

He sighed wistfully. "If I could find love like that, Cynthia, I'd kill for it."

"You'll find someone, Rommy. There's someone for everyone."

"I guess someday lightning could strike. I

would very much like to see lightning strike, I'll tell you."

They dunked and ate.

A drab gray morning rose at the windows, and the kitchen seemed even cozier by comparison to the rainy day.

He said, "Did you know they're in Paris now?"

"Judi and Frankie love Paris."

"Everybody does. I was supposed to go with them this time, but I was hit by an avalanche of work."

"I'll bet they'd be fun to travel with," she said.

"They're an absolute delight. We were in Spain together. We ran with the bulls."

Cynthia's gentian eyes widened. "Judi and Frankie ran with the bulls—like in Hemingway?"

"Well, Judi didn't, but Frankie insisted. And you know, there's no resisting Frankie."

"I'm astonished. But I guess . . . they're both quite athletic."

"Oh, they wear me out sometimes," he said.

"Isn't that dangerous, running with the bulls?"

"Well, it's better to run with them than to be run over by them. My legs were rubber by the end of it."

"The closest I want to get to a bull," she said, "is filet mignon."

"You're marvelous." He patted her arm. "I'm having such fun. This is so nice. Isn't this nice?"

"It is, yes. But I never thought Judi and Frankie would be drawn to dangerous sports. They don't seem the type."

"It's not Judi, really. Frankie's the one who gets a thrill from walking on the edge. I worry about him sometimes."

He dunked and ate, but she sat with a wedge of toast halfway to her mouth, as though she had just remembered that she was on a diet, as though she were clamped between the jaws of appetite and self-denial.

"Have you been to Paris, Cynthia?"

Slowly, she returned the unbitten wedge of toast to her plate.

He said, "Is something wrong, dear?"

"I've got . . . a thing to do. I forgot. An appointment."

When she started to push back from the table, he put a hand over hers. "You can't rush off, Cynthia."

"I have such a sieve for a memory. I forgot—"

Tightening his grip on her hand, Krait said, "I'm curious. What was my mistake?"

"Mistake?"

"You're trembling, dear. You're no good at pretending. What was my mistake?"

"It's a dentist appointment."

"For when—six-thirty in the morning?"

Nonplussed, she looked at the wall clock.

"Cynthia? Cindy? I'd really love to know what my mistake was."

With her eyes still fixed on the clock, she said, "F-Frankie isn't a man."

"Surely Judi isn't a man. Ah. I see. A wonderful **lesbian** couple. Well, that's all right. I have no problem with that. In fact, I'm all for it."

He patted her hand and picked up the wedge of toast from which she had been incapable of taking a bite. He dunked it.

Unable to look at him, regarding her plate, she said, "Did you hurt them?"

"Bethany and Jim? Of course not, dear. They're off to work just like you thought, clawing for bonuses and stock options. I didn't let myself in until they were gone."

He took a bite of toast. Another bite. He finished the wedge.

"May I go?" she asked.

"Dear, let me explain. My outfit was ruined by the rain. I'm waiting here for a delivery of fresh clothes. I have no time in my schedule for the police."

"I would just go home," she said.

"I've never learned to trust people, Cynthia."

"I won't call the police. Not for a few hours."

"How long do you think you could wait?"

She raised her head, met his eyes. "As long as you tell me to. I'll just go home and sit."

"You're a very gentle person, Cynthia."

"I've always just . . ."

"What have you always just, dear?"

"I've always just wanted things to be nice for everyone."

"Of course you have. That's you, dear. That's so you. And you know what? I believe you really might do what you say."

"I will."

"I believe you might go home and sit quietly for hours."

"I give you my word. I do."

Reaching around the end of the table, he retrieved the Glock machine pistol from the chair.

"Oh, please," she said.

"Now don't jump to conclusions, Cynthia."

She looked at the wall clock. He didn't know what hope she saw in the clock. Time was no one's friend.

"Come with me, dear."

"Why? Where?"

"Just a few steps. Come with me."

She tried to get up. She had no strength.

At her chair, he held out his left hand. "Let me help."

Cynthia did not recoil from his touch, but took his hand and held tight to it. "Thank you."

"We're just going to walk across the kitchen to the half bath. That's not so far."

"I don't . . ."

"You don't what, dear?"

"I don't understand this."

Pulling her to her feet, he said, "No. You wouldn't. So many things are beyond understanding, aren't they?"

Thirty-Five

The library, a squat brick structure with narrow barred windows, brought to mind a fortress, as if far-thinking librarians realized that a day was fast approaching when books would have to be defended to the death against barbarian hordes.

Near dawn, Pete Santo parked near the entrance.

Back in February, a troubled youth—as the media tagged him—had hidden in the library overnight. A recent benefit to raise funds for book purchases had taken in forty thousand dollars, and he figured to heist the loot and live high.

An honest media would have referred to him as an ignorant drug-addled youth, but that might have humiliated the child and started him down a path of antisocial behavior.

Although eighteen, the "youth" didn't understand that the money had been contributed in the form of checks and had been deposited in a bank. He didn't trust banks. They were "run by money vampires who want to suck you dry." He preferred a cash stash, and he assumed that anyone as smart as he was—or smarter—would feel the same.

After a search, when he found only a metal box containing petty cash, he decided to wait for the librarian to open in the morning. He would put a gun to her head and demand the forty thousand.

To his surprise, three men from a maintenance company let themselves into the library at 5:00 A.M. to perform a nightly four-hour cleaning. Holding them at gunpoint, he demanded their wallets.

He might have pulled off this robbery if the maintenance men hadn't seen the ruined books. They became incensed.

In the lonely hours after the troubled youth had given up trying to find the forty thousand, he collected books that he felt—based on titles and jacket art—were full of "wrong ideas." He destroyed them.

The maintenance crew was not composed

of three ardent book lovers. They were furious with the youth because instead of tearing the volumes apart or setting them on fire, he had chosen to urinate on them, and it was their job to clean up the mess.

They distracted him, rushed him, took the gun from him, and beat the crap out of him. Then they called the cops.

Pete had given them a stern but not entirely sincere lecture on the inadvisability of taking the law into their own hands.

Now, leaving Zoey in the Mountaineer with the doors locked, he hurried to the shelter of the front overhang. Through the panes in the doors, he saw light, and he knocked loudly.

A maintenance man appeared. Pete held his badge to the glass, but the janitor let him in without examining the ID. "Hey, Detective Santo. What you doin' here? Nobody pissed on no books tonight."

"You hear he's suing the library?" Pete asked.

"He'll probably score a couple million."

"If he does, maybe I'll piss on some books."

"You'll need to get in line."

"Listen, I know the library doesn't open for a few hours, but I've got to use one of the computers here."

"Don't the cops have no computers?"

“This is personal business. I can’t do it at the office, and my computer at home crashed.”

“You sure don’t need my permission. Cops—can’t they go anywhere they want, anytime?”

“That’s not quite how the Constitution puts it, but close.”

“You know where they are, the computers?”

“Yes. I remember.”

The devil of illiteracy had been given a staging post in the temple of the word. Two aisles of books had been displaced to allow the installation of six work stations.

Pete sat down, powered up, and got back on the Web. Soon he was immersed once more in the Cream & Sugar murders.

Thirty-Six

Cynthia Norwood had been a vital sixty-something until their conversation about the running of the bulls. Thereafter, she had seemed to age twenty years in a minute.

Her previous lively eyes were dull. All the charm had gone out of her face, replaced by a slackness that made her look as if she were drugged.

Her legs were weak. She could not lift her feet. Even with Krait's assistance, she shuffled more than walked.

In a meek bewildered voice, she said, "Why are we going to the half bath?"

"Because it doesn't have a window."

"It doesn't?"

"No, dear."

"But why?"

"I don't know why, dear. I would have put a window there if it were up to me."

"I mean what for? Why can't we stay here?"

"You didn't want any more breakfast, remember?"

"All I want is to go home."

"Yes, I know. You love home as much as I do."

"You don't need to do this."

"Somebody has to do it, Cynthia."

"I never did anything to anyone."

"Oh, I know. It's not right. Really, it's not."

As he pressed her through the bathroom doorway ahead of him, he felt her shaking violently under his hand.

"I was going to go shopping later."

"Where do you like to shop?"

"Most everywhere."

"I'm not much of a shopper myself."

She said, "I need a nice summer suit."

"You have taste and flair."

"I've always liked clothes."

"Step over there to the corner, dear."

"This isn't like you, Rommy."

"Actually it is very like me."

"I know you're a good man."

"Well, I'm good at what I do."

"I know you're good at heart. Everyone is, at heart." She stood facing the corner, her back to him. "Please."

"Turn around and face me, dear."

Her voice broke: "I'm afraid."

"Turn around."

"What're you going to do?"

"Turn around."

She faced him. Tears streamed. "I was against the war."

"What war, dear?"

"Malcolm was for it, but I was always against."

"Why, Cynthia—you're transformed."

"And I give to things, you know. I give to things."

"For a moment there, you looked so old, so sad and old."

"To save the eagles and the whales, hunger in Africa."

"But you're not old at all now. I swear, there's not a line in your face now. You look like a child."

"Oh, God."

"I'm surprised you got to that so late."

"Oh, God. Oh, God."

"Very late for that, dear."

He thumbed the selector on the slide, converting the pistol to semi-automatic because he needed only one round. From across the small room, he shot her in the forehead.

Truly, she had appeared to be a child at the end, although not any longer.

Krait left the half bath and pulled the door shut.

After heating more hot chocolate and making two slices of fresh toast, he sat at the table. Everything was delicious, but he didn't feel as cozy as before. He could not recapture the mood.

According to the wall clock, his clothes would not be delivered for another hour and twenty minutes.

He had only done a quick tour of the house. While he waited for the clothes, he could conduct a more intimate inspection.

Incredibly, a man called, "Cynthia," from the front room, and then again, "Cynthia?" Footsteps approached.

Thirty-Seven

Currently vacationing in New York with two girlfriends, Teresa Mendez lived in one half of a duplex in Dana Point. She kept a spare key in a combination key safe secured to the bottom of a redwood chair on the back patio.

Linda led the way into the house by the back door. She took the pistol out of her purse and set it on the breakfast table. She put her carryall and purse in the kitchen sink to let the rain drain off.

Looking down in dismay at the puddle forming around his feet, Tim said, "Got a Creature from the Black Lagoon thing going on here."

"I'll get some towels." She stripped off her jacket, hung it on a chrome-and-vinyl chair, pulled off her shoes, and left the room.

Tim felt awkward, bigger than usual, as if he were a sponge that had swollen up in the storm.

Linda returned barefoot, wearing a robe. She carried a blanket and a stack of towels, which she put on the counter near him.

Pulling aside a pair of folding shutter doors, she exposed a washer and dryer in a laundry nook. "Get out of your clothes, throw them in the dryer. Use the blanket for a robe."

She grabbed one of the towels, went to the sink, and began to dry off her carryall and purse.

"Do I get some privacy?" he asked.

"You think I'm all thrilled to check out your bare butt?"

"Maybe. What do I really know about you?"

"I'm going upstairs to get a quick shower."

"I have my dignity."

"That's the first thing I noticed about you, after your huge head. How long are we safe here?"

"I wouldn't push it past two hours. Ninety minutes is better."

"There's a full bath down here, too, if you want a shower. We can press your jeans and shirt when they come out of the dryer."

"I feel funny about this," he said.

"I promise not to sneak back for a package peek."

"No, I mean using a stranger's house like this."

"She's not a stranger. She's my friend."

"She's a stranger to me. When this is over, I'll have to do something really nice for her."

"You could pay off her mortgage."

"That's an expensive shower."

"I hope you're not cheap. I could never live with a cheap man."

She left the room with her carryall and purse.

For a moment he stood there thinking about two words that she had tossed off so casually: **live with**. If he thought about it hard enough, his clothes would dry on him, without need of the Maytag.

He stripped, loaded the dryer, mopped the floor with a towel, and took the other towels to the downstairs bathroom.

The hot water felt good. He might have stood in the shower longer except that the drain in the floor made him think of Kravet's dilated eyes, greedy for light, and those eyes made him think of **Psycho**.

Scrubbed, dried, wrapped in a blanket, in the kitchen once more, he wanted something to eat, but he didn't feel right about looking through the cupboards and refrigerator.

He sat in a breakfast-set chair to wait, the

blanket pulled around him as if it were a monk's habit.

The previous evening, at Linda's house, before they had gone on the run, there had been a moment when the sight of her had filled him with a complexity of needs but also with dread. He had told himself to remember the tightening knot of terror and the loosening knot of wild exaltation that seemed to bind and to free him at the same time.

He'd had no name for that feeling. But he had realized that when eventually he could name it, he would understand why he was abruptly walking out of the quiet life that he had made for himself and into a new life that had no safety railings.

Now he knew the word. **Purpose.**

He had lived with purpose once. He had thrived on commitment.

For good reasons he had retreated to a life of repetitive work, innocent pleasures, and as little reflection as he could manage.

Back in the day, a kind of weariness of the heart had settled upon him and a kind of disillusionment and something like a sense of futility, none of them the pure thing, all of them alloyed with other feelings that he could not easily define. He might have overcome mere weariness and true disillusionment and a pure sense of futility, but the kind-of-something-like quality of these emotions made them fuzzy at the edges and more difficult to address.

When he retreated to tradesman's labor and simple pleasures, when his greatest purpose was mortaring stone to stone and brick to brick, when his deepest satisfaction came from finishing a book of crossword puzzles or having dinner with friends, weariness lifted from his heart. In this smaller life, no longer committed to any grand enterprise, he had nothing about which to become disillusioned, no challenge great enough to raise doubts and to foster feelings of futility.

The previous evening, in the tavern, his years of retreat had suddenly come to an end. He didn't fully understand why he had chosen to break down the walls behind which he had become so comfortable, but her photograph had something to do with it.

He had not fallen in love at first sight. He had not spent his life looking for someone like Linda. Her face had just been another face, attractive but not enchanting. The feelings he had for her now were nothing he could have imagined then.

Maybe it was this: The name of a person marked for murder is just a name, but the face makes real the cost of violence, for if we have the nerve to look, we can see in any face our own vulnerability.

Looking not in the least vulnerable, Linda returned, dressed in the blue jeans and the black T-shirt that she had brought in the carryall.

She snatched up his wet work boots and said, "There's a gas-log fireplace in the living room. Our shoes should dry on the hearth. While we wait, we can have something quick to eat."

Beyond the windows, the spring dawn had arrived gray and meek, and the angry torrents of rain had receded to a drizzle.

When Linda came back, she said, "You look happier than makes any sense at all."

Thirty-Eight

With a high forehead, bushy white eyebrows, a solid jaw, and weathered skin, the man seeking Cynthia looked like a sea captain from a harder century, one who had chased down a white whale, killed it, rendered it, and brought to port a ship full of barreled blubber oil and ambergris.

He stopped at the threshold of the kitchen, frowned at Krait sitting at the table, and said, "Who're you?"

"Rudyard Kipling. You must be Malcolm."

"Rudyard Kipling—he's some dead writer."

"Yes, I was named after him, and I don't like his work, just a poem or two."

Suspicion knitted the two bushy eyebrows into one. "What're you doing here?"

"Beth and James invited me. We're all terrific friends of Judi and Frankie."

"Judi and Frankie are in Paris."

"I was supposed to go with them, but I had to cancel. Have you had breakfast, Malcolm?"

"Where's Cynthia?"

"She and I have thrown all carbohydrate caution to the wind. We're having hot chocolate and buttered cinnamon toast. She's such marvelous good company, your wife."

Krait needed to entice the old man into the kitchen. The Glock lay on the chair where Cynthia had not seen it. Malcolm couldn't see it, either, from where he stood. If Krait reached for it, however, Malcolm, already suspicious, might back off, and for sure he would bolt when he saw the gun coming up.

Frowning at Cynthia's plate and mug on the table, Malcolm said, "But where is she?"

Pointing to the closed door of the half bath, Krait said, "The call of nature. We were just talking about Cynthia's efforts to save the eagles and the whales. I so admire that."

"What?"

"Eagles and whales. And hunger in Africa. You must be proud of her giving nature."

"Bethany and Jim never mentioned any Rudyard Kipling."

"Well, honestly, I'm not a very interesting person, Malcolm. For every thousand Judi and Frankie stories, they'd have at most one about me."

The old man had steel-gray eyes and a sword-sharp stare. He said, "Something's wrong with you."

"Well," said Krait, "I've never liked my nose."

Malcolm called out, "Cynthia!"

Neither of them looked at the door to the half bath. They kept their eyes on each other.

Krait reached for the Glock.

The old man bolted.

Getting to his feet so fast that he knocked over his chair, thumbing the slide selector to full-auto, Krait brought the pistol to bear on the doorway. Malcolm had fled from sight.

Krait went after him.

Having cleared the dining room as quick as a boy, the old man knocked against an end table in the living room, stumbled, grabbed at an armchair to right himself.

Krait put a short burst in his back, from rump to neck. The sound suppressor absorbed the concussion so completely that a blowgun would have made more noise.

The old man fell facedown and lay there, head turned to one side. His eye was peeled wide; but his stare could not accurately be called sharp anymore.

Standing over Malcolm, Krait emptied the extended magazine into him. The body twitched, not with life but with the impacts.

Wasting twenty or more rounds on a dead man wasn't practical, but it was necessary.

A lesser man than Krait, with less self-control, might have replaced the depleted magazine with a fresh one and emptied that, too. Composure and forbearance were among his most defining character traits, but even **his** singular patience might be tried to the breaking point.

He opened the front door and found Cynthia's raincoat draped over the arm of the glider on the porch. Her umbrella and Malcolm's lay on the floor. He brought everything inside and locked the door.

He hung her coat in the foyer closet. He put the umbrellas there, as well.

In the kitchen, he sat at the table with his cell phone and checked his E-mail. While chatting with Cynthia, he had received word that the Explorer had been abandoned in a restaurant parking lot.

No stolen-vehicle reports had been made from the blocks around the restaurant yet; but somebody might not find his car missing for hours.

Krait thought maybe a bus, and he sent

that message. Not many buses would have been running that route at that hour. They wouldn't have to find and question more than a couple of drivers.

After plugging his phone into its charger, he hand-washed the breakfast dishes, put them away, and wiped off the table.

He had no intention of cleaning up the mess in the half bath or the one in the living room. Cynthia and Malcolm had come nosing around because their daughter and son-in-law had failed to establish privacy rules and boundaries. This was not his business now; it was a family matter.

Having tidied the kitchen, he went upstairs to the master bedroom to learn if Bethany and Jim kept any pornographic videos or interesting sex toys.

He discovered neither erotica nor anything else that gave him any insights into the kind of people they were. Jim folded rather than rolled his socks. A few of Bethany's panties had a cute little pink bunny embroidered at the hip. Not much here for the tabloids.

The most interesting thing in their bathroom drawers were the number of brands—and the quantity—of laxatives. These people either ate no fiber whatsoever or they had colons as inefficient as Third World plumbing.

Bethany and Jim were such a bland pair that Krait wondered why the fabled Judi and Frankie wanted anything to do with them.

The toothbrushes were pink and blue. He used the pink one, assuming it was Bethany's. But he applied the men's rather than the women's deodorant.

Thereafter, he was reduced to passing time in the kitchen with the issue of **O** that had been in the mail.

At 7:15, he opened the front door and smiled at the sight of the hanging travel bag placed neatly on the porch glider and the small carryall standing beside it. His clothes had been delivered.

The rain had stopped altogether. Trees dripped. Sun had broken through the clouds, and the wet street had begun to steam.

Fifteen minutes later, dressed for the day, he inspected himself in a full-length beveled mirror on the back of the master-bathroom door.

When Bethany was naked in this bathroom, perhaps admirers in the mirror world watched her without her knowledge. Krait could not see those who might live in the reversed reality, only himself looking back at him, but that didn't mean the inhabitants of the other realm were likewise limited in their vision.

Downstairs once more, as he approached the front door, he heard a key in the lock. The deadbolt turned, and the door opened.

A woman stepped into the house, made a small sound of surprise at the sight of him, and said, "You startled me."

"And you me. Bethany and Jim didn't tell me to expect anyone."

"I'm Nora, from next door."

She was a petite but buxom woman with a pixie haircut and blue nail polish of which he disapproved.

"This is like a house in one of those sitcoms," Krait said, "where everyone just bursts right in without knocking or ringing the bell."

"Beth pays me to make five dinners every week, put them in her freezer," said Nora. "I stock her refrigerator Monday, cook Tuesday."

"Then it must be thanks to you that we had such a brilliantly scrumptious dinner last evening."

"Oh, you're staying over?"

"I'm a rude, drop-in, ten-minute-warning houseguest, but dear Beth always pretends to be glad to see me. Name's Richard Kotzwinkel, everyone calls me Ricky."

He stepped back to encourage her to enter, but also to block her view of Malcolm in the living room.

"Gee, Ricky, I don't want to intrude—"

"No, come in, come in. Cynthia and I just had a long fabulously chatty breakfast together after the early birds raced off to get the worm or whatever they get at an investment-banking firm."

"Cynthia's here?"

"In the kitchen. And Malcolm stopped in a little while ago." He lowered his voice to a whisper. "Though he's something of a sourpuss compared to dear Cindy."

She stepped farther inside and closed the door behind her. "Was it really scrumptious?"

"Was what? Oh, you mean your dinner. Divine. It was divine."

"Which selection did she heat up?" Nora asked.

Her eyes were a lively blue. She had full lips and smooth skin.

"Chicken," he said. "We had the chicken."

He considered raping her, but he just killed her. For variety, he used his hands.

Collateral damage was frowned upon by

those who solicited him to go on these missions, so he rarely popped bystanders in the process of nailing his target. His generous petitioners would understand. As the bumper sticker says, SHIT HAPPENS.

On the porch, he pulled the door shut and used Nora's key to lock it, although that didn't seem likely to keep out anyone.

Thirty-Nine

As they finished breakfast, Pete Santo called. Tim set his cell on speakerphone and stood it beside the waffle plate.

"I'm not calling from my place," Pete said. "This is strictly cell-to-cell."

"Something happened," Tim said. "What happened?"

"I stayed away from restricted law-enforcement databases, just Googled Kravet's different names. I hit pay dirt, dug in it for a while—and then my cable service failed."

"Maybe coincidence," Tim said.

"Like Santa Claus showing up on Christmas Eve. And talk about showing up—not half an hour later, around five o'clock, three guys pay a visit."

"Not the three wise men."

"More like wiseguys."

"What did they want?" Linda asked.

"I was out when they came. Watched them from up the street. I'm not going back anytime soon."

"You didn't leave Zoey there?" Linda asked.

"Zoey's with me."

Tim said, "So what was the pay dirt?"

Instead of answering, Pete said, "Listen, Hitch Lombard knows my cell number, so these guys have it, too. Maybe they know yours."

"They know it," Tim confirmed. "But you don't mean they can grab our conversation out of thin air?"

"Not your local cops, but maybe these guys. Who knows. They get better at this stuff every week."

Linda said, "And though tracing a cell's location isn't as easy as locating a fixed phone, it's totally doable."

Tim threw a look at her.

She threw it back and said, "Book research."

"You need to go buy a disposable cell phone," Pete said, "so you have a number they don't know. Then call me at another phone they don't know."

"You gonna send me the number by psychic waves?" Tim asked.

"How's this. Remember the guy who lost his virginity while he was dressed up as Shrek?"

"The guy who now has five kids."

"That's the guy who."

"I don't have his number."

"Call him at work. It's in the directory. Ask for him, give your name, they'll put you through. I'll be there in an hour."

Tim terminated the call. Then he switched off the cell phone.

"Who's the guy who?" Linda asked.

"Pete's cousin Santiago."

"Dressed up as Shrek?"

"It was a costume party. I think everybody had to come as a cartoon character. I wasn't there."

"What was **she** dressed as?"

"Jessica Rabbit from **Who Framed Roger Rabbit**. Her name's Mina. He married her. The kids are really cute and green."

Pushing her chair back from the table, she said, "We better be out of here soon."

Tim took his clothes from the dryer and ironed them while Linda cleaned up the breakfast dishes. Their rain-sodden shoes hadn't fully dried, but they were wearable.

In the two-car garage stood Teresa's four-year-old Honda Accord. One of her traveling companions had driven them to the airport.

Linda had found the keys in a kitchen drawer; but she handed them to Tim.

"If there's got to be any stunt driving like last night," she said, "you better be the one behind the wheel."

Although he didn't have adequate legroom, he liked the Honda. It was nondescript, and it didn't have any satellite uplink by which they might be tracked.

As the garage door rolled up, Tim half expected that the hungry-eyed killer would be standing in the driveway, holding a machine pistol.

Blades of sunlight thrust through the torn fabric of the cloud-disheveled sky and liberated the land from the lingering gloom of the recent storm.

"Where do we get a disposable cell phone at this hour?" she asked.

Driving east, heading toward a freeway, he said, "The warehouse clubs open early. I have a membership in one through the union. But I'm not carrying much money."

Withdrawing a fat envelope from her purse, she said, "I've got five thousand in hundreds."

"I missed the moment when you knocked over a bank."

"I've got gold coins hidden at home, too. Last night, when I had to grab something, cash money seemed more practical."

"Don't trust banks?"

"I've got money in the bank. But you can't always get bank money as fast as you might need it. This is my falls-apart money."

"For when what falls apart?"

"Anything. Everything."

"You think it's the End Times or something?"

"Things fell apart last night, didn't they?"

"I guess they did," he acknowledged.

She looked grim when she said, "I'm never going to be helpless again."

"We're in a tight place, but we aren't helpless," he assured her.

"I don't mean now," she said, returning the money to her purse.

"You mean like you were helpless back then . . . with Molly and the other stuff."

"Yeah."

"You want to talk about the other stuff?"

"No."

"You told me about Molly."

"Telling that much hurt enough," she said.

Tim followed a rising freeway entrance. Heavy but unobstructed morning traffic raced at reckless speed through what the real-estate agents would call "another day in paradise."

"In the end," he said, "we're all helpless, if you want to get to the hard truth of things."

"I like hard truth. But damn if I'm near the end yet."

Thereafter, they rode in silence all the way to the exit that would take them to the warehouse club.

The silence was comfortable. Tim suspected that no matter how far and long they might yet go together, they were already past any kind of silence that would feel strained.

The awkwardness would come when they were at last ready to make their separate revelations.

Forty

Sitting behind the wheel of his car in front of Bethany and Jim's place, Krait sent a coded text message informing his support group of the three dead people in the house.

He did not suggest a course of action that should be taken. Decisions of that nature were not in his province. This was only a heads-up call.

He typed REGRET THE MESS BUT UNAVOIDABLE. Then he concluded the message by quoting T. S. Eliot: LIFE YOU MAY EVADE, BUT DEATH YOU SHALL NOT.

Although he had never met any of the men and women in the support group, he imagined that he must be a legendary figure among them, larger than life and as large as Death. From time to time he liked to send them such quotes as the Eliot bit, so they would know that his erudition equaled his skill at execution and would be even more motivated to serve him as required.

If he had ever gone to school, he had done so in childhood and adolescence, but he had no more memory of receiving an education than he had of being younger than eighteen. He was, however, an excellent autodidact, and had taught himself much.

T. S. Eliot was not a writer of whom Krait approved, but even an insistently incorrect man could occasionally pen a pleasing line. If Eliot had been still alive, Krait would have killed him.

The support group most likely would prefer to let Bethany and Jim discover Mom, Dad, and neighbor Nora. As the police investigation proceeded, the support group would destroy or compromise any forensic evidence incriminating to Krait. They also would seed DNA, hairs, and fibers that would confuse the police and ultimately bring them to a blind alley.

Krait knew no name for the organization of which the support group was a department, but he thought of it as the Gentlemen's Club or just the Club. He didn't know what the Gentlemen's Club was or what its members' ultimate purpose might be, or why they wanted certain people dead, and he didn't need to know.

For more than a decade, Krait had done

freelance hits for the mob and for petitioners who had been referred to him by grateful people for whom he had killed quarrelsome spouses and rich parents and other impediments to the good life. Then seven years ago, a member of the Club had approached him with the sincere hope that he would kill for them on a regular basis.

Their conversation had taken place in the back of a moving superstretch limousine at night, in Chicago. The interior lights had never been turned on, and to Krait the representative of the Club had been only a shadow in a cashmere topcoat, sitting at the farther end of the luxuriously upholstered passenger cabin.

The man had spoken with what Krait took to be the accent of a Boston Brahmin. He was articulate, and his manner suggested that he had been born to wealth and social position. Although the Brahmin referred to his mysterious associates only as "our people," Krait thought of him as a gentleman and of his group as the Gentlemen's Club.

When the gentleman described the level of support that would be provided, Krait had been impressed. And he knew this counted as further evidence that if he was not a species different from human beings, he was at least superior to and separate from them.

The best thing about the support group was that they served Krait not only when he was engaged in a kill for the Gentlemen's Club, but also when he undertook a mission on behalf of the mob or any other petitioner. They did not want exclusivity, yet they were **always** there for him.

They had two reasons for this generosity, the first being that they recognized Krait's singular talent. They wished to ensure that he would never be unavailable to them by reason of imprisonment.

Second, they did not want Krait to be able to detect a pattern in the kinds of people whom he was asked to kill, or to deduce from that pattern the possible goals and the ultimate purpose of the Gentlemen's Club. Therefore the Club paid him in cash, delivered by guys whom he could not distinguish either from the bagmen of various mobs or from treacherous husbands and sons and businessmen.

They paid him in cash also to keep a financial firewall between themselves and their assassin, just in case one day, in spite of all their heroic efforts on his behalf, he took a fall.

After that limousine ride in Chicago, Krait had never again met face to face with anyone who he could be certain was a Club member.

In fact it didn't matter to him who was and who wasn't a courier for the Club. He loved to kill, he was well-rewarded for it, and he felt that forgetfulness was a grace that he owed to every one of his petitioners. He wiped from his mind forever the faces of those who had passed the cash to him.

Krait had a remarkable ability to cast off beyond recovery any memory that he wished to set adrift. The faces of men who petitioned him or who served as couriers on the behalf of petitioners were as irretrievable to him as any astronaut, severed from a tether to his spacecraft, is lost forever to the eternal depths of space.

Life was so much simpler when you could send out beyond the stars, with no risk of recovery, not only things like couriers' faces but also dreary episodes and even whole great swaths of time that had been occupied by unsatisfactory experience.

He never spoke to any member of the Club by phone. Communication remained strictly by coded electronic messaging. Voice analysis could be submitted as evidence in a court of law, but no one could prove beyond doubt whose fingers had typed a message.

In the Lamplighter Tavern, when he had

mistaken Timothy Carrier for the correct petitioner, he had assumed that this mission was not on behalf of the Gentlemen's Club. The Brahmin and his people would never tell Krait to keep half the money as a no-kill fee. They didn't change their minds. When they wanted someone dead, they wanted him or her dead the hard way and without hope of resurrection.

Krait still doubted that the Paquette woman might be a target of the Club. She seemed to be a nobody. Gentlemen of wealth and power did not turn their heads for a woman like her, let alone pull a trigger on her by proxy.

After sending his message, he drove to the Pacific Coast Highway and then south to the restaurant at which Carrier had abandoned the Explorer. He went through the vehicle end to end but found nothing helpful.

As he finished that task, his cell phone vibrated. The support group reported that a bus driver remembered dropping off in Dana Point a couple that matched the description of Carrier and Paquette.

Krait drove to Dana Point while the support group reviewed the woman's phone records in the hope of identifying anyone she might know in that seaside town.

The clouds relented, blue sky insisted, and the sun gilded the coastal hills and the beaches and the squamous sea.

Krait felt brilliantly alive, full of a gratifying fire, as a forge is filled with fire but not consumed by it. Dealing death did that for him.

Forty-One

The **warehouse club offered an irre**sistible price on one-gallon jars of mayonnaise, six to a carton, and for a modest sum, you could buy enough bricks of tofu to build a two-bedroom house.

On their quest for a disposable cell phone, Tim and Linda did not bother with the shopping carts that were, in a pinch, large enough to transport a lame horse. Other customers had piled their carts with multiple twelve-packs of toilet paper, panty hose by the half gross, and barrels of cocktail onions.

A young couple piloted two pushcarts with adorable identical three-year-old girls facing backward in the kiddie seats, as if they had taken advantage of a two-for-one child sale in Aisle 9.

Sometimes Tim worried that Americans

were so accustomed to abundance that they thought this level of affluence and choice had always been the norm and was even now the norm in all but the most insistently backward corners of the world. Sudden falls can come to societies that know too little history or that have furnished their minds with easy one-note propaganda in place of the true complexity and terrible beauty of the storied past.

They purchased a cell phone suitable to their needs and an electric razor for Tim. The cashier, clearly puzzled by a mere two-item sale, did no more than raise an eyebrow in disapproval of their un-American restraint.

Tim drove the Honda to a nearby auto center as Linda used his phone to make a call to activate the disposable cell they had just bought. Because the telephone came with prepaid minutes, she was not required to give a credit card or a name to trigger service.

This system, not yet prohibited by law, was a great convenience to terrorists whether they bought one disposable phone to facilitate untraceable conversation or acquired them in bulk to be employed as bomb timers.

Fortunately, even honest citizens were permitted to make use of this user-friendly technology.

The auto center was comprised of numerous dealerships, hawking almost every make of wheeled transport, situated side by side along a large figure-eight roadway. Pennants fluttered in the faint breeze, banners proclaimed bargains, and thousands of vehicles stood on blacktop sales lots like gems on jewelers' velvet display boards.

Every dealership needed all of its on-lot parking spaces for inventory, for vehicles awaiting repair, and for potential customers. Consequently, employees' cars, repaired vehicles awaiting pickup, and trade-ins not yet refurbished for resale were parked along the auto center's communal roadway.

Tim pulled to the curb behind a two-year-old silver Cadillac. From Linda's carryall, he withdrew his zippered vinyl kit of tools.

She remained in the Honda to monitor whether the touted "instant activation" would be minutes or hours later than promised.

Openly rather than furtively, quickly but not with an air of haste, Tim removed the front and back plates from Teresa's Honda. He put them in the trunk.

No passing motorists would think twice about a man with tools attending to a car in the middle of an auto center.

The showrooms were set so far back behind the sales lots that the vehicles parked along the communal roadway were out of sight of the dealership employees.

He walked forward to the silver Cadillac. The doors were locked. Peering through the windows, he saw no personal effects inside. The glove box hung open, looked empty.

Evidence suggested this was a recent trade-in, not yet sent for service prior to resale, so it might sit here undisturbed for a few days. In California, license plates remained on a trade-in, and the buyer drove with no plates on the new vehicle until he received them in the mail.

If the Cadillac had seemed to be an employee's car, Tim would have moved up the line until he found a possible trade-in, because the sooner someone drove the car, the sooner the missing plates might be noticed.

He removed the tags from the Cadillac and put them on the Honda Accord.

When Tim got behind the wheel again, Linda said, "No service yet. If I were still a writer, I'd write about a psychopath who tracks down someone who failed to keep a guarantee of instant activation."

"What's the psycho do when he finds the guy?"

"Deactivates him."

"You're still a writer," he said.

She shook her head. "I don't know anymore. And if I don't know, how would **you** know?"

Starting the Honda, he said, "Because we are what we are."

"That's very deep. If I ever write another book, I'll use that for sure."

"I thought I could be just a mason. I'm a mason, all right, but I'm still what I was, too."

As he pulled away from the curb, he could feel that green gaze all over his face.

"And what is it that you were?" she asked.

"My dad is a mason, too, and a damn good one. Being a mason defines him like it doesn't seem to totally define me, though I wish it did."

"Your dad is a mason," she said almost with wonder, as if he had revealed something magical.

"Why's that surprising? Tradesmen tend to pass the trade on to their kids, or try to."

"This is going to sound stupid. But since you showed up at my place, everything's been going so fast . . . it never occurred to me to think did you have a father. Do you like him?"

"Do I like him? Why wouldn't I like him?"

"Fathers and sons, it's not always a sure thing."

"He's a great guy. He's the best."

"My God, you have a mother, too, don't you?"

"Well, my dad's not an amoeba, he didn't just divide in two and there I was."

"Oh, my God," she said softly, with a kind of awe, "what's your mother's name?"

"Oh, my God, her name is Mary."

"Mary," she said, as though she had never heard the name before, as though it were musical and sweet upon the tongue. "Is she really wonderful?"

"She's about as wonderful as you could stand."

"What's your dad's name?"

"Walter."

"Walter Carrier?"

"It would be, wouldn't it?"

"Does he have a huge head like you?"

"I don't remember it any smaller."

"Walter and Mary," she said. "Oh, my God."

Perplexed, he glanced at her. "What're you grinning about?"

"I thought you were this foreign country."

"What foreign country?"

"Your own country, an exotic land, so much to learn about it, so much to explore. But you're not a foreign country."

"I'm not?"

"You're a **world**."

"Is that another crack about my big head?"

"Do you have any brothers or sisters?"

Departing the auto center, Tim said, "No sisters. One brother. Zach. He's five years older than me, and he's got a normal head."

"Walter, Mary, Zach, and Tim," she said, and seemed delighted. "Walter, Mary, Zach, and Tim."

"I'm not sure why it should matter, but suddenly everything seems to matter, so I should say Zach is married to Laura, and they have a little girl named Naomi."

Linda's eyes shone as if with restrained tears, but she didn't look like a woman on the verge of weeping. Quite the contrary.

He sensed that he might be walking a ragged edge with this question, but he said, "What about your mom and dad?"

The disposable cell phone rang. She took the call and said, "Yes," in answer to a question, and then "Yes," and then "Thank you."

Service had been activated.

Forty-Two

From the contents of the desk in Teresa Mendez's den, off her living room, Krait learned a great deal that he did not like about her. She had all the wrong values.

The most important fact concerning this thirty-two-year-old widowed medical assistant, which Krait discovered from the simple day-planner she had left behind, was that currently she could be found vacationing in New York City with women named Gloria Nguyen and Joan Applewhite.

She had left the previous Sunday. This was Tuesday. She would return home on the coming Sunday.

On the back of the cabinet door under the kitchen sink hung a dishtowel. He found the towel damp.

The shower floors in both bathrooms, upstairs and down, were beaded with water, and the tile grout was dark with moisture.

In the living room, the gas-log fireplace had been ablaze early in the day. The bricks lining the firebox were still slightly warm to the touch.

The two-car garage contained no vehicles. The widow Mendez might have driven to the airport to catch a flight to New York. But if she owned a second car, Carrier and the woman possessed it now.

He sent a text message to his support group, seeking information on motor vehicles registered to Mendez.

A short while later, as he satisfied his curiosity by inspecting the contents of the widow's freezer, he received a coded-text reply to the effect that Mendez owned only a Honda Accord.

They had the license number, but that was of little use to a man who worked without full legal sanction. Krait could not issue an all-points bulletin.

For the moment, he'd lost track of his quarry. He wasn't unduly concerned. They could find only temporary sanctuary. This was Krait's world. He was secret royalty, and they were commoners; and he would find them sooner rather than later.

Having gone sixteen active hours without

sleep, he realized this might in fact be fate working on his behalf, giving him a chance to refresh before the final showdown.

He brewed a pot of green tea.

In the narrow pantry, he found a package of simple biscuits. He arranged half a dozen of them on a plate.

In a high cupboard, he discovered a lovely little decorative thermos, blue with black-and-white harlequin bands at top and bottom. When the tea was ready, he filled the thermos.

The well-earned respite he had hoped to enjoy at Bethany and Jim's house waited for him here, in the humbler residence of the widow Mendez.

He carried the thermos of tea, a mug, the plate of biscuits, and two paper napkins upstairs to the master bedroom. He put them on the nightstand.

After undressing and carefully laying out his clothes to prevent wrinkling, he found two robes in the widow's closet. Neither could have belonged to her deceased husband.

The first was quilted, pink, floral, and without style. He found a disgusting wad of used tissues and half a roll of throat lozenges in one pocket.

Fortunately, the second choice, a blue silk

number, while small for him, fit well enough and felt delicious.

After turning down the bed and making a backrest of four plump pillows, Krait discovered unwashed laundry in a basket in her closet. She had not been able to catch up with chores before leaving for New York.

In the dirty laundry, he turned up one stretch bra without hard couplings, two T-shirts, and three pair of panties. He draped these over the top pillow on his stack, against which he would lean while enjoying his tea, and on which he would eventually rest his face when the time came to sleep.

The sole reading material in the widow's bedroom consisted of magazines that Krait found unappealing. He remembered seeing a few shelves of books in her den, and in a thrilling silken shimmer, he went downstairs to review them.

Evidently, Teresa was not a reader. Most of the volumes in her den fell into the genres of pop psychology, self-help, spiritual search, and medical advice. Krait found them all jejune.

The only books of interest were what, judging by the spines, appeared to be six novels. The titles intrigued him: **Despair, The Hopeless and the Dead, Heartworm, Rotten . . .**

The title **Relentless Cancer** particularly appealed to Krait. He slipped the book off the shelf.

The author's name, Toni Zero, had a nice nihilistic flair to it. Clearly, it was a pseudonym, and it seemed to say to the reader **You are a fool if you pay for this, but I'm sure you will.**

The cover illustration struck him as sophisticated, brutal, and bleak. It promised a blistering portrayal of humanity as worthless, duplicitous ruck.

When he turned the book over to look at the back jacket, the author's photo rocked him. Toni Zero was Linda Paquette.

Forty-Three

As Tim braked to a stop in an empty shopping-mall parking lot, more than an hour before stores opened, Linda called 411 for the number to Santiago Jalisco, the restaurant owned by Pete Santo's cousin, alias Shrek.

When she used Tim's name, the receptionist at once sent her through to Santiago Santo in his kitchen office, but in fact Pete took the call. He was surprised to hear her voice instead of Tim's.

"I'll put you on speakerphone," she said.

"Hey, wait, I gotta know."

"Know what?"

"What do you think?"

"Think what?"

"Of him. What do you think of him?"

"Why's that your business?"

"It's not, you're right, but I'm dyin' to know."

Tim caught her attention, raised his eyebrows quizzically.

"I think," she told Pete, "he's got a lovely head."

"Lovely? We can't be talking about the same sand dog."

"Sand dog. What's that mean, anyway?"

"Speakerphone," Tim said impatiently. "Speakerphone."

She obliged, and told Pete, "You're public now."

Tim said, "Maybe I see why there's nothing left of your marriage except a stuffed marlin."

"Maybe what I've got is a dead fish and a shy dog, but neither one of them ever nags me."

"So that's what you've got, you poor schlump, but what do you have for us?"

"You remember the Cream and Sugar Coffeehouse in Laguna?"

"Drawing a blank," Tim said.

"I know it. Knew it," Linda said. "I used to go there. It was like three blocks from my house. They had a nice patio."

"Terrific apple cake," Pete said.

"With the almonds."

"My mouth's watering. Anyway, early one morning a year and a half ago," Pete said, "just before Cream and Sugar would have been opening for business, the place burned to the ground."

"An inferno," Linda recalled.

"Fire marshal thinks accelerants were used, but they weren't the usual crap, mondo sophisticated, hard to get a chemical profile on them."

Tim said, "Yeah, I got it now. Never went there. Half remember driving past it."

"When they put out the fire," Pete said, "they found four badly burned bodies."

"Charlie Wen-ching, he was the owner," Linda said. "He was the sweetest man, never forgot a name, treated all his regular customers like family."

"Real name, Chou Wen-ching," Pete said, "but he used Charlie for more than thirty years. Immigrated from Taiwan. Smart businessman, good man."

"Two of the other bodies were his sons," Linda said.

"Michael and Joseph. Family business. The fourth victim was a niece, Valerie."

Although they were surrounded by acres of empty blacktop, Tim continuously surveyed the parking lot, checked the mirrors.

Barely a breeze stirred at ground level, but a high-altitude wind drove a ragged fleet of clouds eastward, and the shadows of ghost galleons sailed across the pavement.

Pete said, "They all died in the walk-in cooler where the milk and pastries were stored. Coroner later determined they'd been shot to death before being set afire."

"This is why I don't follow the news," Tim said. "This is why I just want to build some wall each day."

"It's a business district, a populated area, but no one heard any gunfire."

"He's a pro," Tim said. "He has the right equipment."

"Two people **did,** however, see someone leave the Cream and Sugar about ten minutes before it went up in flames. He crossed the highway to a motel directly opposite the coffeehouse, turned in his room key, and drove away. He had stayed there overnight, in Room 14. His name was Roy Kutter."

"Those initials," Linda said. "One of Kravet's aliases."

"I've got a printout of his driver's license. San Francisco address. The same smiley-faced prick."

Tim said, "But if someone saw him—"

"Forty-eight hours, he was a person of interest. Police wanted to talk to him. So they find him, and he says the witnesses have it wrong.

Says he didn't **leave** the Cream and Sugar, didn't come out of it, because he never got into it. Says he went over there to get some take-out coffee, but they weren't open yet, the door was locked. He couldn't wait another twenty minutes till they started serving, he had to get to an important appointment."

"What appointment? What's his business?" Tim asked.

"Crisis management."

"What's that mean?"

"Who knows. He supposedly worked for some federal agency."

"Which one?"

"It's always vague in the news stories."

"But he looked credible?" Linda asked. "They set him loose, clean?"

"Here's where I started reading between the lines of the news stories," Pete said. "You can tell that the detective on it, also the chief, they wanted to lean on this Kutter some, even find a way to hold him."

"So why didn't they?"

"This is maybe reading too deep between the lines, but I get the feeling someone heavy leaned hard on **them** when they tried to lean on Kutter."

"Like someone leaned on Hitch Lombard," Tim said.

"Just like. Pretty soon, Roy Kutter wasn't a person of interest anymore."

A scattering of cars entered the vast lot, parked in different rows. The people who got out of them and walked to the mall might have been store employees, perhaps managers, coming in an hour ahead of the public. None of them seemed to have any interest in the Honda.

"So," Linda said, "why does it matter that I went there for coffee? I didn't go there the day of the fire. I don't think I'd been there during the week before the fire, either. Why does somebody want me dead because I used to go to the Cream and Sugar?"

From the humble kitchen of Santiago Jalisco, where surely the world seemed more ordered and sane than it did out here where Kravet was probably even now seeking Teresa's Honda by some sorcerous means, Pete said, "Are you trying to gut-kick me for fun, girl, or do you mean that, for real, someone wants you dead?"

"Feels like maybe it's time I tell you what this is about," Tim suggested.

"Yeah. Like maybe."

Succinctly, Tim recounted the events at the tavern, the two instances of mistaken identity.

"Sweet Jesus, Doorman."

"So here we are," Tim said, "nothing to prove it happened, and now it seems even if we had video of him shooting at us, we might not get anyone to so much as wag a naughty-boy finger at him."

"Something's happened since," Pete guessed.

"Yeah. A bunch of something."

"Gonna share?"

"I'm too tired for a blow-by-blow. Let's just say Linda and me—we earned the right to still be breathing. Truth is, I'm surprised we are."

"I know this can't be news. But say you get lucky and punch his ticket, it's still not over till you also punch whoever's ticket he's working for."

"I have a hunch they've got a steel ticket."

"And where do we go from here?" Linda asked. "We're two mice, and a hawk is coming, and there's no tall grass anywhere."

No fear strained her voice, and she appeared calm.

Tim wondered about the source and the depth of her strength.

"I got one thing more," Pete said. "It might be something. This friend on the Laguna PD, Paco, he's as reliable as sunrise. I talked to him half an hour ago, on the QT, felt him out about the Cream and Sugar case. I know it's an open file, but is it active? He says no, not active. Then Paco tells me Lily Wen-ching, she's still so crazy with grief, she thinks it's not done yet. She thinks whoever whacked her family is still taking care of whatever business those killings were part of."

"Lily is Charlie's wife," Linda told Tim. "His widow."

"What do you mean—still taking care of business?" Tim asked.

"She's got it in her head that some regular customers of Cream and Sugar have died suspiciously over the past year and a half, since the fire."

Linda hugged herself and shivered, as if a quirk in time had folded January into May.

"Died suspiciously?" Tim asked. "Who?"

"Paco didn't say, and I didn't want to push so hard his antenna popped up. What's totally clear is, they don't take Lily seriously. After everything the poor woman has lost, it's easy to believe the crazy-with-grief angle. But what you might want to do is talk to her."

"Soon," Linda agreed. "I know where the family lived. If she's still in the same house."

"Paco says she is. She can't let go of anything. Like if she holds on stubborn enough, she can bring them back."

Tim saw in those expressive green eyes the fullest understanding of the obstinate sorrow that Pete had just described.

"Give me your new cell number," Pete said. "I'm going right out and buy a disposable of my own. I'll get back to you. Don't call here again. I shouldn't have involved Santiago, not even this much."

Tim said, "I don't see what more you can do for us."

"If I can't do a lot more than what I've done so far, then I'm a sorry-ass sonofabitch. Let me have your new number."

Linda gave it to him.

"And one more thing you need to know, though you probably know it already."

"What?" Tim asked.

"I'm not talking to you, Doorman. I'm talking to the pretty one. Are you listening, pretty one?"

"With both ears, holy one."

"You probably know this already, but you couldn't ever be in better hands than the hands you're in right now."

Meeting Tim's eyes, Linda said to Pete, "I've

known that since he walked into my house last night and said he didn't understand modern art."

"I guess you had to be there," Pete said.

"The thing is," she explained, "he could have said something else or nothing at all, and I'd still have known I was safe."

Forty-Four

Sitting up in bed, reading Toni Zero's Relentless Cancer, Krait soon forgot his green tea and biscuits.

Her narrative drive was strong, her prose luminous and assured. She understood the necessity of understatement but also the value of hyperbole.

Most of all, he liked the seductive despair, the deeply settled hopelessness, the corrupting bitterness that gave no quarter to any optimist who might wish to debate this dark worldview.

From Zero's book, the apprentice demon Wormwood could have learned much about turning innocent souls away from the light. And even old Screwtape himself might have picked up a trick or two.

Krait also approved of her anger. The anger remained always subordinate to despair, but she served it up in small doses that were enthrallingly vicious and vindictive.

For a while, he thought she might be the writer of the century, or at least that she would become his favorite above all others.

Gradually, however, she revealed a frustration with the willful ignorance that is an abiding human trait, an indignation at the cruelty that people visit upon one another. She might see the world as hopeless, but she believed it did not have to remain that way.

Worse, she yearned for a world in which promises were kept, in which trust was not betrayed, in which honor mattered, and in which courage inspired courage. Because of this, she finally forfeited Krait's adoration.

Clearly, the despair on the page was not what she sincerely felt, but was what rough experience or a good professor had convinced her that she **ought** to feel. By contrast, the moments of anger burning in the book were real, but they were neither intense enough nor numerous enough for Krait's taste.

Touring Paquette's house the previous evening, he had reviewed the shelves of books in her living room, but he had not seen her Toni Zero novels. The fact that she had consigned them to a closet or had boxed them in the attic suggested that she might have recognized her own lack of conviction in the writing.

Indeed, the '39 Ford coupe, her collection of novels by other writers, and her decor suggested an annoyingly hopeful heart.

He took her book into the bathroom and dropped it in the toilet. He emptied his bladder. He did not flush, but closed the lid to let the novel marinate.

This act did not harmonize with his penchant for cleanliness, but it was necessary.

In bed again, he found that the thermos had kept the tea warm. The biscuits were tasty.

When he settled down for a two- or three-hour nap, he kept the Glock under the covers with him, and he held the cell phone loosely in his hand.

He would wake in the precise position in which he had gone to sleep, and the phone would remain in his hand. He never dreamed and he was never restless in his slumber. He truly did sleep like the dead.

Forty-Five

While Linda drove the Honda, Tim plugged his new electric razor in the cigarette lighter, and shaved without benefit of a mirror.

When he finished, he said, "I just can't stand that feeling."

"What feeling?"

"Stubble, the way it itches. Clothes so full of sweat and stink you feel you're in a pot of boiling cabbage—that doesn't bother me."

"Maybe it should."

"Lice, lips so cracked they bleed, prickly heat, that dry gray fungus, the fancy cockroaches they have—give me all that and more if you can spare me stubble itch."

"Most guys don't reveal their affection for dry gray fungus on the first date."

Returning the razor to its travel case, he said, "Most first dates aren't this long."

"Fancy cockroaches?"

"You don't want to know. What is Mrs. Wen-ching like?"

"A petite dynamo. She worked at Cream and Sugar like the rest of the family. She was usually there lunch to early evening. She wasn't scheduled to work the morning it happened."

The Wen-ching residence was a sleek Moderne-style home in the hills of Laguna, cantilevered over a canyon.

Queen palms flanked the diamond-cut slate walkway and cast wings of raven-feather shadows on the variegated stone.

Lily Wen-ching answered the doorbell. Fiftyish, with porcelain-smooth skin the color of aged ivory, slender, wearing black silk pants and a matching blouse with a high collar, she stood perhaps five feet tall but had a presence bigger than her weight and height explained.

Speaking before they had a chance to introduce themselves, Lily said, "Is it . . . Linda? Double espresso, lemon peel on the side?"

"Exactly," Linda said. "How do you do that, especially after all this time?"

"It was our lives, and such a satisfaction to see people happy with what we provided to them."

Her voice was mellifluous. She made even common words sound like spoken music.

"You weren't a regular," she said to Tim, "and even if you came once in a while, I wouldn't forget what a giant drank. How do you like your coffee?"

"Black or espresso, or intravenously."

Smiling at Linda, Lily Wen-ching said, "I would remember him if he had come even a few times."

Linda said, "He leaves an impression like a sudden silent falling stone."

"How perfectly put," Lily said.

Linda made introductions, and then said, "Mrs. Wen-ching—"

"Lily."

"Thank you. Lily, when I tell you why we're here, I hope you won't think I'm crazy. Most people would. I suspect someone is trying to kill me . . . because I had coffee at the Cream and Sugar."

The widow's eyes, as dark and clear as a fresh-brewed Jamaican blend, neither widened nor narrowed. "Yes. The possibility exists."

Lily Wen-ching led them into a living room with a stepped ceiling one shade lighter than the glazed apricot walls.

Lustrous bronze-colored drapes were gathered at each end of a wall of windows with a view of the purple morning sea and Catalina Island and a sky wrung dry of all but a few tangled scraps of scrim.

Linda and Tim sat facing the view in dark zitan-wood armchairs with red seat cushions and peony medallions in the wide back splats.

Their hostess excused herself without explanation. Her slippered feet made no sound either on the area rugs or on the wood floor.

A red-tailed hawk rose out of the canyon over which the house was suspended, and glided in a widening gyre.

In the living room, a pair of carved-stone chimeras displayed on tall incense stands seemed to watch Tim as he watched the hawk.

Silence of the kind with weight pooled in the house, and Tim felt it would be impolite, even coarse, to disturb the quiet.

So quick that she must have had an espresso machine standing by for service, Lily returned with three double servings in white cups on a red-lacquered tray. She set the tray on a zitan-wood table with recessed legs, elongated brindle joints, and decorative struts.

With her back to the view, she sat on a Luohan bed used as a sofa. Hornless dragons were carved on the back and arms, and a red cushion matched those on the chairs.

After a sip of espresso, she said, "Dear Dr. Avarkian was a regular customer."

"We chatted a few times on your patio, when we sat at adjacent tables," Linda remembered.

"Professor at UCI," Lily told Tim. "He was a regular customer, died young of a heart attack."

"How young?" Tim asked.

"Forty-six. Three months after the fire."

"That's young, all right, but men that young do sometimes have fatal heart attacks."

"Lovely Evelyn Nakamoto."

"I knew her, too," Linda said, leaning forward on her chair. "She had that art gallery on Forest Avenue."

"Five months after the fire," Lily said, "visiting Seattle, Evelyn was killed in a crosswalk by a hit-and-run driver."

"But Seattle," Tim said, playing devil's advocate, suggesting that if these deaths were related, they might be expected to have occurred in Laguna Beach or nearby.

"Somebody dies far from home," Linda said, "it seems less connected to other deaths here. That's exactly why they might have gone after her in Seattle."

"Sweet Jenny Nakamoto," said Lily Wenching.

"Evelyn had a daughter, they often had coffee together," Linda said. "A pretty girl."

"Yes. Jenny. So sweet, so bright. She was a student at UCLA. Had a little apartment above someone's garage in Westwood. Someone waited in her apartment, raped her when she came home. Then murdered her."

"Horrible. I hadn't heard," Linda said. "When did it happen?"

"Eight months ago, five months after her mother in Seattle."

The rich espresso, beautifully brewed, had begun to taste bitter to Tim.

After returning her cup to the lacquered tray, sitting forward on the Luohan bed, hands clasped in her lap, Lily said, "An ugly thing about Jenny's murder."

Spotting prey, the circling red-tail plunged into the canyon, leaving the sky hawkless.

Staring at her folded hands, Lily said, "She choked to death on quarters."

Not sure that he had heard correctly, Tim said, "Quarters?"

As if unable to meet their eyes when recounting this atrocity, Lily continued staring at her hands. "He tied Jenny's hands behind her back, bound her ankles, held her down on the bed, and forced a roll of quarters down her throat."

"Oh, God," Linda said.

Tim felt certain that the last thing Jenny Nakamoto had seen, as her vision blurred with tears, had been the fierce dilated eyes, greedy for light, all light, her light.

"A heart attack, one vehicular manslaughter, one rape-murder," Tim said. "The police might not see connections, but I think you're right, Lily."

She met his eyes. "Not just three. Two more. Nice Mr. Shotsky, the lawyer, and his wife, they came to Cream and Sugar together."

"I didn't know them," Linda said, "but I know the story from the news. He shot her, then committed suicide with the same gun."

"I don't believe it," said Lily Wen-ching. "Mr. Shotsky left a note saying he caught her naked in bed with a man. There was . . . I'm sorry, but I must say . . . there was semen in her, the police say didn't come from her husband. But if Mr. Shotsky could shoot his own wife, why not the man? Why let the man go? Where is the man?"

Tim said, "You ought to be a detective, Lily."

"I ought to be a wife and mother, but I'm not anymore."

Although a tremor of emotion marked those words, her porcelain-smooth face and dark eyes remained serene.

Grief might be a thickening agent of the profound silence that pooled in this house, but a stoic acceptance of the adamantine rule of fate gave substance to it, as well.

The stone chimeras had pricked ears, as if listening for the footfalls of the man with gargoyle eyes.

Forty-Six

In a field of golden grass, among clusters of black bamboo, stood cranes with black-stick legs and black necks and black beaks.

Shades of gold defined this six-panel screen in Lily Wen-ching's living room, the black elements almost calligraphic. Otherwise there were the white feathered bodies of the cranes and their white heads, and a sense of peace.

"To the police," Lily said, "these five deaths are less than coincidence. One of them told me, 'There's no conspiracy, Lily. It's just life.' How do they come to think this way—that death is life? That unnatural death and murder are somehow a natural part of life?"

Tim asked, "Have they made any progress in the investigation of your family's murders?"

"You can't make progress in a bear hunt if

you only follow the tracks of deer. They're looking for a thief, but there was no thief."

"No money taken?" Linda asked.

"The fire took it. There wasn't anything worth stealing. We began each day with just enough in the cash-register drawer to make change. Who kills four people for forty dollars in coins and small bills?"

"Some kill for less. For hate. For envy. For nothing. Just to kill," Tim said.

"And then they prepare a fire with great care? And lock the door behind them, having timed the fire to start after they're well gone?"

"The police found a timer . . . an incendiary device?" Linda asked.

"Such intense heat. Nothing left but a **suggestion** of a device. So they argue among themselves—there was, there wasn't."

In the vastness of sky beyond the window, a last fragile skiff of cloud was coming apart and sinking in the high blue.

Lily said, "How do you know someone wants to kill you?"

After glancing at Tim, Linda said, "A man tried to run me down in an alleyway. Later, he took shots at us."

"Have you gone to the police?"

Tim said, "We have reason to think he may

be in law-enforcement somehow, somewhere. We want to know more before we make a move."

Leaning forward on the sofa, she said, "You have a name?"

"We have a name, but it's phony. We don't have his real name."

"How did you know to come to me, that I have such suspicions?"

"Under this false name, the man was briefly a person of interest in the murders of your family."

"Roy Kutter."

"Yes."

"But he was real. Roy Kutter. They cleared him."

"Yes," Linda said, "but that turns out to be a fake identity."

"Do the police here know that?"

"No," Tim said. "And I beg you not to go to them with anything we've told you. Our lives may depend on your discretion."

"They wouldn't listen anyway," she said. "They think I'm crazy with grief."

"We know," Tim said. "We heard you'd gone to them about these other five deaths. And so we came."

"Grief has not made me crazy," she assured them. "Grief has made me angry and impatient and determined. I want justice. I want truth."

"If we're lucky, we may turn up at least the truth for you," Tim said. "But justice is even harder to find in this world, these days."

Rising from the sofa, Lily said, "I pray each night and morning for my lost sweetheart, for my lost boys, and my niece. I'll pray for the two of you now, as well."

As he followed the women out of the living room, Tim looked once more at the six-panel screen of graceful cranes and black bamboo. He saw something in it that he had not noticed previously: hidden in the golden grass—a golden, crouching tiger.

Although not sure that it was appropriate, at the front door, he bent to Lily Wen-ching and embraced her.

She must have thought it appropriate, for she stood on her toes to kiss his cheek. "Earlier, I saw you admire the screen."

"Yes. And again just now. I like it very much."

"What do you like—the beauty of the cranes?"

"At first, yes. But now I more like the calm of the cranes in the presence of the tiger."

"Not everyone sees the tiger," she said. "But he is there. He is always there."

In the Honda again, Linda said, "Five more

murdered since the fire. For something they didn't know they knew?"

"Something happened while you were all there one day at the same time. Having coffee at the same time on the patio, at your separate tables."

"But nothing ever happened on the patio," she protested. "Nothing remarkable. We had our coffee. A pastry, a sandwich. Had our coffee and read a newspaper and enjoyed the sun—and went home."

Driving away from the Wen-ching house, Tim said, "The tiger was there, but no one saw."

When they descended through hills to the coast, she wondered, "What now?"

"I'm not sure yet."

"We only slept two hours. We could find a motel where they don't raise their eyebrows when you pay in cash."

"I don't think I could sleep."

"Me neither. So . . . why don't we go to a coffeehouse with a patio? Let's sit in the sun on the patio. Maybe enough sun and espresso can melt a memory out of me."

Forty-Seven

At 10:44 A.M., having slept little more than two hours, Krait was roused from dreamless sleep by the vibrating cell phone that he still cupped in his hand.

Instantly awake, he threw back the covers and sat on the edge of Teresa Mendez's bed to read what proved to be an annoying coded text message from his support group.

They had two questions. First, they wished to know why the three people at Bethany and Jim's house had been killed.

Never previously had he been asked to explain collateral damage. He took offense at this query, which seemed to suggest that he might have unnecessarily terminated someone.

His first impulse was to reply that the three were better off dead, that everyone now alive would be better off dead, for the sake of the world they burdened, and that if the support group was arrogant enough to question him, then they should ask not why he had killed Cynthia and Malcolm and Nora, but instead why he had not yet killed **everyone.**

They also wanted to know how his pursuit of the Paquette woman had led him to the house where three now lay dead.

He would not answer that question because it was an impertinent violation of his privacy. They **petitioned** him to grant them a certain **grace.** They didn't **own** him. He had a **life,** a good life in the art of death.

As long as ultimately they received the grace they sought—the death of Paquette—they had no right to make him account for his actions or his time. Outrageous.

Besides, Krait couldn't tell them why he had gone into that house, because they didn't know that he was homeless. They thought that he kept the whereabouts of his home a secret, which made sense for a man of his bloody calling.

If he explained his unconventional living arrangements, they would not understand. They would sever relations with him. They were mere men, after all; none of them was a prince of the earth like he was.

Instead of a home of his own, he had millions of homes. Usually, he lived in the residences of others with such circumspection that they never knew he had been there.

Once in a while, he found himself in a situation out of which he could not talk his way. Then he killed through the problem.

In the past, the Gentlemen's Club had shown no curiosity about such matters. The difference this time might be quantity: three collateral casualties in one incident.

He decided to ignore both questions and to reply with only a line from Wallace Stevens, a poet he liked but did not understand: THE ONLY EMPEROR IS THE EMPEROR OF ICE-CREAM.

Sometimes, reading Wallace Stevens, Krait not only wanted to kill everyone in the world but wanted also to kill himself. This seemed to him to be the ultimate proof of great poetry.

THE ONLY EMPEROR IS THE EMPEROR OF ICE-CREAM.

Let them reflect on that and, if they were bright enough, reach the conclusion that they had trespassed with their questions.

Krait was now alert to the likelihood that the Paquette woman was in fact a target specified by the Gentlemen's Club and not by one of his other petitioners. Their irritation over these recent three deaths might be merely a reflection of their concern that his quarry had repeatedly escaped him, which had never happened before.

If he moved quickly to locate and destroy the woman, he would allay the Club's concern. With Paquette dead, the murders of Cynthia and Malcolm and Nora would be accepted as unavoidable collateral damage, and soon forgotten.

He returned Teresa's undergarments to the laundry basket in the closet, and made the bed. He took the mug, thermos, and biscuit plate to the kitchen, washed them, and put them away.

In the bedroom once more, he dressed. The reproduction art from Paquette's bedroom had been soaked with rain, and he had earlier unfolded it on the carpet. He found it dry now; once more he folded the print and returned it to an inside coat pocket.

With the Glock machine pistol, he returned to Teresa's small den. He switched on her computer and went on-line.

The don't-ask rule had served Krait well. The less he knew about the targets of the Club, the better. If he ever understood why these people were wanted dead, he would know too much. He had considerable experience regarding what happened to men—perhaps even to princes—who knew too much.

Although he had been petitioned to kill

Paquette, not Carrier, he'd thought it wise to apply the don't-ask rule to the man, as well. Having been outfoxed more than once, however, and in consideration of the sudden restiveness of the Gentlemen's Club, Krait decided to amend his strategy.

He composed a simple search string to seek whatever information about Carrier might exist. He didn't expect to find a great deal more than what he already knew. Wrong.

Forty-Eight

The **wide-spreading branches of a** New Zealand Christmas tree sheltered that half of the coffeehouse patio closer to the street. Its majestic limbs were not cloaked in crimson flowers at this time of year.

Tim and Linda sat in the sun, at the table farthest from the street, next to a whitewashed wall of sand-mold bricks on which climbing vines were adorned with Mexican blood flowers.

As they nursed cups of espresso, the sun warmed an increasing aroma from a plate of small chocolate-pistachio cookies.

They were talking about the blood flowers when, after a pause, Linda said, "My father's name was Benedict. Everyone called him Benny."

Tim heard the **was** and waited.

"He had a master's degree in child development."

"He did all right with you."

A thin smile came and went. "My mother's name was Renee."

On a hunch, he said, "Do you carry pictures of them?"

From her purse, she took her wallet, and from the wallet an insert of plastic photo windows.

He said, "I like their faces."

"They were gentle and sweet and funny."

"You resemble her."

"She had a degree in education," Linda said.

"Teacher?"

"They worked in day-care, founded a preschool."

"Sounds like they should have succeeded at it."

"Eventually they owned three."

She turned her face up to the sun and closed her eyes.

A hovering hummingbird sought the nectar of a blood flower.

She said, "There was this five-year-old named Chloe."

In one photo, Benny in a funny hat was mugging for Linda.

"Chloe's mother already had her on Ritalin."

In the same photo, Linda laughed with delight.

"My folks were counseling her to stop the Ritalin."

The spring sun made her face seem luminous from within.

"Chloe was a handful. The mother wanted her on the drug."

He said, "They say half the kids are on it now."

"Maybe my folks made the mother feel guilty."

"Maybe they didn't try. Maybe she already felt guilty."

"Whatever. Anyway, she resented them for raising the issue."

The hummingbird was an iridescent green, its wings a blur.

"One day on the playground, Chloe fell and scraped a knee."

The photos had begun to look sad to him. Souvenirs of loss.

"Mom and Dad cleaned the abrasion."

Tim returned the photos to her wallet.

"They used iodine. Chloe cried and fussed about the sting."

Moving to a new bloom, the hummingbird went **zrrr-jika-jika**.

"She told her mom, she didn't like the way they touched her."

Tim said, "Surely she knew the girl meant iodine."

"Maybe she misunderstood. Maybe she **wanted** to misunderstand."

Linda's face seemed to darken even as the sun waxed brighter.

"Chloe's mother complained to the police."

The blur of wings produced a soft solemn threnody.

"The police questioned my folks, and cleared them."

"But it didn't end there?"

"The district attorney was facing a hard re-election battle."

Tim said, "So the law became just politics."

She lowered her face from the sun, but kept her eyes closed.

"The D.A. hired a psychiatrist to interview the children."

"All of them, not just Chloe?"

"All of them. And the wild stories started."

"And then no going back," he said.

"Naked games. Naked dancing. Animals killed in the classroom."

"Animal sacrifice? People believed that?"

"Dogs and cats killed to scare the children into silence."

"My God."

"Two kids even said a little boy had been chopped apart."

"And they never mentioned this to their parents?"

"Repressed memories. Chopped apart, buried in the schoolyard."

"Then dig it up, find out."

"They did, found nothing."

"And that wasn't the end of it?"

"They tore open the school walls, looking for kiddie porn."

"And found none," he assumed.

"None. Also looking for items used in satanic rituals."

"This sounds like Salem in another century."

"Kids said they were forced to kiss pictures of the devil."

"And children never lie," he said.

"I don't blame them. They were little . . . and malleable."

"Psychiatrists can unwittingly implant false memories."

"Perhaps not always unwittingly. Ceilings were torn out."

"All this from a knee abrasion."

"Floors ripped up, looking for secret basement rooms."

"And nothing ever found," he said.

"No. But my folks were indicted on the strength of testimony."

She opened her eyes. She was looking into the past.

"I think," he said, "was there a lot of this back then?"

"Yeah. Scores of cases. A nationwide hysteria."

"Some must have been true."

"Ninety-five percent eventually proved bogus, maybe more."

"But lives were ruined, people went to prison."

After a silence, she said, "I had to see the psychiatrist."

"The same one interviewing the preschool kids?"

"Yeah. The D.A. required it. And the child welfare department."

"Had they taken you away from your parents?"

"They were trying. The psychiatrist said he could help me."

"Help you what?"

"Help me remember why I had bad dreams."

"Did you have bad dreams?"

"Doesn't every child? I was ten. He had a forceful presence."

"The psychiatrist?"

"A forceful presence, a seductive voice. He made you like him."

The ascension of the sun shrank the cup shadows on the table.

"He made you want to believe in things . . . hidden, forgotten."

She folded both hands around the small espresso cup.

"The lights were soft. He was patient. His voice hushed."

She lifted the cup but did not drink.

"He had a way of making you meet his eyes."

A fine sweat chilled the back of Tim's neck.

"He had such lovely, sad, sad eyes. And soft gentle hands."

"How far did he lead you toward . . . false memories?"

"Maybe farther than I want to remember."

She drank the last of her espresso.

"In our fourth session, he exposed himself to me."

As she spoke, she rattled her cup back into the saucer.

With a paper napkin, Tim blotted the cold damp nape of his neck.

She said, "He asked me to touch it. Kiss it. But I wouldn't."

"Good God. You told somebody?"

"No one believed me. They said my parents put me up to it."

"To discredit him."

"I was taken from Mom and Dad. I had to live with Angelina."

"Who was she?"

"My mother's aunt. Molly and I, my dog Molly—to Angelina."

She stared at the backs of her hands. Then at her palms.

"The night I left, they stoned our house, broke the windows."

"Who stoned it?"

"Someone who believed in secret rooms and devil-kissing."

She folded her hands, one over the other, on the table.

Her remarkable calm had not deserted her.

"I haven't talked about this in fifteen years."

He said, "You don't have to go on with it now."

"Yes. I do. But I need the courage of caffeine."

"I'll get two more espressos."

"Thank you."

Weaving between tables, he carried their soiled cups across the patio. At the coffeehouse door, he paused and looked back at her.

The beneficent sun seemed to favor her above anyone and anything in view. Judging solely by appearances, you might have thought this world had never been unkind to her, that a life of steady happiness explained the innocent beauty that drew your eyes, as if magnetized, to her face.

Forty-Nine

On the road again, Krait drove with a happy heart. Events were proving him to be the king of this world, not a mere prince.

Timothy Carrier might be a formidable adversary. But the mason had a weakness that would be the destruction of him.

No longer did Krait need to track down this elusive pair. He could make Carrier—and the woman—come to him.

As he drove to Laguna Niguel, a thought occurred to him that he found electrifying. Perhaps the reversed world that he saw in mirrors and that he longed to explore might be his true world, the one from which he had come.

If he had no mother, as memory assured him that he did not, if his life had begun suddenly at eighteen, and if prior to that his life remained a mystery, then it made sense that he had come into this world not by way of any womb, but through a mirror.

His yearning for the mirror world might be a yearning for his true home.

This further explained why he had never purchased a house of his own in this world. Subconsciously, he had realized that no place on this side of the mirror could fully satisfy his need for hearth and haven, because here he would be forever a stranger in a strange land.

He was superior to and apart from the people of this backward world because he hailed from a land where all was as it should be, everything familiar and eternally unchanging and clean, where nobody needed to be killed because everyone had been born dead.

In Laguna Niguel, he drove the streets of a solid middle-class neighborhood, where handsome tract homes were well maintained with quiet pride, and where families owned more cars than their garages could contain.

At a few houses, basketball hoops were fixed above garage doors. The nets hung ready, in expectation of after-school games.

No fewer but no more flags flew than basketball hoops waited, not gloriously undulant, but solemn and draped, stars folded into stars, and stripes curled into furrows.

Close-cropped green lawns, bordered beds of impatiens in lush red and purple plenitude, geometric trellises entwined with climbing roses eloquently spoke of a love for home and a need for order.

Krait, a stranger here, wished all these people dead, street after street of them, mile after mile, dead by the millions, and wished all the houses to ashes, and all the lawns to dust.

This world might be the wrong place for him, but at least he found himself here at the right time, on the brink of an age of great violence and mass murder.

He located the particular house that had drawn him to these suburban hills. Two stories of butter-yellow stucco and white wood. Dormers. Shake roof. Bay window. Potted geraniums on the porch.

After parking at the curb and rolling down the window in the passenger's door, he put on a set of headphones. He picked up from the seat a hand-held directional microphone and pointed it at one of the windows on the second floor.

Earlier, he had retrieved the sophisticated mike from the suitcase in the trunk of the car.

It was one of several items he had been perspicacious enough to order from his support group following the unfortunate loss of his first vehicle.

At a maximum distance of fifty yards, through a closed window, the directional microphone could pick up conversations that were inaudible to the unassisted ear. Wind diminished its usefulness, and heavy rain rendered it worthless. But now the sky was clear, and the air had a mortuary stillness.

One by one, he tried the second-floor windows, but none gave forth a sound.

From the ground floor came singing. The woman had a light sweet voice. She sang softly, with a casualness that suggested she might be entertaining herself while doing household chores. The song was "I'll Be Seeing You," an American standard.

Krait heard a series of clinks, a soft rattle. They might have been kitchen sounds.

He heard no other voice but hers. Evidently, she was home alone, which was what he expected based on what he had learned.

After switching off the directional microphone and rolling up the car window, he drove two blocks and parked on a different street in the same neighborhood.

Carrying a small cloth satchel, he walked back toward the yellow-and-white house.

The sun-washed residential streets had a dreamy quality: bees buzzing lazily over festoons of yellow lantana, the lacy foliage of California pepper trees seeming to shimmer with pleasure as they basked in the warm light, a calico cat sleeping on a front-porch step, three larks perched on the rim of a birdbath as if studying their reflections in the water. . . .

At the target house, the front walkway was paved with quartzite cobblestones laid in an intricate and pleasing pattern.

The deadbolt in the front door was not engaged. The simpler lock popped instantly to the pick of the LockAid, making little noise.

He put away the LockAid and carried the satchel into a small foyer, and softly closed the door behind him.

From the back of the house came the woman's fair voice. Now she sang "I Only Have Eyes for You."

Krait stood for a moment, enjoying.

Fifty

The hummingbird remained busy at the Mexican blood flowers.

Clean white cups held fresh black espresso.

"How many children were at that day-care?" Tim asked.

"Fifty-two."

"How many were induced to remember things like naked games?"

"Seventeen. The D.A.'s office leaked the salacious details."

"Were the kids given physical exams?"

"First the psychiatrist said exams would be traumatizing."

"If the D.A. bowed to that, he suspected there was nothing."

"Maybe he planned to drop the case after it got him re-elected."

"But it gained too much momentum in the media," Tim guessed.

Quivers of sunlight curled like lemon-peel oil on the espresso.

"The psychiatrist spent months drawing out the seventeen."

"The same one who exposed himself to you."

"Eventually he okayed pre-trial physical exams."

A dog on a leash led its whistling owner past the patio.

Linda watched the tail-wagging mutt until it was out of sight.

"Two little girls showed evidence of prior molestation."

At another table, chair legs shrieked against the stone deck.

"Soft-tissue scarring," she said. "One of the girls was Chloe."

"The one whose mother started it all."

"By then Chloe was on more than Ritalin."

"What do you mean?"

"Her parents hired the psychiatrist to treat her long-term."

"My God."

The crimson flowers bobbed their heads in a stir of air.

"He medicated Chloe. As part of her therapy."

"The girls claimed more than . . . naked games?"

"Graphic claims of molestation," she said.

The laughter of young women rose from a table under the tree.

"They said my mother held them down while my father . . ."

One of the laughs was silvery, the others shrill.

Disturbed from their branches, three sparrows flew.

"The girls' testimony was recorded by the D.A."

The sparrows soared, vanished in the throat of the sky.

"The psychiatrist was present for the recording," she said.

"Are recordings like that admissible in court?"

"Shouldn't have been, but the judge steamrolled it."

"Grounds for appeal."

"No hope of that, as it turned out."

Like a scimitar, a brown feather carved down through the air.

"My father got twenty years. He went to San Quentin."

"How old were you?"

"Ten when it started. Almost twelve by the verdict."

"Your mother?"

"She got eight to ten years. A women's prison in Corona."

Espresso occupied her for a while.

Tim wanted to reach out to her, but he sensed that she would refuse comforting. The hardness of the injustice had long sustained her. Anger was her only comfort.

"Dad served five months before an inmate killed him."

Her story had a weight that bowed Tim's head.

"Stabbed four times in the gut, twice in the face."

Tim closed his eyes but did not like the darkness.

"My mother developed pancreatic cancer. Misdiagnosed in prison."

Looking up, he saw her staring at the feather on the table.

"In the hospital, she had no strength to hold my hand."

A young man with a bouquet of roses crossed the patio.

"I held her hand in both of mine, but she slipped away."

The bearer of flowers joined the laughing women.

"Their legal defense bankrupted them. Angelina had little."

A woman rose to kiss the young man. He looked happy.

"Our name had been Locadio, but that was notorious now."

Tim realized: "I was young then, but I remember the name."

"Kids called me the monsters' daughter. Some boys were obscene."

"Is Angelina's last name Paquette?"

"Yes. I took it legally. Changed schools. But that didn't work."

The hummingbird had gone. Now it returned.

"So I was home-schooled."

"You seem to have thrived on that."

"Because I wanted to know everything. To understand **why**."

"But there is no why," he said. "Just—evil is."

"The second girl who'd been molested found me two years ago."

"She began to shed the false memories?"

"She never had any. She lied about my dad, as she was led to."

"Led by . . . the therapist? Afraid of him?"

"In blind terror of him. He molested her in their sessions."

"The soft-tissue scarring."

"She suffered. Shame. Fear. Guilt over the death of my dad."

"What did you say to her?"

"That I loved her for making the effort to find me."

"Has she accused him?"

"Yes. And he says he'll sue her for defamation of character."

"What about Chloe? Could she support the other girl?"

"When she was fourteen, Chloe committed suicide."

The sun warm on the skin and all of Nature reaching up to it, the hummingbird and the crimson flowers, the tail-wagging dog and its whistling owner, the young man with roses and the laughing women: For all the beauty and joy of life, the world is nonetheless a war zone.

Fifty-One

While the woman sang in the kitchen, Krait toured the living room.

The pale-yellow of the exterior walls had been repeated on the interior, and all the molding and built-in cabinets had been painted glossy white. The reddish Santos mahogany floor anchored the space, and on it floated a yellow-and-aubergine area rug with palmettes and feathery leaves, a cheaper modern version of a Persian carpet.

The furnishings were nothing special, but not hideous, either. The room had not been feminized with floral prints and ruffles and fringe; yet it felt warm and womanly.

Most people might think of this as a family-friendly style. Having had no experience of a family, Krait could not make that judgment himself.

The woman stopping singing.

Krait put the cloth satchel on an armchair, unzipped it, and removed from it an instrument with which he could instantly subdue her.

He listened for approaching footsteps, and he imagined that the woman was standing still, also listening, but after a while she began to sing again. The song was "Someone to Watch over Me."

Above the fireplace hung a painting of children in swimsuits running on a beach. Sun made luminous a rising arc of surf. The children looked exuberant.

Krait had no use for children, of course, but he found this painting so repellent that, paradoxically, he was drawn to it.

The style of this work could not be criticized as precious, not even as sentimental. The artist had a realist's eye not only for form and proportion and detail, but also for the subtleties of light.

The longer Krait studied the painting, the more he detested it. But study did not bring him any closer to an understanding of the reason for his antipathy.

Instinctively, he knew that this painting represented something against which he must always be in opposition, something that he must resist with every fiber of his being and to which he must respond with merciless violence.

In the kitchen, the woman segued from "Someone to Watch over Me" into "These Foolish Things," and Krait moved on from the painting, counseling himself to smooth away the hostility that spiked his nerves and to recover his usual placidity, which was more befitting a person of his gifts and stature.

The family had a bookcase. Of the titles with which Krait was familiar, he approved of none.

In addition to books, some shelves held framed photographs of the family, both group shots and portraits.

Although the mother and father were in some group pictures, the most frequently featured faces were those of the children, Timothy and Zachary.

The boys were captured by the lens as young as three or four, as old perhaps as twenty. Some photos were posed, and others were candid shots.

Krait could not recall having seen so many smiles, so many faces alive with laughter in one collection of images. The Carrier family seemed always to be full of delight and merriment.

Well, that would soon change.

Part Three

The Wrong Place at the Wrong Time

Fifty-Two

Krait walked along the hallway to the kitchen and stood in the open doorway.

At the sink, the woman stood with her back to him, coring and peeling apples.

She was doing a nice job with "These Foolish Things," singing it slow and easy, almost talking the lyrics, giving it a melancholy note like it ought to have.

The kitchen and family room flowed together. Between those two spaces, six captain's chairs surrounded a big pine table.

He could picture Tim at that table. As a boy, Tim must have eaten a lot of meals there, putting some pressure on the family budget, big as he was.

Over the table hung a handsome copper chandelier. Stylized birds flew in a circle around eight candleform lights with copper shades patterned like feathers.

Having finished peeling an apple, the woman used a different knife to halve it and then to slice it into a metal bowl on the cutting board next to the sink.

She had long-fingered, nimble hands. He liked her hands.

When the woman finished the song, Krait said, “Mary?”

He expected her to be startled. Instead, she turned to him with no more reaction than a slight widening of the eyes.

In her mid-fifties, she was old enough to be Krait’s mother, if he’d ever had a mother, but she was nonetheless a trim and attractive woman.

“Do you know ‘As Time Goes By,’ from **Casablanca**?” he asked.

She did not say **Who’re you** or **What’re you doing here,** but only stared at him.

“I’ve seen that movie forty-two times,” Krait said. “I like watching the same movies. You always know what you’re going to get.”

He could see her thinking about the knife in her hand. She was calculating the distance to the back door, too, though she didn’t glance at it.

Before she complicated the situation, Krait shot her. The air gun that he had taken from the cloth satchel spoke **pop-whoosh**, not loud, and the hypodermic dart stung her in the right breast.

She wore a checkered blue-and-yellow blouse and most likely also a bra. That much clothing would not interfere with the delivery of the drug.

The bite of the dart pricked a hiss of pain from Mary. She plucked it out of her breast and dropped it on the floor, but the hyperfast-acting tranquilizer had been injected in an instant.

"Maybe later you can sing 'As Time Goes By,'" he said. "I'm sure you know the words."

She snatched the combination peeler-corer from the cutting board and threw it at him. Her aim was wide.

Holding the knife, she turned to the back door, but her ankles wobbled and her legs sagged under her. She grabbed at the counter for support.

Krait walked around the kitchen island, toward her.

As her head began to loll forward, she raised it with an effort. Her eyes glazed.

The knife slipped from her hand and clattered on the tile floor.

Krait kicked away the blade and, as Mary swooned, he caught her before she hit the floor.

He carried the unconscious woman to the large pine table. She was so limp that she wanted to slide out of the dining chair. Krait leaned her forward, folded her arms on the table, and rested her head on her arms. In that position, she seemed to be stable.

In the living room, he drew shut the draperies. He retrieved the cloth satchel.

After engaging the deadbolt on the front door, he returned to the kitchen. He put the satchel on the pine table.

In respect of the possibility that the Carriers had sitcom drop-in neighbors à la Bethany and Jim, Krait closed the blinds in the kitchen and draperies in the family room.

He withdrew two sets of police handcuffs from the cloth bag. He cuffed Mary's left wrist to the left arm of her chair.

Head still on the table, she began to snore.

Using the second handcuff, he shackled one leg of the chair to a leg of the table.

He quickly toured the house, not to satisfy his curiosity about how these people lived, but to make sure that he and Mary were alone.

Except for himself in a few mirrors, he saw no one. He winked at one reflection of himself, gave another a thumbs-up sign.

Two vehicles were registered to the Carriers: a six-year-old Suburban and a newer Ford Expedition. Walter had taken the Suburban to work, but in the garage, the Expedition stood ready for Krait.

In the kitchen once more, he selected a slice of apple from the metal bowl on the cutting board. Crisp and delicious. He savored a second slice.

At the table, Mary made a choking sound and stopped snoring.

On rare occasion, an allergic reaction to the drug could result in anaphylactic shock and death.

When he checked, he found her still breathing. Her pulse was slow and steady.

He sat her up straight in her chair. This time she didn't sag forward, though her head tipped to one side.

Sitting in the chair beside hers, he brushed the hair back from her face. She had clear skin, only a few lines at the corners of her eyes.

He peeled back both eyelids. She had gray eyes flecked with green. The lids stayed open a moment when he released them, but then slid slowly shut.

Her jaw still sagged. Her lips were parted. She had full lips.

Krait traced the shape of her mouth with his fingertips, but she did not respond.

From the cloth satchel, he took a flexible rubber tube and a blue plastic case. The case held two hypodermic syringes and ampules containing an amber solution.

He stripped the sheath off one of the hypodermics and pierced the cap of the ampule and drew a measured dose of the solution and squirted some of it on the floor to be sure no air remained in the needle.

He turned her right arm palm-up and used the flexible tubing as a tourniquet to make a vein clarify in her flesh. He stuck the vein and slowly pressed the plunger and slipped loose the tourniquet and watched as the amber solution receded from the clear barrel of the hypodermic.

He had not swabbed the injection site with alcohol. If a blood infection developed, Mary's crisis wouldn't come for a couple of days at least, and he would be done with her by then, anyway.

Her arms were quite feminine, shapely, but not soft. She had good muscle tone.

When he withdrew the needle, a bead of blood appeared. He stared at it, intrigued.

This was blood from the mother of the most formidable adversary whom Krait had ever encountered or was ever likely to encounter.

Breathing in the scent of her skin, he bent to the crook of her arm and licked the blood away.

Reason could not explain why he felt compelled to taste this crimson essence, but he was convinced that he had done the right thing.

The amber fluid was a counteractive drug to the tranquilizer that she had received in the air-gun dart. She would wake not only faster with this chemical assistance but also with immediate clarity of mind.

Krait leaned back in his chair and watched her eyes begin to twitch beneath her lids.

She worked her mouth as if grimacing at a bad taste. Her tongue appeared and licked her lips.

When her eyes opened the first time, they were unfocused, and she closed them. She opened them again, and again closed them.

"Don't pretend," he said. "I know you're with me now."

Mary sat up straighter in her chair and looked at the handcuff that shackled her left wrist to the arm of the chair and looked at her right arm where he had injected it and stared at the used syringe that lay on the table.

When finally she met Krait's eyes, he expected her to ask what he had done to her, but she said nothing. She stared at him, waiting for what he might have to say.

Impressed, he favored Mary with a smile. “Girl, I gotta say, you’re a different kind of animal.”

“I am not an animal,” she said.

Fifty-Three

Breaking waves flung spray across the tortoise-shell rocks. The rhythmic crashes and intervening susurrations sounded like multitudes whispering in different languages at once, as though all the ancient dead claimed by the sea spoke forever in its voice.

The park extended for several blocks along the bluff. Workers on break opened their bagged lunches at the picnic tables under the palm trees, and dedicated joggers followed the pathways, wincing and grim.

Tim and Linda strolled from viewing point to viewing point, and leaned against the railing, watching the shore receive the sea and the sea surmount the shore.

They were metabolizing nerve-tightening quantities of caffeine, and he was assimilating everything she had told him, while she was adapting to the fact that she'd spoken about her family's destruction for the first time in more than fifteen years.

"Funny," she said, "how just when I feel like I'm ready to live, really live, someone is coming to kill me."

"He may be coming, but he's not going to kill you."

"Where do you get your confidence?" she asked.

He held up a bag containing the last of the chocolate-pistachio cookies, which they had brought with them and which they had eaten while they walked.

"Sugar," he said.

"I'm serious, Tim."

He watched the waves, and she did not press him, but at last he said, "More than seven years now, I've known there's a thing coming I've got to deal with."

"What thing?"

"It sounds too grand to call it destiny."

"We all have a destiny."

"This is more like—what's in the blood."

"So what's in your blood?" she asked.

"It's nothing I take pride in. I didn't earn it. It's just a thing that's there."

She waited.

"It scared me some when I discovered it," he said. "It scares me still. And then there's the way people react to it, which can be embarrassing."

With sudden shrieks, gulls kited through the sky. One dived, and the sea took him.

"I told myself being a mason is a good and honest trade, and being a mason is the best thing for me, and I do believe it is."

The bird broke from the water or from the shelter between two waves, and soared with its fish.

"But sooner or later, the part of yourself you try to keep down, it won't be held down any longer. It's in the blood, and blood will have its way, I guess."

In the sea spray but beyond the reach of the waves, two men and a woman navigated the rocks below, plucking up crabs and putting them in bright-yellow plastic buckets.

"And anyway, things have a way of happening that force you to be what you are."

The disposable cell phone rang.

"Don't answer it," she said. "Just finish."

"It'll be Pete," he said, and it was.

"Got my own disposable cell," Pete said.

"You have something to take down the number?"

"Pen and paper?" Tim asked, and Linda produced them from her purse, and Tim said to Pete, "Go ahead."

After giving the number and repeating it, Pete said, "Have you seen Lily Wen-ching yet?"

"We did. And it was something."

"I've got to hear it. But let's get face to face."

"Have to break your legs to keep you out of this, wouldn't I?"

"That wouldn't do it. I was a high-school gymnast. I can walk on my hands."

"So where you want to meet?"

Pete asked where they were. "I'll meet you there. Half an hour."

"We'll be at a picnic table."

He pocketed the disposable phone and began walking again along the bluff path.

At his side, Linda said, "Hey, big head, you owe me some talk."

"Yeah, but I can't get my tongue around the words."

"I tore down my wall," she reminded him.

"And I know how hard it was. But my wall has a lot of rebar in it. Let's just go a ways up here while I brood a little."

She walked with him.

He said, "I don't want to change what you think of me."

She walked with him. The sun passed its zenith, and the trees began to grow east-leaning shadows, and she walked with him.

Fifty-Four

"That's **quite some boy you've got,"** said Krait.

Mary did not reply. Her mouth appeared less full than it had been previously. Her lips were set tight.

"I'm sure Zachary, he's quite some boy, too," Krait said. "But I mean Tim."

Those people who were charmed by Krait's smile and by his easy manner, when he chose to pour on the honey, seldom met his stare, as if subconsciously they knew that they were deluding themselves about him and wished to avoid his eyes in order to remain deluded.

When someone did engage his eyes, they tended not to meet his stare for long.

Mary had the probing gaze of an ophthalmologist. Each time she blinked, she seemed to be turning another page in Krait's mind.

"Dear, just because I disabled you in a painless fashion does not mean that I won't hurt you if I must."

No reply.

"If you're stubborn, then I'll get cooperation by subjecting you to pain beyond your imagination."

She continued to read his eyes.

"Only fools aren't afraid," he said, "and fools die."

"I'm afraid," she acknowledged.

"Good. I'm pleased to hear that."

"But afraid isn't the only thing I am."

"Let's see if we can work with that."

She still didn't ask who he was or what he wanted. She declined to waste time on questions that would not be answered or on those that he would answer without being asked.

"My name is Robert Kessler. You can call me Bob. Now, Mary dear, your boy Tim has something I want, and he won't give it to me."

"Then you probably shouldn't have it."

He smiled. "I'll bet when he was a boy, you defended him to every teacher who ever gave him a bad report."

"Actually, I never did."

"What if I told you that he hijacked a substantial amount of cocaine that belongs to me?"

"If you were stupid enough to tell me that, I'd know you were lying."

"Mary, Mary, you don't strike me as a naive woman."

"Then don't treat me as if I am."

Krait persisted: "No one can know another person's deepest secrets. Even a mother can't know her son's true heart."

"This mother does."

"So it didn't surprise you that he could murder people?"

Regarding Krait with contempt, she said, "That's pathetic. **Murder?** That's less than sophistry."

He raised his eyebrows. "**Sophistry?** That's quite a word for a mason's wife and a mason's mother."

"We try to be just dumb working stiffs, but our brains get in the way."

"Mary, I've gotta say, under other circumstances, I might get to like you."

"I can't imagine any circumstances where I'd like you."

He studied her in silence for a while.

She said, "You can't make me doubt my son. The more you try, the more I'll doubt your seriousness."

Krait said, "This is going to be interesting."

He went into the kitchen and got the bowl of sliced apples from the cutting board and returned to his chair.

After munching a slice, he said, "What are the apples for?"

"You didn't come here to talk about apples."

"But they're what interest me now, dear. Were you going to make a pie?"

"Two pies."

Munching another slice, he asked, "Do you make your own crusts from scratch or buy them ready-made at the supermarket?"

"I make my own."

"As much as possible," Krait said, "I try to eat homemade food. It's healthier and more flavorful than restaurant food or frozen entrees, and when you have as many homes as I do, there's infinite variety."

He took a third crescent of apple from the bowl and threw it at her face.

She flinched. The apple stuck for a moment on her forehead, then slipped off and fell onto her blouse.

He threw another slice, which struck her cheek and dropped onto her right arm. She flicked it to the floor.

"Try to catch this one in your mouth," Krait said.

The piece of apple bounced off her tightly pressed lips.

"Come on, be a sport. Go for it."

Because she kept her mouth shut and raised her head, the slice of apple hit her chin.

"Whatever you want," she said, "humiliating me won't help you get it."

"Maybe not, dear. But I'm enjoying myself."

He ate another slice of apple, and then he threw two more.

"What time does Walter get home from work?"

She didn't answer.

"Mary, Mary, so contrary. Maybe you don't care if I go find a razor blade and start carving your face to make you cooperate."

He withdrew the Glock 18 machine pistol from the shoulder rig under his coat and put it on the table.

"But," he continued, "if Walter walks in here unexpected, I'll shoot him dead when he comes through the door, and that'll be your fault."

She stared at the weapon.

"It's fitted with a silencer," Krait explained. "And it's a machine pistol. From point-blank, I could put four, five, six rounds in his neck and face with one squeeze of the trigger."

Reluctantly, she said, "Usually between four and four-thirty."

The quickest way at her was through those she loved.

Krait said, "Sometimes he comes home earlier?"

"Not unless the weather turns bad."

"Are you expecting anyone else?"

"No."

"All right. Fine. I'll have you out of here long before four o'clock."

He saw her react to the news that he would be taking her away from home, but she said nothing.

"I'm going to place a call to Tim," he said. "Timmy. Do you call him Timmy?"

"No."

"Did you call him Timmy when he was a little boy?"

"It's always been Tim."

"All right. But certainly never Tiny Tim. I'm going to place a call to Tim and offer him a trade. I need you to speak to him."

"What trade?"

"Ah, curiosity at last."

"Tell me the truth. Not the cocaine nonsense."

"I've been hired to kill this bitch, this writer,

rape her if I have the time, and he's hiding her from me."

The mason's mother searched Krait's eyes, then lowered her attention to the weapon on the table.

"It was supposed to look like an intruder in her house, but that probably can't be made to work now. But if I can, I'm still going to rape her because she's made me wait so long for it."

Mary closed her eyes.

"Does that sound like more nonsense to you, Mary?"

"No. It's crazy, but it sounds true."

"When you're reunited, Tim can tell you all the details. They're fascinating. He's led me on quite a chase."

He threw a slice of apple at her to make her open her eyes.

Scooting his chair closer to her, he said, "Stay with me, Mary. You need to understand a couple things."

"I'm listening."

"Later, I'm going to tie you up, carry you out to the Expedition in the garage. We'll leave in the Expedition. I'm going to put you in the cargo space, on your back. Are you afraid of needles, Mary?"

"No."

"Good. Because I'm going to hook you up to a clever little intravenous-infusion pump. Do you know what that is?"

"No."

"It's like an IV drip in the hospital but more compact, and it's battery-powered instead of gravity-fed. It'll administer a continuous measured dose of sedative. Are you allergic to any drugs, dear?"

"Allergic? No."

"Then it'll be perfectly safe. You'll sleep until this is done with. That'll make things easier for both of us. I'll cover you with a blanket, arrange some other things in the cargo space, and anyone who happens to glance in won't even know you're there. But I've got one problem. Look at me, dear."

She had lost interest in reading his eyes because she knew now what he was. She knew that he would not be in the least vulnerable to a mother's wiles.

"After the air-gun dart, I administered a counter-sedative so we could have this little tête-à-tête. It's still in your system. It'll interfere with the effect of the next sedative I give you for"—he consulted his wristwatch—"about another hour and a half, hour and fifteen minutes. So we've got to wait. You follow me?"

"Yes."

"So when we call Tim, I'll tell him I've spirited you away. And I'll have instructions for him. You'll play that game. You're long gone, and you want to come home, and please will he do what the bad Mr. Kessler tells him to do."

Earlier her cheeks had flushed with anger and humiliation. At last she had paled.

"I can't do it," she said.

"Of course you can, dear."

"Oh, God."

"You're a trouper."

"I can't put him in that position."

"What position?"

"Choosing who's going to die."

"Are you serious?"

"What a horrible thing for him."

"You're serious."

"I can't do it."

"Mary, she's a skank he met just yesterday."

"It doesn't matter."

"**Just yesterday.** You're his **mother**. It's an easy decision for the boy."

"But he'll have to live with it. Why should he have to live with a decision like that?"

"What the hell? Are you afraid he'll choose the skank over you?" Krait asked, and warned himself against the anger that he heard in his voice.

"I know Tim. I know he'll do what he thinks is right and best. But there's no right here that doesn't have a wrong attached to it."

Krait took a deep breath. He took another. Calm. He needed to remain calm. He stood up. He stretched. He smiled down at Mary.

"And if he chooses me," she said, "**I'll** have to live with that girl on my conscience, won't I?"

"Well, life sucks, Mary, but most people feel it's better than death. I don't feel that way personally. I think all of you would be better off dead, but that's just me."

She met his eyes. She looked bewildered.

He picked up the Glock and walked slowly around the table. "Let me explain something, dear. If you can't do this for me, I'll kill you and leave you for Walter to find. Do you believe me?"

"Yes."

"And next I'll go after your boy Zachary. I'll give Tim that choice—his brother or the skank. Do you believe me?"

She said nothing.

"Do you believe me?"

"Yes."

"If Zachary is stupid enough to have moral

reservations, I'll kill him. Is that what you have, Mary—moral reservations?"

"I just care about my son."

"After I kill Zachary, I'll go for his wife. Her name's Laura, isn't it?"

Mary finally asked, "Who are you?" by which she meant **What are you?**

"Robert Kessler. Remember? You can call me Bob. Or Bobby if you want. Just don't call me Rob. I don't like the name Rob."

The woman did not appear any less self-possessed, but the seed of fear in her had bloomed nicely.

"And if Laura has some crazy-assed righteous attitude, if she's been infected, then I'll rape her and kill her and move on to Naomi. How old is Naomi?"

Mary did not answer.

"Dear, I know this is difficult, you were just making apple pies and singing old songs and having a nice day, and then **this**. But tell me how old Naomi is, or I'll blow your brains out right now."

"Seven. She's seven."

"If I ask a seven-year-old girl to plead with her uncle Tim to save her life, do you think she will? I think she will, Mary. I think she'll cry and sob and beg, and she'll break her uncle's heart.

He'll give up the skank or maybe even kill her himself to get his little niece back safe."

"All right," she said.

"Do I have to go all the way to Naomi?"

"No."

Having circled the table, he went to the sink and pulled a few paper towels from a dispenser and lightly dampened one of them and returned to his chair.

He smiled at her. When he used the damp paper towel to wipe the apple juice from her face and used the dry towels to pluck the slices from her clothes, she wouldn't give him the satisfaction of a flinch.

He cleaned up the chunks of apple that had fallen on the floor and put everything in the trash can.

At the table again, he said, "I like your home, Mary. I'd be happy to live here a few days, except for the painting in the living room, the brats running on the beach. I'd have to cut that in pieces and burn it in the fireplace, or otherwise I'd probably wake up in the night, screaming, just knowing it was there."

Fifty-Five

Some argued that the youth of today were poorly educated and insufficiently industrious, but one of them had sought to validate his generation by spending considerable time and effort chiseling an obscene word in the concrete picnic table, and he had spelled it correctly.

Tim and Linda sat on a bench, backs to the table, watching in-line skaters, dogs and their owners, couples hand in hand, a priest reading from a breviary as he walked, and a stoned fifty-something guy who wandered through the park trying to strike up whispered conversations with the palm trees.

Still brooding about how to tell her what she waited patiently to hear, Tim finally said, "Here's the thing. I'll go through it once and not with a lot of detail. You'll have some questions, and that's all right. But when we're done with it, we don't talk about it again. It's not something, years from now, we meet new people, and you say, **Tim, tell them what you did back then**. Because I won't."

"'Years from now.' I like the sound of that. All right. Once and once only. You sure know how to tease the moment. Maybe you should write books, I'll do the bricklaying."

"I'm serious, Linda."

"So am I."

He took a deep breath, blew it out, took another—and his cell phone rang.

She groaned.

This was his personal cell, not the disposable. The screen did not reveal a caller number.

"It's gotta be him," Tim said, and took the call.

"How's my girl?" the killer asked.

Watching the tree whisperer, Tim said nothing.

"Did you do her yet, Tim?"

"I'm going to hang up before you can trace my location," Tim said. "So say what you have to say."

"I don't have much to say, Tim. Are you on speakerphone there?"

"No."

"Good. You'll want to keep the skank out of this. But we're on speakerphone here, and Mary wants to talk to you."

"Mary who?"

His mother said, "Tim?"

"Oh, my God."

In the suddenly too-bright sun, in air too thick to breathe with ease, he rose from the bench.

"You be yourself, honey."

"Mom. Oh, God."

"You be yourself. You hear me?"

He couldn't speak. Linda had risen to her feet beside him. He could not look at her.

"Be yourself," his mother said, "and you'll do fine."

"If he's hurt you—"

"I'm all right. I'm not scared. You know why I'm not scared?"

"I love you," he said.

"You know why I'm not scared, honey?"

She was focusing him. "Why?"

"Because I'm sitting here thinking of you and Michelle."

Tim became very still.

"I want to be there for your wedding, honey."

"You will," he said. "You'll be there."

"She's so sweet. She's perfect for you."

"She reminds me of you," he said.

"I love the ring she made for me."

The killer said impatiently, "Tell him, Mary."

"I'm looking at the ring right now, honey, it gives me hope."

"Mary," the killer warned.

"Tim, oh please, Tim, I want to come home."

"What has he done, where has he taken you?"

"He wants to make a trade."

"Yeah, I know what he wants."

"Honey, I don't know who this woman is he wants."

"It's a mistake I made, Mom. A big mistake."

"Think of me and Michelle. I love you."

"It's going to be all right, Mom."

"You be yourself. Do what you think is right."

"I'll get you home. I swear."

The killer said, "We're off speakerphone, Tim."

"Don't touch my mother."

"I'll do anything I want to your mother. We're shacked up in a lonely place, nobody to hear her scream."

Tim bit back everything that he could think to say, for none of it was productive.

The killer said, "So you're going to be married."

"Tell me what I have to do."

"What's Michelle's last name, Tim?"

"That's none of your business."

"I could torture it out of your mother."

"Jefferson," Tim said, giving Michelle Rooney's maiden name. "Michelle Jefferson."

"What's Michelle going to think about you risking everything for the skank?"

"You leave Michelle out of this."

"That's up to you, Tim."

Across the park came Pete Santo, smiling, waving. He had Zoey on a leash.

Tim sensed that he could not pretend to cave easily to the killer's demand. He would not be believed, and his quick fold would generate suspicion. He needed to resist. He needed to offer an alternative. He needed to **think**.

"How could I trade? How could I do that?"

"You've got a weakness, Tim."

"It would be like killing one of them myself."

"You're one of the good guys, Tim. That's your weakness."

"I'm not a good guy. I just get along."

"Good guys finish last, Tim."

"Maybe not if they stay in the game. Listen, let's find another way here. I can't do this."

"You can do it."

"No. Not this."

"You've done harder things."

"Not ever. Nothing like this. Good God. I can't."

"Then your mother's dead."

"**I can't do this!** Give me a minute to think."

"Your family belongs in a carnival freak show."

"I can't. Just let me think."

"Under glass in a museum," said the killer.

As Pete drew near, Linda moved forward to intercept him and to prevent him from saying anything that might carry on the phone.

"Tim, get real. I need to kill her, you know."

"You could just walk away."

"No, Tim. I've got an image to protect."

"And I've soiled that image, haven't I?"

"Don't flatter yourself."

"How much do you hate me?"

"Oh, Tim, beyond measure."

"Then kill me instead."

Linda heard, and she turned back to Tim, eyes as bright and sharp as beveled emeralds.

"Kill me instead," he repeated.

"Exactly how does that work?"

"You pick a place to meet. I'll come unarmed."

"I've already chosen a place for the swap."

"As my mother walks away from you, toward a waiting car, I'll walk toward you. It has to be timed so just as she's driven away, I come within shooting range."

"You're setting up a shootout."

"No."

"You'll be armed, all right."

"No. I'll come in a pair of briefs. Nothing else. Nowhere to hide a weapon. I have a friend I'll want to drive the car. But he won't be anywhere near you."

"Aren't you afraid of death, Tim?"

"Hell, yes. But it's not at the top of my list."

"You're a crazy sonofabitch, Tim. You're an original."

"My mother gets to live. Linda gets a head start on you, she can run, and that's as much as I can do for her. If I'm lucky, if Linda's lucky, I've bought both their lives."

"She won't get far without you," the killer said.

"Maybe she will. She's tough. Do we have a deal?"

Out beyond the trees, a boy and his dad were flying a tubular kite. The kite was a raging dragon. The dragon undulated in the sky, its roar as silent as the silence on the phone line.

Finally the killer said, "I've read about you now, Tim."

"Don't believe everything you read."

"I do believe it. That's why I think you're serious about this."

"It's what I can do. Please. It's what I can do."

"You must have read too many boys' adventure books, Tim. Your head is screwed up. You're a crazy sonofabitch."

"Whatever. Do we have a deal? Kill me instead."

"All right, that works for me."

"Now what?" Tim asked.

"Do you know Fashion Island in Newport Beach?"

"The shopping plaza. Everyone knows it. That's too public."

"It's not for the swap. It's just a first step. You be at the big koi pond in Fashion Island in forty-five minutes."

"Okay. I can make that."

"I'll have someone watching. He better see you at the koi pond in forty-five minutes. Then you wait there. I'll call you about what comes next."

"All right."

"Better be there, Tim."

"I will."

"Be there or I'll slit your mother's throat."

The killer terminated the call, and Tim pocketed his phone.

The tree whisperer raised his arms toward the dragon in the sky, as if the bright beast had come for him. And the thing that had been coming for Tim all these years had now also fully arrived.

Fifty-Six

An engagement ring and a wedding band graced Mary's left hand, which remained cuffed to the dining chair.

"The diamonds aren't that impressive, dear."

"Walter didn't have much when I married him."

Her right hand displayed a ring with a large clear purple stone surrounded by smaller stones of the same kind.

"What gem is this?" he asked.

"Opalite," she said. "It's rare."

"Never heard of it. So Tim's fiancée made this?"

"Yes. She makes jewelry. She's very talented."

"What's Michelle's last name?"

"Tim didn't want to tell you."

"But he did. I'm just confirming."

She hesitated.

"I could take that ring," Krait said, "and the finger with it."

"Jefferson," said Mary.

"When is the wedding?"

"August."

"I thought women want to be June brides."

"Most do. That's why every place you could have a reception is booked in June. So it had to be August."

"You like Michelle very much, do you?"

"I love Michelle. Please don't bring her into this."

"I won't, dear. There's no need for Michelle. Perhaps I've made a deal with your Tim. I'm still thinking about it. Would you like to know what it is?"

"No," she said. Then: "Yes. All right."

Krait's cell phone vibrated. "Give me a moment, Mary."

Sitting at the table, he discovered that he had received a text message from his support group. ARE YOU AT CARRIER RESIDENCE? CONFIRM. WHY IS CARRIER FAMILY INVOLVED THIS MISSION? EXPLANATION REQUESTED.

Such an intrusion into his operations so astonished Krait that he read the message again from the top. This was unprecedented.

The don't-ask rule by which he abided was supposed to apply also to the support group. If he had any lingering doubts, this proved that the Paquette woman was indeed a target of the Gentlemen's Club.

Worse than their attempt to question his strategy and tactics: They were monitoring him. They knew where he was. They were looking over his shoulder. Intolerable.

Evidently, the blue sedan had been delivered with a satellite-readable transponder attached. When he had stopped in front of the Carrier house to use the directional microphone, the support group had identified the address, and then had taken note of him parking two blocks away.

Krait could think of only one explanation for this outrageous development. The Gentlemen's Club must have recently assigned some ambitious young snot to the support group, and he had taken it upon himself to exert an authority his bosses had not given him.

With a self-possession that he himself could not help but admire, Krait granted the snot a reply: MISSION NEARLY ACCOMPLISHED. WILL REPORT WITHIN HOURS.

Then, to remind them that they were dealing with an intellectual superior who did not

need to consult with a gaggle of bureaucrats, he added four lines from Wallace Stevens: THEY SAID, "YOU HAVE A BLUE GUITAR/ YOU DO NOT PLAY THINGS AS THEY ARE."/ THE MAN REPLIED, "THINGS AS THEY ARE/ ARE CHANGED UPON THE BLUE GUITAR."

After sending the message and putting the cell phone away, he realized that Mary was staring at him. "What's wrong?" she asked.

"Nothing you should worry your pretty head about."

"The deal," she reminded him. "You made a deal with Tim."

Getting up from his chair, he said, "He'll come to a meeting stripped down to prove he's unarmed. When he arrives, you walk away from me to a waiting car."

She stared, perplexed. "I don't understand."

"As you reach the car, he's walking toward me, into shooting range. And as you're being driven to safety, I kill him."

Dread contested with despair for possession of her face.

Krait said, "He buys your life with his, and he buys the skank a chance to run. Does that sound like your son?"

"Yes." A flood rose in her eyes.

"What kind of mother are you, Mary, raising a son to die for you? What twisted values did you teach? You give new meaning to the term **domineering mother.**"

Fifty-Seven

They talked on the move, Zoey lead-ing at the end of her leash, returning to the south end of the park, where both Tim and Pete had left their cars.

"Michelle gave Mom and Dad a chandelier. Copper birds flying in a circle. A circle is a ring. She said, 'I'm looking at the ring right now, honey, it gives me hope.' She's still at home."

"Maybe not for long," Pete said.

They cut across the grass to avoid the skaters and strollers on the pathways.

"I can be there in twenty minutes," Tim said. "Twenty-five."

"But if she's not there," Linda worried.

"She's there."

"Maybe. But if she's gone by the time you get there, we can't make it all the way to Fashion Island for his next call."

"Fashion Island is bullshit. Misdirection. Just to keep me busy and off balance. It's too public for **any** phase of this. He doesn't have anyone watching the koi pond."

"That math works the same for me," Pete agreed.

"What if you're both wrong?"

"He won't kill her just because I'm late to Fashion Island. She's the best leverage he's got."

"That's a cold equation," Linda said.

Tim recognized the mood he was in. Fear and anger were part of it, but they did not define it.

His fear rose to the level of controlled terror, and the anger might better be called wrath, and the former forged in him a steely resolution, while the latter sharpened a desire to deal retribution, which was in truth a need for vengeance more than justice, but also justice. Emotion of this intensity ought to have clouded his thoughts and hobbled him physically, but as the terror and the wrath became purer and more intense, his thoughts grew clearer and he became acutely aware of his body and its capabilities.

This was in his blood, this clarity in crisis and this dogged purpose in a pinch, and he could take no credit for it and no blame.

They arrived at the Mountaineer before the Honda, and Pete said, "We'll take my car."

"I'm going alone," Tim said.

Opening the tailgate of the SUV, Linda said, "Screw that."

"She's **my** mother."

"Don't give me any territorial crap, big head. I don't have a mother. I think I'll like yours. So I'm staking a claim."

As Zoey leaped into the back of the SUV, Tim said, "Get real. You can't go with me."

Confronting him, she said, "I'm not going into the house, for God's sake, I wouldn't know what to do in the house, like I think you **will** know, but I'm not gonna sit in the freakin' park, wondering what's happened to you, watching that spaced-out acidhead talk to the palm trees."

"Since both of us know what to do in that house," Pete said, "we're going in together."

"Mom and Dad's house, a guy with a machine pistol, it's gonna be tight quarters," Tim protested.

"Isn't it always tight quarters, Doorman?"

Slamming the tailgate, Linda said, "We're wasting time." She opened a door, climbed into the backseat.

Offering the key, Pete said, "You want to drive?"

"You know the way."

In the shotgun seat, Tim pulled the door shut as the Mountaineer began to roll.

He asked Linda for her pistol. She took it from her purse and passed it forward to him.

"Is that a lady gun?" Pete asked dubiously.

"It's a strong little piece," Tim assured him.

From the backseat, Linda said, "It has a really low bore axis. So there's almost no muzzle jump. It's loaded with 147-grain JHPs. It'll do the job."

Tim didn't need to ask if Pete was carrying. On duty or off, he would be armed. "I don't want it to come to guns," he said. "Not in those close quarters, my mother in the room."

"If we can get in there, he doesn't know we're in there, we can come in behind him with a clear shot," Pete said.

"That's the only way. But let's hope we can take him alive. We have to know who hired him."

Linda said, "You think it's gone too far now, we should go to the police, a SWAT team or something?"

"No," Tim and Pete said simultaneously, and then Pete said, "A for-hire killer doesn't structure jail time in his career plan."

"Especially not this guy," Tim said. "He's

way bold. He's all or nothing, he'll go out shooting."

"SWAT protocols, you start with a hostage negotiator," Pete said. "In that situation, Mary's an instant liability to a guy like this. He knows they'll never give him free passage with her. She's dead the moment he hears a bullhorn. He wants to be able to move fast."

"Speaking of fast," Tim said, "step on it some."

Fifty-Eight

Lovely, the tears that flowed freely. Lovely, too, the sobs that she refused to voice, which expressed instead as thick choking noises and brief spastic shudders.

After slipping the Glock into his shoulder rig, Krait moved the cloth satchel, the rubber-tube tourniquet, the hypodermic syringes, and the bowl of sliced apples to the kitchen island. He left nothing on the table within the reach of Mary's free right arm.

He stood beside her chair, gazing down at her as she wiped at her damp cheeks.

"Tears beautify a woman," he said.

She seemed to be angry with herself for weeping. Her damp hand tightened into a fist, which she pressed to her temple, as if she could quell her distress by an act of will.

"I like the taste of tears in a woman's kiss."

Her mouth was loose with anguish.

"I'd like to kiss you, Mary."

She turned her face away from him.

"You might be surprised to find you enjoy it."

With a sudden fury, she looked up at him. "You might enjoy having your lip bitten off."

The meanness of her rejection would have caused a lesser man than Krait to strike her. He merely stared at her and, after a while, found his smile.

"I've got a little something to do, Mary. But I'll be nearby in another room. If you shout for help, no one will hear you but me, and I'll have to shove a rag in your mouth and seal your lips with duct tape. You don't want that, do you?"

The murderous intent in her eyes had seared away all tears.

"You are a piece of work, dear."

He thought she might spit at him, but she did not.

"Raise a son to die for you." He shook his head. "I wonder what kind of man your husband must be."

She looked as though she had a withering response to make, and he waited for it, but she chose silence.

"I'll be back soon, to put you to beddy-bye

in the Expedition. You just sit here, Mary, and remember what a good thing it is that you've decided not to get yourself and Zachary and his whole family killed."

He left the kitchen and stood in the hallway, listening.

Mary made no sound. Krait expected subtle rattling noises as she tested and examined the handcuffs, but she remained quiet.

In the living room, Krait took down the oil painting of happy children running on a sunny beach. He put it on the floor and knelt beside it.

From a pants pocket, he withdrew a switchblade and flicked open the knife. He cut the canvas from the frame, then sliced the painting into strips.

He considered taking from the frames on the bookshelves all the photos that included Tim, and cutting those to pieces, as well. But because he would soon be killing the real Tim, his remaining minutes in the Carrier house would be more enjoyably spent elsewhere.

Fifty-Nine

Pete Santo did not slow down as he drove by the Carrier house.

Nothing about the place appeared different except that the draperies were drawn shut at the first-floor windows. Tim's mother always kept them open.

At the end of the block, Tim said, "Park here."

Pete pulled to the curb, screened from the house by trees. He put down the backseat windows and switched off the engine.

During the drive, Zoey had clambered forward from the cargo space to be with Linda. The dog lay now with her head in her new mistress's lap.

Linda said, "When do I know something might've gone wrong?"

"If you hear a lot of gunfire," Tim said.

"But how long?"

He turned in his seat to face her. "If we don't have him in ten minutes, it's gone bad."

"Wait fifteen," Pete said, "then drive away from here."

"Leave you?" she asked. "I can't do that."

"You do it," Tim insisted. "Wait fifteen, then do it."

"But . . . drive where?"

He realized that she literally had nowhere to go.

Reaching between the front seats, holding the disposable phone, he said, "Take this. Get out of the neighborhood. Park somewhere. If one of us doesn't call you in an hour, two hours, we're both dead."

She held fiercely to his hand for a moment before taking the phone.

Pete got out and closed the driver's door.

"You have all that cash," Tim said. "You can decide whether to go back to your place, get those gold coins. Don't think I would, but that's up to you. What you've got is what you start a new life with, a new name."

"I'm so damn sorry, Tim."

"Nothing to be sorry about. If I'd known what was coming, I'd have done it all the same anyway."

He got out of the Mountaineer, closed the door, and checked to be sure the pistol tucked under his belt was adequately concealed by his Hawaiian shirt.

Her face was at the open window. In all his life, he had never seen a better face.

He and Pete were not going in by the front door. Houses on these streets backed up to one another, without benefit of an alleyway. They would have to go around to the parallel street and approach his folks' place through a neighbor's backyard.

Walking away from the SUV, toward the nearby corner, Tim wanted to glance back, to take one last look at her, wanted it almost more than he could bear, but this was business now, this was the thing.

Following Pete around the corner, to the cross street, he nearly collided with an old man whose pants were hitched so high above his waist that if he kept a watch in his watch pocket, the ticking would tickle his right breast.

"Tim! Morning glory and evening grace, if it isn't our Tim!"

"Hi, Mickey. What a sight you are."

Mickey McCready, closing on eighty with thickets of bristling white ear hairs to prove it, lived across the street from Tim's folks. He was wearing bright-yellow pants and a dazzling red shirt.

"These are my walking clothes. Damn if I'm gonna be hit in a crosswalk. How you been, Tim? How's work? Got a special girl yet?"

"I do, Mickey. A really special one."

"Bless her, the lucky girl, what's her name?"

"Mickey, I gotta go. Have an appointment. You gonna be home?"

"Where do I ever go?"

"I'll come visit. A little later, okay?"

"I want to hear about this girl."

"I'll come visit," Tim promised.

Mickey clutched his arm. "Hey, I been transferring my videos to DVD. Made a disc about you, our Tim, from when you were a toddler."

"That's great, Mickey. I gotta go. I'll come visit." He pulled away and hurried to catch up with Pete.

"Where does he get shirts that're only eight inches long?" Pete asked.

"He's a nice old guy. Everybody's favorite unrelated uncle."

At the next corner, they turned right. They were on the street that ran parallel to his parents' street.

The sixth house featured a sign at the front

walkway that said THE SAPERSTEINS' and showed two teddy bears, male and female, with names on their coveralls, NORMAN and JUDY.

"They'll both be at work," Tim said. "Kids are grown. Nobody home."

He led Pete through a side gate into the Sapersteins' backyard.

Filigrees of sunlight rippled across the water in a swimming pool, and a cat sunning on the brick patio was surprised into flight, vanishing into the shrubbery.

The property ended at a six-foot-high privacy wall all but concealed by purple trumpet vines.

Pete said, "Doorman, did I ever tell you, you're the ugliest man I've ever met?"

"I ever tell you, you're the dumbest?"

"We ready?"

"We wait till we're ready, we'll be as old as Mickey."

The trumpet vines were mature and thick, so firmly secured to the stucco-coated concrete blocks that they made a good ladder. Tim climbed about a foot and peered over the top of the wall into his parents' backyard.

Blinds covered the kitchen windows and the kitchen door. The draperies were drawn shut at the family-room doors.

At all the second-floor windows, the draperies were open. He didn't see anyone up there, keeping watch.

Controlled terror, channeled wrath, that roaring in the blood that he could hear but that didn't mask other sounds, all told him that the moment was his to seize.

He climbed the wall, knocking off a cascade of purple blooms behind him, dropped onto the grass beyond, and Pete followed fast to his right.

Pulling the pistol from his waistband, Tim hurried to the house, to the back wall next to the kitchen door.

Carrying his service pistol, Pete flanked the door, and they looked at each other, listening. The house lay quiet, but that didn't mean anything. Duck hunters in a blind were quiet. Morgues were quiet.

From a pants pocket, Tim fished a small ring on which he kept his apartment key and the key to the toolbox on his work truck. He also had a key to his folks' place because he always looked after things when they were away.

Brass sliding in the keyway made a crisp sound. His dad kept the locks well lubricated, and the Schlage deadbolt retracted with little noise.

This was when you could take a bullet or a bunch of them, going through a door, doors were never easy, but he had an okay instinct for them, could usually tell the safe ones from the doubtful, usually knew the doors behind which one kind of hell or another waited.

He was having trouble reading this one, maybe because this was not an ordinary search-and-clear, his mother was in there, his mother and the guy with the hungry eyes, so he had even less room for error than usual.

Heart rapping a little now, still breathing low and slow, hands dry, nice and dry, he was at that cusp where you did or you didn't, further delay was bad tactics, so he pushed the door open.

He went in low and fast, pistol in a two-hand grip, wishing the gun were bigger, better sized for his hands, and nobody waited for him in the kitchen.

Sweeping with the muzzle left to right, kitchen to family room, he glimpsed syringes on the island and what looked like a hypodermic-dart pistol, and then he saw his mother over the gun sight, sitting at the table, just sitting there at the table, in the coppery light of the chandelier with the circling birds, and she raised her head, only now aware that someone had entered, and what a look she gave him.

Sixty

Considering that he most likely had come out of a mirror into this world, Krait wondered if he might one day return to his native realm by way of another such portal.

In the master bedroom, he stood before a full-length mirror that was mounted on the inside of the open closet door. He put his right hand upon his reflection, half expecting the silvered surface to quiver and then to relent, offering no more resistance than the surface tension of pooled water.

The glass was cool but firm beneath his hand.

He raised his left hand, as well, and pressed it to the reaching hand of the other Krait who gazed out at him.

Perhaps in the reversed mirror world, time

ran backward. Instead of aging, he might grow younger, until he became eighteen, the age at which his memories began. Thereafter, descending into his youth, he might learn where he had come from and of what he had been born.

Eye to eye, he peered down into the darkness of himself, and he liked what he saw.

He thought that he was exerting only a light pressure, but the mirror cracked before him, split top to bottom, though it remained secure within its frame.

The halves of his reflection were now slightly offset from each other, one eye a fraction higher than the other, the nose deformed. One side of the mouth hung askew, as though he had suffered a stroke.

This other Krait, this fractured Krait, disturbed him. This broken, imperfect Krait. This unfamiliar Krait whose smile was not a smile anymore.

He took his hands off the mirror and quickly closed the other Krait in the closet.

Unnerved and not sure why, he calmed himself by opening dresser drawers and examining the contents, learning what he could about the lives of his hosts, seeking secrets that would illuminate.

Sixty-One

The door between the kitchen and the downstairs hall stood open, and Pete covered it.

Putting a finger to his lips to signal silence, Tim knelt by his mother and whispered, "Where is he?"

She shook her head. She didn't know.

When she put her right hand to his face, he kissed it.

A leg of the chair was shackled to a leg of the table. On the chair, a stretcher bar prevented him from slipping off the handcuff. On the table, a large ball-and-claw foot would not allow him to lift the leg out of the other half of the cuffs.

Her left arm was cuffed to the arm of the chair.

These were double-lock cuffs. He might be

able to bend a paper clip or something into a pick with which to spring the locks, but he couldn't do it quickly.

Between the arm and the seat of the pine chair were supporting spindles. The spindle nearest the end of the arm was thicker than the others, but it alone prevented the cuff from being slipped free of the chair.

Although he did not want to leave the hallway unguarded, Tim hissed for Pete's attention, and gestured for assistance.

Both of them had to put down their guns.

Tim wanted to avoid dragging the chair, the loud stutter of its legs barking against the wood floor.

Pete put one hand on the right arm of the chair, one on the rounded back rail, and bore down with all his weight.

Holding the left arm of the chair with one hand, Tim gripped the forward support spindle. He pushed on the arm and pulled hard on the support, then harder, with all the strength that he could muster.

The spindle was in fact a dowel rod, glued into bores in the seat and in the underside of the arm. In theory, the joints were points of weakness, and the vertical dowel might crack loose from the holes in which it had been fitted.

Tim's right arm seemed to swell with the effort, and he felt the cords rising and pulling taut in his neck, his pulse throbbing in his temples.

His folks had bought this pine suite at least thirty years ago, in what might as well have been another world from this one, when furniture was made in places like North Carolina and made to last a lifetime.

The threat of the unguarded hallway at his back insisted on his attention, but he had to block it from his mind and focus on the chair, the chair, the too-well-made damn chair.

Sweat popped at his hairline, and the support spindle cracked away from the chair arm with an unavoidable splintering sound that might have carried to the next room but not much farther.

Snatching his pistol off the table, Pete returned to the hallway door.

Tim retrieved the 9-mm, put an arm around his mother, glanced at Pete for an all-clear, and Pete nodded, and Tim guided her across the kitchen to the back door.

Outside, he hurried with her through the bright sun to the walkway that led along the north side of the house.

He whispered, "To the street, turn right—"

"But you—"

"—Pete's SUV, near the corner—"

"—you're not—"

"—a woman, a dog, wait with them."

"But the police—"

"Just us."

"Tim—"

"Go," he insisted.

Another mother might have argued or clutched, but she was **his** mother. She shot him a fierce look of love and hurried toward the front of the house.

Tim returned to the kitchen, where Pete watched the hallway. He shook his head. The splintering spindle had not betrayed them.

Tim left the back door standing open behind him. If things went wrong more ways than you could ever figure, you wanted to have an easy exit.

Forward from the kitchen, on the left side of the hall, were the dining room, a closet, and then the stairs. On the right were a half bath, a small study, and the living room.

Pete had been here many times since they had grown up fast together in their eighteenth year, since they had come home in their twenty-third. He knew the layout almost as well as Tim knew it.

They stood listening, and the house was

full of silence and threat and blind fate, and then together they did what they had done often before, although not recently, went forward quietly into the silence, door by door and room by room, with blood racing and hackles up and their minds as clear as distilled spirits.

Sixty-Two

Having found nothing enlightening in the dresser drawers, Krait moved toward a promising highboy. Passing a window, he saw Mary on the front lawn.

She ran to the sidewalk, turned right, and fled out of sight, shielded by the street trees. From her left wrist dangled the set of handcuffs.

However she might have gotten free of the chair, she had not engineered her own escape. The fact that no one ran at her side confirmed for Krait the identity of her rescuer. Tim had come home.

Why and how could wait for later. This was not a time for questions but for a final answer to the problem of the mason.

Drawing the Glock from his shoulder rig, Krait quickly crossed the bedroom, hesitated at the open door, and sidled into the upstairs hall.

If Tim had come to the second floor, he

would already have found Krait, perhaps would have shot him as he turned away from the window after glimpsing Mary.

Krait could see down the upper flight of stairs to the landing. The lower flight turned out of sight.

Aiming at the landing, he waited for a head to appear, a face to look up and receive a splash of bullets.

Thunders of silence rose from below, the kind of silence that quakes through you and breaks your sweat and promises lightning.

Krait decided that Tim would not come up the stairs without a strategy and proven tactics. He would know the danger of stairwells.

Standing here at the head of the stairs, from what seemed to be an unassailably superior position, Krait sensed that he was also vulnerable. He eased back until he could neither see down the stairs nor be seen from the landing.

He looked along the hall toward the back of the house. Besides the master-bedroom door, five doors waited. One would be a bathroom. Perhaps one was a closet. At most, there were three other bedrooms.

Although Krait had always been a decisive man, he stood for a moment in uncharacteristic indecision.

The silence rose like a drowning flood, though this was **only** silence, not stillness, for through it moved a predator unique in Krait's experience.

—

Tim and Pete, on opposite sides of the downstairs hall, staying out of each other's forward line of fire, toed open doors that were ajar, cleared the spaces beyond, scanned the dining room from the archway, the living room, and came to the stairs.

If the killer believed he had the house to himself, it seemed that he would not be this quiet. Even if he were playing both sides of a game of chess, a pawn would once in a while clatter as it was set off the board; in a game of solitaire, some cards were laid down with a snap.

They had several sets of tactics for taking a stairwell, though they might have been better armed for this job. No matter how often they had ascended guarded stairs in the past, Tim was not keen to make an assault on these. Here were stairs that felt like a **series** of dangerous doors.

With gestures, he indicated to Pete a simple plan of action, and a nod confirmed that the message had been understood. Leaving Pete at the stairs, Tim moved toward the back of the house, from which they had just come.

—

In the master bedroom, Krait unlocked the double-hung window through which he had seen Mary on the run. He raised the lower sash, which squeaked faintly on waxed tracks.

Over the sill, onto the front-porch roof, he expected a hail of bullets in the back. He stepped immediately sideways, out of the window.

Two cars passed in the street, but the drivers didn't notice a man with a gun on the Carriers' porch roof.

Krait went to the edge, looked down, and jumped to clear a row of shrubs, and landed in the grass.

—

In the living room, Pete snared a decorative pillow from the sofa and a larger seat cushion from an armchair. He returned with them to the foot of the stairs.

Glancing back down the hall, he saw that Tim had already gone out the open back door.

The staircase featured an inlaid carpet runner. He wondered how much the treads creaked.

Still no sound came from the second floor.

Maybe the guy felt so sure of himself that he was taking a nap. Maybe he had died of the most conveniently timed heart attack in history.

With the pistol in his right hand, the seat cushion under his left arm, and the throw pillow in his left hand, Pete tried the first step. It didn't squeak, and neither did the second.

—

The south end of the back porch was enclosed with a trellis that Tim had long ago built with horizontal two-by-fours and vertical two-by-twos. His mother would not have tolerated quaint lattice.

Joseph's Coat climbing roses were far from their peak growth this early in the season, but they offered enough thorns to make him glad that his hands were well callused.

The horizontals easily took his weight, and the vertical two-by-twos held even though they protested more than he would have liked.

On the roof, he drew the pistol from under his belt and went to the nearest window. Beyond lay his former bedroom, which he still used when he stayed overnight on holidays or when house-sitting.

The room appeared to be deserted.

As a kid, he had spent countless evenings

on this porch roof, lying on his back to study the stars. A fiend for fresh air, he had never locked his bedroom window, and maybe fifteen years ago, the latch had corroded in the open position.

On his most recent overnight visit, his father had still not replaced the latch, so of course he expected now, in the crunch, to find that it had been repaired. But Dad respected tradition, and the unlocked sash slid up with ease.

Like a cat burglar, he entered his bedroom. A couple of creaks lived in the floor, but he knew where they lurked, and he avoided them as he circled the room to the hall door, which was ajar.

He listened for movement, and when he heard none, he pulled the door inward and cautiously looked out. He expected to see the killer toward the front of the house, near the stairs, but the hallway was deserted, too.

—

Pete stopped halfway up the first flight of stairs and waited. When he felt sure that he'd given Tim enough time to reach the second floor, he tossed the decorative pillow onto the landing.

A nervous gunman might fire at any movement, but no one blew the crap out of the pillow.

He counted to five and threw the much larger cushion, because a nervous gunman, not on edge enough to have fired at the small pillow, might expect a subsequent and larger target to be the charge behind the fake-out. Silence. Maybe this guy wasn't nervous.

—

Bedroom to bedroom to closet to bedroom to bath, Tim traveled the upstairs hall, clearing rooms, finding no one.

As he approached the master bedroom, he heard the heavy chair cushion **flump** on the landing. He snatched a decorative pillow from a hallway chair and threw it into the nearby stairwell.

Having worked with Tim enough to be able to interpret the return pillow as an all-clear, Pete came up fast, but quiet and alert, with his pistol at arm's length, backlit by golden afternoon sunlight streaming through the high round window in the stairwell.

Tim indicated the master bedroom, and they flanked the half-open door, Tim on the side away from the hinges. This was it now, the guy had to be here, so they were in the dead zone.

Push the door wide, through fast, sweep the room with the gun. Move right, Pete to the left, no one on the far side of the bed.

The window open, the draperies limp in the motionless air, not good, the window open, not good, if the guy had been at the window at the wrong moment, when she had crossed the front lawn.

Or it was a ruse. If they went to the window, their backs would be to the master-bathroom door, now ajar, and to the closet door, now closed.

He wanted the window, knew it was the window, but you go by the book for a reason, and the reason is it keeps you alive more often than it gets you killed.

If the guy was gone from the house, hunting her, every second counted, but there were two doors, so the doors first.

Pete took the closet, standing aside, reaching for the knob, throwing it wide, but no fusillade responded. In the closet ceiling, a trap to the attic. Closed as it should be. Anyway, he wouldn't have gone to the attic.

Tim slammed back the bathroom door, went in fast, small space, just enough light from the curtained window to see there was no one.

In the bedroom, heart hammering now, a metallic taste in the mouth, maybe the taste of disaster, he said to Pete, "He went after Mom, he'll find her with Linda."

Window, porch roof, lawn was faster than down the stairs and out, so he headed toward the raised sash, Pete with him, but from the corner of his eye, he caught movement, turned.

Beyond the open door, a large distended oval of golden light bright on the hallway wall, thrown by the high round window in the stairwell, and into it a shadow creeping, twisted shadow of a demon in a dream.

Not after Mom and Linda, after all, but out the front window, around the house, in the kitchen door, and up the stairs, behind them now and closing.

Open door, machine pistol, he'd come in spraying. Nothing to shelter behind, they'd be cut down dead, whether they nailed him or not.

Tim dropped the pistol, grabbed the highboy, and he didn't know where the strength came from. He was big but so was the highboy, full of folded sweaters and spare blankets and whatever the hell else it was full of, yet he lifted it off the floor, lifted it away from the wall, swung it toward the door, and high-velocity slugs chopped into it even as he set it down, rapped it, drilled it, and a round came all the way through the drawer fronts, through the stuff inside, punching out the board back, two inches from his face, a splinter biting his cheek.

Pete flat on the floor, maybe hit, no, firing back from under the highboy, which stood on six-inch legs. Hell of an angle, all skill useless, just squeezing off rounds, but luck happens just like shit happens, and the guy in the hall screamed.

The pistol with the sound suppressor had made little noise, but the incoming rounds had chopped wood, pocked walls, smashed lamps. It all stopped, and there was just the scream, which diminished into a high thin keening.

Maybe the scream was a trick, maybe the guy was jamming a new magazine into the pistol, but when you can't go by the book because the situation isn't covered in it, then you go by the gut. Tim snared his gun from the floor. He broke from the cover of the highboy and saw no one in the open doorway and went for the hall.

The air ripe with gun stink. A litter of shell casings. Blood on the carpet.

Hit in the left leg, the shark from the tavern had backed off toward the stairs, still standing but leaning against the newel post. The clack of a fresh magazine locking in place. The black-hole eyes came up, found Tim, and in spite of the thin keening, here was the smile.

Tim squeezed off two rounds, and the shark took one in the left shoulder, but his right arm was still on the clock, and the machine pistol rose, the muzzle wavering but as deep as the dilated pupils of the hungry eyes. Wanting the guy alive, Tim went at him fast, because you have to walk straight into what you don't dare run away from. The muzzle jumped, a burst of fire sliced past his head, and hot pain bloomed.

The second burst went wide because the shark needed two hands to hold the target, and Tim reached him and took the machine pistol away from him, the barrel hot in his callused hand, and the killer fell backward down the stairs, collapsed on his back on the landing, knocking the pillows aside, not dead but not ready to run a marathon.

Tim touched the right side of his head, where pain throbbed, and it was wet with blood. Something wrong with his ear. He could hear, but blood trickled down the ear canal.

Wanting the name of the guy with the parachuting dog named Larry, the guy who had paid for Linda's murder, Tim went down the stairs. He squatted beside the fallen man, reaching out with the intention of lifting the killer's head off the floor by a twisted handful of hair.

A switchblade flashed open, slashed, Tim felt a faint pressure across the palm of his reaching hand, the shark was rising, levering up on his good leg, he wasn't a quitter, so Tim shot him twice point-blank in the throat, and that was the end of it.

—

Krait fell back into an infinite maze of mirrors, the light yellow and dim. Strange figures moved in countless silvered panes, aware of him, approaching and circling, from one glass to the next. He strained his eyes to get a better look at them, but the harder that he sought to see them, the faster the light faded, until at last he lay in a palpable dark, in a wilderness of mirrors.

—

The switchblade had merely grazed his left palm, scoring the skin but leaving the meat of the hand intact.

His right ear had fared worse.

"A piece of it's missing," Pete said.

"Big piece?"

"Not so big. Your head won't hang out of balance, but you need to see a doctor."

"Not yet." Tim sat on the hallway floor, his back against the wall. "You can't lose a life-load of blood from a torn ear."

He fumbled his phone from his pocket and keyed in the number of the disposable cell that he had left with Linda. He put it to his damaged ear, flinched, and pressed it to his left.

When she answered, Tim said, "He's dead, we're not."

Relieved, she let out her breath in an explosive expletive. "I never even kissed you."

"We can do that, if you want."

"Tim, they want us out of the car. Your mom and me, we put up the windows and locked the doors, but they're trying to get us out."

Confused, he said, "Who, what?"

"They came in so fast, sealed off the street, like just after we heard the gunfire. Look out a window."

"Hold on." He got up and said to Pete, "We have some kind of company."

They went to the open window in the master bedroom. The street was full of black SUVs with bold white letters on the roofs and front doors: FBI.

Armed men had taken up position behind the vehicles and at other points of cover.

"Stall them two minutes," Tim told Linda, "then tell them it's over, and we'll walk out to them."

"What the hell?" Pete wondered.

"I don't know," Tim said, terminating the call.

"Feels right to you?"

"Feels something."

He stepped away from the window and keyed in the number for directory assistance. When the operator came on, he asked for a listing for Michael McCready.

They offered to connect the call automatically for an extra charge, and it was not a day for pinching pennies.

Mickey answered, and Tim said, "Hey, Mickey, I'm going to have to postpone that visit for a while."

"Angels in Hell, Tim, what's happening over there?"

"You got your videocam on this?"

"It's better than any of your kiddie birthday parties, Tim boy."

"Listen, Mickey, don't let them see you with the camera. Shoot from inside the house. Use the zoom, try to get as many of their faces as close up and clear as you can."

Mickey was silent for a moment. Then: "Are they a bunch of bastards, Tim?"

"They might be."

Sixty-Three

He said he was Steve Wentworth, which might in fact be his name or only one of his names.

His photo ID, complete with convincing holographic details, said FEDERAL BUREAU OF INVESTIGATION.

Tall, athletic, with close-cropped hair and the ascetic features of a handsome monk, he looked plausible. Perhaps too plausible.

His generic Southern accent had been polished by an Ivy League education.

Wentworth wanted to talk to Tim alone in the small study off the downstairs hall. Tim insisted that Linda be present.

Resisting, Wentworth said, "This is a courtesy I can't extend to anyone but you."

"She is me," Tim said, and would not compromise.

They brought her from the dining room, where they were holding her, ostensibly for questioning.

The house swarmed with agents. If they were agents.

Tim thought of them as orcs, as in **The Fellowship of the Ring.**

Entering the study, she said to Wentworth, “He needs treatment for his ear.”

“We have medics present,” Wentworth said. “He won’t let them touch him.”

“It’s hardly bleeding anymore,” Tim assured her.

“Because it’s all a clotted mess. My God, Tim.”

“It doesn’t hurt,” he said, though it did. “I had two aspirin.”

His mom and Pete were being held in the family room.

Supposedly somebody intended to take statements from them.

His mom probably thought they were safe now. Maybe they were.

The killer’s corpse had been bagged and wheeled from the house on a gurney. No one had taken photographs of it before it had been moved.

If CSI types were present, they must have

forgotten to bring their gear. Evidence collection did not appear to be under way.

As Wentworth closed the study door, Tim and Linda sat together on the sofa.

The agent settled in an armchair and crossed his legs. He had the relaxed air of a master of the universe.

"It's an honor to meet you, Mr. Carrier."

Tim felt Linda's analytic Egyptian-green eyes regarding him, and he said to Wentworth, "I don't want any of that."

"I understand. But it's true. If you weren't you, I wouldn't be here, and this wouldn't be over for you or for Ms. Paquette."

"That surprises me," Tim said.

"Why? Because you think we're not on the same side of things?"

"Are we?"

Wentworth smiled. "Whether we are or not, even in this world, the way it's changing, some things must remain above assault. In the interest of principled reconstruction, some things must be respected, including men like you."

"Principled reconstruction?"

Wentworth shrugged. "We need our jargon."

"I'm at sea here," Linda said.

"He's going to tell us some truth," Tim said.

"Some?"

"As little as he has to."

"I'd prefer not to tell you any," Wentworth said. "But **you**—you'll never stop until you know."

"You're not FBI, are you?" Linda asked.

"We are what we need to be, Ms. Paquette."

His suit had the cut and finish of expensive hand-tailoring, and his wristwatch was worth a year of an agent's salary.

"Our country, Tim, must make certain concessions."

"Concessions?"

"We cannot be what we once were. In the interest of prosperity, there must be less of it. Too much freedom assures less peace."

"Try selling that at the ballot box."

"We do sell it, Tim. By inciting false fears in the people. Remember Y2K? All computers would crash at the stroke of midnight! The collapse of high-tech civilization! Nuclear missiles would launch uncontrollably! Thousands of hours of TV news and uncounted miles of newsprint sold the Y2K terror."

"It didn't happen."

"That's the point. For a long time now, has not the news been nothing but doom? Do you think that just happens? Electric power lines cause cancer! But of course they don't. Most everything you eat will kill you, and this pesticide, and that chemical! But of course people lead longer and healthier lives decade by decade. Fear is a hammer, and when the people are beaten finally to the conviction that their existence hangs by a frayed thread, they will be led where they need to go."

"Which is where?"

"To a responsible future in a properly managed world."

Wentworth was a man completely without gesture. His hands rested unmoving on the arms of the chair. His manicured nails gleamed as if coated with clear polish.

Tim mulled the phrase: "Responsible future."

"The people elect mostly fools and frauds. When the politicians make policy that leads this country toward the needed reconstruction of its systems, they can be supported, but when they make bad policy, they must be sabotaged at every turn, from within."

Tim stared at the thin crust of blood that

the switchblade had drawn across the palm of his left hand.

"Just wait," Wentworth said, "till—oh, say—the threat of the asteroid impact builds in the years ahead. You would see unthinkable sacrifices quickly embraced by the people as we united the planet to establish a massive asteroid-deflection system in deep space."

"Is there an approaching asteroid?" Linda asked.

"There could be," Wentworth said.

Still looking at the dried blood in his hand, Tim said, "Why was Linda targeted?"

"Two and a half years ago, two men met for an hour over coffee on the patio of Cream and Sugar."

"What men?"

"One was secretly in the employ of a United States senator. He was a liaison to foreign parties with whom the senator would not want to be known to have contact."

"Foreign parties."

"I'm already being too generous with you, Mr. Carrier. The other man was a deep-cover agent for one of those foreign interests."

"Just having coffee at the Cream and Sugar."

"Their mutual suspicions required a safe public meeting place."

"And I was there that day?" she asked.

"Yes."

"But I didn't notice them that I remember," she protested. "And I certainly didn't overhear anything they said."

Tim first pegged Wentworth as about forty, but longer inspection suggested he was in his mid-fifties, as much as fifteen years having been Botoxed from his now too-smooth forehead and crinkle-free eyes.

"Charlie Wen-ching," said Wentworth, "loved his wall of fame."

Linda frowned. "You mean those photos of his regular customers?"

"He was always snapping away with his digital camera, updating the wall. That day, he snapped you and other regulars on the patio."

"He photographed me more than once," Linda said, "but I think I may know the day you mean."

"The senator's man and the foreign agent were not regulars and were not approached by Charlie for a photograph. The quick photos he took of others hardly drew their attention."

"But they were in the background of those pictures," Tim said.

"So what?" Linda said. "No one knew who they were."

"But over the next year, four things happened," Wentworth said.

"First," Tim guessed, "it came to be known in political and media circles that the secret liaison was the senator's associate."

"Yes. And the foreign agent eventually was publicly identified as a key strategist of a major terrorist organization."

"What was the third thing?" Linda asked.

Wentworth recrossed his legs. He wore designer socks with a blue-and-red geometric motif.

"Charlie's sons, Michael and Joseph, built a website. Very well done. A first step toward developing a chain of Cream and Sugars."

"They got some business-magazine attention," Linda remembered.

"And the website started getting hits. The regular-customer gallery featured two hundred of Charlie's favorite photos—some with the liaison and the agent in the background, totally identifiable."

"The senator's man, meeting secretly with the equivalent of Osama bin Laden—that could wreck a political career," Tim said.

"Even a political party," said Wentworth.

"But with all your resources," Linda said, "you could have hacked their website, somehow purged the photos."

"We've done our best. If it's on the Web, it's out there somewhere forever. Besides, Charlie had discs of the photos in a safe at the Cream and Sugar."

"Burglarize the place. Steal them."

"He often gave copies to the customers he photographed."

"So burglarize them, too. Why kill all these people?"

"If an ambitious prosecutor or a rebel journalist came to one of them, who knows what they might remember—or **pretend** to remember. 'Oh, yes, I heard them talking about an embassy bombing, and months later it happened.' People love the spotlight, their moment of fame."

"So the decision was made," Tim said, "to liquidate everyone who could have **pretended** to overhear them on the patio that day."

Wentworth drummed his elegant fingers on the arms of his chair, which was the first movement of his hands since he had sat down.

"Much is at stake, Mr. Carrier. The fourth thing that happened is that the senator's star ascended. We may be looking at our next president. Which would be a fine thing. The senator has been with us for twenty years, since our earliest days."

"You mean with this shadow government of yours."

"Yes. We thrive in bureaucracies, in law-enforcement agencies, in the intelligence community, in Congress—but now the opportunity exists to extend our reach into the Oval Office."

Wentworth consulted his wristwatch and rose to his feet.

"The man I killed," Tim said.

"A tool. A good one for quite a while. But his wiring seemed to be coming apart."

"What was his real name?"

"He was no one special. There are multitudes like him."

"Multitudes," Linda murmured.

Lacing his fingers, cracking his knuckles, Wentworth said, "When we discovered he was targeting you and your family, Mr. Carrier, we had to intervene. As I said—some things must be respected for the sake of principled reconstruction."

"But that's just jargon."

"Yes, all right, but behind the jargon is a philosophy in which we believe and by which we try to live. We are principled men and women."

As Tim and Linda got up from the sofa,

Wentworth adjusted the knot in his tie, shot his cuffs.

He smiled. "After all, if men like you had not so valiantly defended your country, we would have nothing to reconstruct."

Tim had been both respected and put in his place.

Before opening the door to the hall, standing with one hand on the knob, Wentworth said, "If you try to go public with what I've said here, you'll look like a paranoid fool. We'll make sure of that, with all our opinionmakers in the media. And then one day, you will snap, kill Ms. Paquette, your entire family, then commit suicide."

Linda was quick to Tim's defense. "No one would believe he could do that."

Wentworth arched his eyebrows. "A war hero, having seen such horrible things, suffering posttraumatic stress disorder, finally cracks, perpetrating a bloodbath? Ms. Paquette, considering all the impossible things that the public has been persuaded to believe these days, **that** one will go down as smooth as a spoonful of ice cream."

He left the room.

Linda said, "Tim? War hero?"

"Not now," he said, and led her into the hallway.

Wentworth departed the house by the front door, leaving it open behind him. Tim closed it.

All of the orcs seemed to have gone.

Tim's mother and Pete were in the kitchen.

She had a haunted look, and Pete said, "What the hell was that?"

"Take Mom and Linda to your place."

"I'm staying," she said. "And you have to get your ear treated."

"Trust me. Go with Pete. I have a couple things to do. I'll call Dad, have him come home, take me to an emergency room. We'll all meet at Pete's later."

"And then what?" she wondered.

"And then we'll have our lives."

The phone and doorbell began to ring simultaneously.

"Neighbors," Tim said. "We're not talking to any of them until we've talked among ourselves and decided on a story."

When Pete had left with Linda and Mary, Tim went into the garage and got a carpet knife from his father's tool cabinet.

He cut out the bloodstained sections of carpet on the stairs and in the upstairs hall. He bagged them and put them out with the trash.

The doorbell and phone rang periodically, but not as frequently as before.

Surprisingly, neither the small decorative pillow nor the chair cushion was bloodstained. He returned them to the living room.

He collected the ragged strips of the ruined painting and upstairs retrieved all the ejected shell casings and threw those things in the trash, as well.

With some effort, he walked the highboy against the wall where it belonged. He gathered up the broken lamps. He used the vacuum to sweep the wood chips and other debris from the master-bedroom carpet.

In a day or two, he would repair the bullet holes in the drywall and give the room two fresh coats of paint.

He closed and locked the open window, then closed but did not lock the window in his bedroom at the back of the house.

The orcs had taken with them all of the killer's paraphernalia that had been on the kitchen island. They had taken the handcuff from the table leg.

The sliced apples in the metal bowl had turned brown. He put them down the garbage disposal with the peels that were in the sink.

He washed the bowl and the peeler and the knife, and he put them in the drawers where they belonged.

Later, he would repair the broken chair.

This was his home, where he had grown up, a sacred place to him, and he would put it right.

After calling his dad, he went across the street for a brief visit with Mickey McCready.

Sixty-Four

Pete's cable service had been restored, and no one had taken his computer. He switched it on, encouraged Linda to sit at the keyboard, gave her the website address, and left the room.

On the website, this was the citation she found when she typed in Tim's name:

Sergeant Timothy Eugene Carrier, for conspicuous gallantry and intrepidity in action at the risk of his life above and beyond the call of duty. A platoon of Sergeant Carrier's company, while on operations, discovered a warehouse in which mass executions of civilians sympathetic to the democratic movement were under way. As the platoon fought to seize possession of the building and rescue the prisoners therein, which included scores of women and children, they were attacked from the rear and

surrounded by a large enemy force. Realizing that the unit had suffered casualties depriving it of effective leadership, and aware that the platoon was even then under attack, Sergeant Carrier took eight men and proceeded by helicopter to reinforce the beleaguered platoon. Sergeant Carrier disembarked with his men from the helicopter, which was disabled on landing by enemy action, and braving withering fire, led them and the helicopter crew to the trapped platoon, where indeed every ranking officer had perished. For the next five hours, he moved fearlessly from position to position, directing and encouraging the troops. Although painfully wounded in the leg and back by fragments of an enemy grenade, Sergeant Carrier directed the valiant defense through repeated enemy assaults, apprising headquarters of the platoon's plight. When the warehouse was breached by enemy forces, he personally held them off at the critical doorway for a grueling forty minutes, collapsing of his numerous wounds only when the enemy retreated upon the arrival of reinforcements for which he had called. Sergeant Carrier's actions saved his fellow Marines from capture and minimized the loss of life. A full inspection of the warehouse complex revealed 146 dismem-

bered and beheaded civilians, 23 of them women, and 64 of them children. Sergeant Carrier's valiant devotion to duty and indomitable fighting spirit had helped to save another 366 civilians being detained there, 112 of them women, and 220 of them children, some of them infants. His leadership and great personal valor in the face of overwhelming odds reflect great credit upon himself and are in keeping with the highest traditions of the Marine Corps and the U.S. Naval Service.

This man with his big sweet head and his tender heart had been presented with the Congressional Medal of Honor.

She read the citation once, shaking with awe. She read it again, through tears, and then again.

When Pete decided that she no longer needed to be alone, he came to her, sat on the edge of the desk, and took her hand.

"My God, Pete. My God."

"I was in the original platoon at that warehouse, when he came with his eight men."

"When you grew up together."

"Later this evening, at dinner, you'll meet Liam Rooney, who was one of the men Tim brought with him. And Liam's wife, Michelle—

she was the pilot of the downed helicopter. You know in the citation, where it says he led his men and the chopper crew through withering fire?"

She nodded.

"What it doesn't say is first he put a tourniquet on Michelle's arm. And when he led them through withering fire, he was sheltering her and half carrying her."

For a while she could not speak, and then she said, "Every idiot from coast to coast knows who Paris Hilton is, but how many know **his** name?"

"One in fifty thousand?" Pete guessed. "But he wouldn't have it any other way. That's a small club he's in, Linda. I've met several other men who've received the medal. They're all different in many ways, and different ages going back to World War II, but in some ways they're all the same. One thing, and it really impresses you when you meet them, one thing none of them does is talk about what they did back then, and if you press them on it, you see it embarrasses them to be thought of as a hero. There's this humility that I don't know if they were all of a type born with it or it came from the experience, but it's a humility I know damn well I'll never have."

They went into the kitchen.

Mary stood at the sink, peeling apples for a pie.

Linda said, “Mrs. Carrier?”

“Yes.”

“Thank you.”

“For what, sweetheart?”

“For your son.”

Sixty-Five

The sky was vast, and the plains, and the green fields of early corn, and across the vastness lay the quiet of things growing and of men patiently tending.

Tim had been stopped at the turnoff out at the highway, where he had been delayed awhile, and then he had driven a half mile along the lane to the farmhouse.

Two stories, roomy, but in no sense palatial, the house met the world through a veranda that encircled all sides of it. The white clapboard walls were so impeccably maintained that in the flat clear Midwest sun, he could detect no peeling paint, no smallest weathered patch.

Previously he had seen the house in photographs, but he had never been here before.

He had dressed in his only suit, one of two white shirts that he owned, and a new necktie that he had bought especially for this occasion. When he got out of his rental car, he had adjusted the knot in the tie, brushed his hands down the front of the coat to get rid of lint, if there was any, and looked down to be sure he didn't need to spiff up the polish on his shoes with a quick rub on the back of each pant leg.

A pleasant young man in more casual dress had come out from the house and led him to the front porch, asking if he would like a glass of iced tea.

Now Tim sat in a handsome rocking chair on the veranda, with a glass of excellent tea.

He felt big, clumsy, costumed, but not out of place.

Every length of the veranda was furnished with bentwood rockers and wicker armchairs and wicker sofas and small wicker tables, as if in the evening neighbors came from all around to enjoy the commodious porch and talk about the weather.

She didn't keep him waiting. She arrived in boots, tan jeans, and a crisp white blouse, much more casually dressed than on the one previous occasion when he had been in her company.

He said that it was a pleasure to see her again, and she said the pleasure was all hers, and made him feel that she meant it.

At seventy-five, she was tall and trim, with thick gray hair cut short, and her blue eyes were as direct as they were clear.

When she shook his hand, her grip was firm, as he remembered it. Her hands were strong and darkly tanned and well used.

They drank tea and talked about the corn and about horses, which she loved, and about the joys of a Midwest summer, here where she had been born and raised and hoped never to leave. Then he said, "Ma'am, I have come here to ask you for a favor of great importance to me."

"Just ask, Sergeant Carrier, and I'll do what I can."

"I've come here to request a private meeting with your son, and it's vital that you yourself directly speak with him about it."

She smiled. "Fortunately, he and I have always been on excellent speaking terms except for a month when he was in the Navy and thought he had to marry a girl I flat-out knew was wrong for him."

"How did that turn out, ma'am?"

"To my relief and considerable amusement, he discovered that the girl had no interest in marrying him."

"I'm getting married myself in a month," Tim said.

"Congratulations, Sergeant."

"And I'm flat-out sure that she's the right one."

"Well, you're older now than my son was then, and I daresay more sensible."

They talked about Linda for a while, and then they talked about the meeting he wanted, and why he wanted it, and he didn't tell her all of it, but he told more than he had intended.

Sixty-Six

In the red twilight, the evergreen forest stood in a fragrant vaulted hush, like a cathedral in which only owls worshipped with a one-word prayer.

With consummate grace, the large shingled house shared the last slope with the trees and faced onto a long lake that burned with the reflected fire of the sky.

A man escorted Tim down a set of softly lighted stairs from the deck, to the shore, to a pier that led out about a hundred feet into the water.

"You're on your own from here," he said.

Tim's footsteps were hollow on the planks, and waves lapped gently at the pilings, and in shadowed water somewhere to his right, a fish jumped and splashed.

At the end of the pier stood an open pavilion large enough to seat eight for dinner. This evening, the table was small, and only two chairs were provided, both turned to face the western sky and the sky repeated in the water.

On the table were a tray of sandwiches covered by a glass lid, and a small silver-plated chest full of crushed ice in which four bottles of beer were nestled.

Tim's host stood to greet him, and they shook hands. His host opened two beers. They sat to watch the fading twilight, drinking from the bottles.

Red bled to royal purple, and as the purple darkened, stars rose to crown the night.

At first Tim felt awkward and could not easily think of small talk and wished that nearby had been a nice work of masonry on which he could have commented favorably, but there was not a stone or brick in sight. Soon, however, he had been made to feel comfortable.

The pavilion lights were not on, but moonlight bounced off the dark water, and the night was bright enough.

They spoke of their mothers, among other things, and they both had stories as funny as they were tender.

Over sandwiches and the second bottle, Tim told about the killer with the hungry eyes and Wentworth and all that had happened. There were many questions, and he answered them, and then there were more, for this son of the Midwest was a thorough man.

Putting Mickey McCready's DVD on the table, Tim said, "What I ask, sir, for the sake of my family, is you do your best to go at them from a direction that doesn't look like you started from what I've brought to you."

He secured a promise to that effect, and he believed that he could trust it.

In a sense, he was opening a door here. He had an instinct for doors, and this one felt safe.

"Sir, that video shows twenty men, all their faces clear enough, including Wentworth's, whatever his name might be. They all work in law enforcement or in government somewhere, so they have photo ID on file. Run a comparison using facial-recognition software, you'll find them. I figure each of those twenty will give up twenty more, and so on. But I'm telling you how to do what you know better than me."

A while later, an aide approached along the pier. He nodded to Tim, and to his boss, he said, "Mr. President, that call you were hoping for is coming in five minutes."

Tim rose with his host, and they shook hands.

The President said, "We've been a long while at this. My limit's two, but would you like to have another beer before you go?"

Looking around at the black lake and every wavelet silvered with moonlight along its crest and the black trees rising at every shore and the black sky pierced at a thousand points, Tim said, "Thank you, sir. I don't mind if I do."

He stood until the President had walked back the entire length of the pier, and then he sat once more.

A maid brought the beer and an icy glass on a tray and then left him alone. He didn't use the glass, and he nursed the beer.

From far away across the lake came the enchanting call of a loon, and the echoes were likewise enchanting.

Tim was as far away from home here as he had been at that white farmhouse on the plains, but he felt at peace because it was all home, really, from sea to sea.

Sixty-Seven

They could not afford the prices in the south or in the Bay Area, so they found a small town that they liked along the central coast.

Even there, they could not afford to live on the water or with a broad view of the sea, but they bought a 1930s house with good bones.

While they remodeled the property, keeping it true to its period, they lived in an on-site trailer. They did most of the work themselves.

His family—which in his definition included Pete, Zoey, Liam, and Michelle—came north for the housewarming between Thanksgiving and Christmas. Michelle brought the finished lion chandelier, and Linda cried at the sight of it, and cried again at the news that Michelle was pregnant.

He found a job building a wall, and then a

patio deck, and each project led to another. Soon most people in town knew him: Tim the mason, he cares about his work.

With the house finished, Linda had begun to write again. A story that was not full of anger, in which the sentences did not drip with bitterness.

"This will go somewhere," he said, after she gave him the first few chapters to read. "This is the real thing. This is you."

"No, big head," she said, shaking the pages at him. "This isn't me. This is us."

They did not have a TV, but they bought a newspaper some days.

In February, nine months after Tim had killed Linda's would-be murderer, the media was full of stories about conspiracies and indictments. Two prominent politicians committed suicide, Washington quaked, and political empires fell.

They followed the news for a week, then didn't.

In the evenings, they played swing music and old radio programs—Jack Benny, Phil Harris, Burns and Allen.

They had sold her '39 Ford, in which the killer had left them a remembrance, and they talked about buying another one if her book did well.

Like Pete, Tim had sometimes dreamed of the severed heads of babies and of a distraught yet grateful mother who had lost one child but not two others, and who had in a fit of conflicting emotions torn her hair out by the roots to plait it into simple ornaments because she was poor and had nothing else to give to signify her gratitude. He dreamed of those things no more.

The wide world remained dark, and greater darkness threatened. But he and Linda had found a small place of light, because she knew how to endure and he knew how to fight, and together they were whole.

About the Author

DEAN KOONTZ is the author of many #1 **New York Times** bestsellers. He lives with his wife, Gerda, and their dog, Trixie, in southern California.

Correspondence for the author should be addressed to:

Dean Koontz
P.O. Box 9529
Newport Beach, California 92658

In an auction benefiting Canine Companions for Independence, Linda Paquette—of Pasadena, California—won the dubious honor of having a character named after her in this book.